Stephen Foster was bo
spent time as a chef, cab-driver
Norwich. His collection of stories *It Cracks Like Breaking Skin*, which was nominated for the Macmillan PEN award, was published by Faber in 1999.

Acclaim for *It Cracks Like Breaking Skin*:

'Fresh, raw and vital . . . we have a very good and original writer in the making.' Kate Figes

'Stephen Foster has a crisp new tone, and an unusual talent for telling stories which take the reader deeply into the consciousness of the narrator. His book is a pleasure to read.' Alan Sillitoe

'His carefully observed minutiae bring back the moment in a way that is instant and identifiable.' *Sunday Times*

'In these hard-won acts of memory and imagination, humour, nostalgia and pathos and blended with considerable success.' *Times Literary Supplement*

'Foster has a nicely tuned ear for the inflections of casual speech. He can write with easy poignancy about real emotion and real life.' *Independent on Sunday*

by the same author

IT CRACKS LIKE BREAKING SKIN

STEPHEN FOSTER

Strides

faber and faber

First published in 2001
by Faber and Faber Limited
3 Queen Square London WC1N 3AU
This paperback edition first published in 2002

Photoset by Faber and Faber
Printed and bound in Great Britain by
Mackays of Chatham plc, Chatham, Kent

A CIP record for this book
is available from the British Library

ISBN 0–571–20919–X

2 4 6 8 10 9 7 5 3 1

for Jack

Strides

1

You couldn't make zabaglione with fried eggs, that's what I'm saying. The state of the raw material has changed. Irrevocably. I mean, it couldn't be done. Could it?

Alan chalks-up, raises his eyes. I've been banging on for long enough, trying to say something to him, trying to explain this feeling. Alan doesn't like conversation over the Old Green Baize, because conversation over the Old Green Baize can only be regarded as an unwanted interruption to the will-to-win force which is the core-centre of his life.

'Yours.' He nods at the table.

I begin a slow circuit, pretending to study the balls but actually not seeing them. If I thought about it, which I don't, I wouldn't like the look of things. It was a bad break. The reds, which should be easy, should be on, are loitering about the cushions. The colours are all over the place. It's a mess. I try a double and miscue – the supremely unsatisfying squeak as the tip crosses the cue ball at one of a million possible wrong tangents, for the cue ball to miss the red entirely, for the cue ball to skim off the brown. Alan sips his drink, marks up his four and tosses me one of his questions. They're quite smart, these questions, well judged. They're of the kind which will shut me up.

'How much are you putting into your fund these days?'

Anchoring himself, chin on cue, he kisses a red and trundles behind the black. These days I haven't even got a fund, which he well knows. It *is* a snooker and it *was* a fluke, but he's good enough to glance at me like he meant it. I cashed my fund in months ago, which he well knows. I grind the chalk cube over my tip. Specks of blue powder mote under the light. Nothing. Except, not only is this dust attracting my attention disproportionately c/f its mass, I'm actively transforming it into something else. Snow caught in headlights. I wonder if snow in Scandinavia is a different colour to snow here. It might be, I don't know. I've never been.

Alan is tapping his foot. I should be able to concentrate better than this. I used to be able to concentrate better than this.

I have to stretch to play the shot and I send the white in off the pink. Minus six. Or plus six if you're him: the two ways of looking at it. There's a phone by the table, just an internal one. You use it to order a drink. The people from the bar bring the drinks through. Very plush. Just lift the handset, and they answer, you don't have to dial. A pint of Guinness and a . . .

'Just Guinness?'

No. Not just Guinness. A woman's voice; if I look, I can see her through the smoked glass. The partition. It's Alan's club – we play here often enough, but I don't like the place, I don't like the smoked-glass partition. What's it supposed to be, Rear Window or something? I'll have a vodka, that's what I should be drinking, that's what Nat's probably drinking now. It's tonic you have with vodka normally, isn't it? Yeah, that's right. I'll have a vodka and tonic.

'I'll have a vodka and tonic.'

I'd like a cold peppered one with frosting on the glass actually, and some caviar, and some people – Russians – to toast with, to raise glasses, to say Ha! Nazdaroveeyeh!

There's a restaurant somewhere near Farringdon tube where me and Natalie went on our third date. It's a sort of Jewish/East European place. It was Natalie who knew it, not me. The tables were laid out like a canteen, and there were benches, not seats, so you were sitting with the other diners, not separate from them. Four old men were beside us, eating a stew-like soup which they mopped up with bread. About every three mouthfuls, they had some reason to celebrate, they had something to drink to: Ha! (glasses up) Nazdaroveeyeh! (down the hatch, comrades). It didn't take long for them to begin joining the two of us into their toasts. It was almost certainly Nat they really wanted to join in, they probably all fell in love with her at once.

'A pint of Guinness and a vodka and tonic then?'

'Yes. Please. And two packets of salt and vinegar.'

Alan polishes the white on his logoed sweatshirt, leans over the arc and deposits the ball. It falls from him oddly, like a laying bird. A swan? No, it can't be that. He relocates it by rolling the cue over the surface, a professional gesture. His backside in the stabilizing position, he cues straight, elbow firm, shoulder steady. He plays a sharp red off two cushions and into the middle pocket. It's an ostrich, that's what it is. I lean against the wall, casting my eyes down.

There's something not quite right about these trousers I'm wearing, something off. The drop on to the shoes is about, what, let's say ten, eleven millimetres too much. So they over-crease, there's like a concertina too many, or the concertinas are the right number, but too wide or too fat depending on how they're hitched. That's one thing. Another: there's slightly too much material around the hips. They're not exactly baggy, they're more . . . marginally over-generous. If you get a pair which are good on the hips, snug but not too snug, then more often than not the waistband will be too tight. Not too too tight, but over-tight enough to cause discomfort, to leave a mark. This is partly because trouser waists only come in even sizes (I'm talking off-the-peg here). I mean, there are no odd sizes, or rather, there are odd sizes now, but they're no better; they're not a better fit, not at all. You'd think they would be, but they're not. They make no difference.

The way in which the fly sits on this pair is okay. It's not too prominent or bumpy, which you can get. That's one good thing, one thing in their favour. Button up, or through, as some people say. Neat. It's not a zip at least, I've stopped making that mistake. The buttons have good buttonhole-clearance clearance too – they're the kind that rattle a bit. I quite like that.

Alan is wearing jogging pants, the tasselled ends of the pullcord hang below their bow in a way which is just comically wrong vis-à-vis the genital area. Whatever else happens, I'm never going to make that mistake. He romper-suits around the table. I'm sure Jenny sends him out in them deliberately, to keep him safe from all the hot girls. Yeah, right. I hate being seen in public with him, it seriously embarrasses me.

I can't concentrate any more.

I mean, I really can't concentrate any more, and I'm spending far too much time thinking about trousers again. I hate shopping for them, it gives me a lot of problems, unresolvable problems I think, and I shy away from a tailored pair for the fear that that won't be any better. I mean, if a made-to-measure trouser didn't fit perfectly, I couldn't face that level of disappointment, and the subsequent loss of hope. And I wouldn't be able to face the thought of going through it all again, of finding a different tailor and reaching the same potential outcome. Because, bespoke, I would expect an absolutely perfect trouser, a trouser that was uncomplainable about in any way.

No, it's just too risky.

I'm breaking a basic rule of trouser-etiquette here, tonight, because in my right-leg pocket I'm carrying an Alaskan face mask. It looks like a mask, anyway, but actually it's a pair of snow goggles. There's only one of it, but, like trousers, it's called a pair. The pockets in these trousers are good, well made, nearly satisfactory. Deep enough to get your whole hand in, while not being the kind from which all the money rolls out when you sit down – the worst trouser pocket design of all, if you could even call it a design. (Although you should keep your money somewhere else, of course: coins have no place messing up the lines of your trousers.) It's not such a problem for me, this, because, usually, I haven't got any. Money, that is.

They're carved from walrus ivory, the goggles, they're hard and delicate and fine and I stole them this morning from a museum. There was a museum employee who'd taken everything out of the cabinet, to clean it. This item, this mask/goggle – I often go down there to look at it, it's a habit – was with some other *objets* on a trolley just behind the employee. He had his back to this trolley and I whipped it like it was nothing and slid out quick and hailed a taxi. It looks like something somewhere between Catwoman's mask and that protective shield footballers sport when they've bashed their cheek up. I guess it was probably used by Stone Age Eskimos to keep the snow out of their eyes. The period of origin is all the information they give on the label beside the display case, apart from the material – walrus ivory. I think it's Stone Age anyway, I'm not very sharp on dates. I've been fingering it all night. There are tiny nicks and carvings over the surface which you can catch with the tip of your nail, if you want something to go right through you. The texture is cold and hard like eggshell. I was quite cool about it, this theft, until the taxi was a few streets away, when my heart started banging and my fingernails went white and my palms went into a sweat.

'Yours.'

Somehow we're on to the colours already. The barmaid arrives carrying one of those metal trays with a lip. I pause while she places the drinks, removes the empties. Her smell reminds me how much I prefer the company of women to the company of men. Actually, you do get women in snooker halls much more now, I've noticed that, but like the odd trouser sizes, it doesn't make any difference. I can't concentrate. I'd rather be somewhere else. It's not Alan's fault, or the barmaid's. It's mine. Chin down. The cue ball's a way off the long yellow. Whack it. I'm happy enough to see it make contact, but get a much better result as the yellow slams into the far-right bottom, no hint of a touch on the jaws, like it was deliberate, like I meant it.

'Shot.'

Keep my eyes lowered in false modesty. Ah, it was nothing.

Alan takes the green and the brown. He leaves me a chance on the blue. And now, finally, I am interested. I *can* just about concentrate when the only ball you can play for is worth five. Worth more than a standard foul. It's too late, this effort of concentration. I need the blue, the pink and the black plus three snookers to draw level and have the black respotted. But the blue is just sitting there, hanging over the middle, asking for it. I play it gently, and in it trickles. The pink, on the opposite cushion – I've got no positional play, I can only imagine beginning to consider the possibility of actually plotting where the cue ball will end up – invites a double, which I execute with what could look like aplomb. It's the best shot of all, that, totally satisfying, flying in clean and hard and sharp and giving the appearance that you actually *have* worked out an angle, double-decoded the situation. Now of course I can't win – you can't play a snooker when there's only the black and the white left, when there's nothing to put between the last two balls – but, not pausing to catch Alan's eye, I sweep to the baulk-end, the white nestling right on the cushion, and hammer it at the black, on its spot, which cuts into the bottom left, as the cue ball follows an equal and opposite trajectory into the bottom right.

'Story of your life, mate. Three in a row.' He shakes his head sadly. 'D'you fancy another?'

Sure. *I'll* take the next three and we'll make it the best of seven, eh? I unscrew the cue and slide the halves into the red plush lining of the carry-case.

'Pub?'

He just wants to string it out, Alan, he can be like this.

'Sulking?'

No. Just waiting, like I have to.

'What was that you were on about . . . zabaglione?'

'I was saying, once it's done you can't change it back. Not ever. You know. And about how it's changed altogether, so even if you did want to change it back, you couldn't. A cooked egg's devoid of possibilities, isn't it, it's done, fixed. It's a chemical thing. It's undoable. In your language it'd be like you crashed the hard disk and had a system failure. Probably.'

'What do you mean, *in your language*?'

'I mean like an idea you'd get.'

We've passed through the smoked glass, into the foyer-part. Alan's offering the balls back over the counter, packed in their plastic tray.

'It's a bit rich, you giving it the condescension, under the circs, isn't it? Why d'you *always* want to be such a prick? Why don't you just grow up and get a proper job, eh? Then you might have money of your own, and not talk such shit.'

The plastic shakes in his hand. He's quick to lose his cake, Alan, touchy. To be honest, the reason I give it the condescension is that I don't actually like him, even though we are so-called friends. It's nothing all that personal, it's just that I can't get on with anything he stands for, like belonging to this club, for example, when he's only the same age as me. We should be too young for this, we should have better things to do. That shaking tray, I think he wants to stove it into my head. But I'll tell you what I don't want, I'll tell you what I hate. Scenes. I hate them. I don't want a scene in front of Rear Window Girl, I'd hate *that*.

Pull a fiver out and hold it across the bar, at least pay for the drinks. Distract attention. She's growing some colour out of her roots, shoulder length, so it's about half and half, brown to blonde. A bit lank, that's okay, that's something I quite like. The same length as Natalie's hair, but different otherwise. She's there before me.

'It's a vodka and tonic and a pint of Guinness, is it?'

Please. Thanks.

I keep my non-concentration fast on her. Low-cut hipsters, smokes a lot. I can't bring myself to pass a single word outside of the routine of purchase. There's enough in the way of off-duty and assorted other wankers about to do that.

'Here, Alan. Drink. There's a table free in the corner.'

His body's lost the tension, the moment's passed. We're back. We can talk, about Alan's work, and, eventually, he can write me the cheque.

42. That was the number that was the meaning of life, wasn't it, or was that a different number? Can't remember. It's the number on the door I'm double-unlocking now anyway. Or rather, no, it's the number on the door I'm double-locking now. Which means I forgot to double-lock when I left. I thought I came back to do that? Yes. Or rather, no. I did, but then I remembered that I'd forgotten the cue, and so I came back inside to get it. The usual – remembering something *else* I'd forgotten – made me forget what I came back to do in the first place. At least I've still got the keys with me, which isn't always the case. And the cue too, I've still got that, which is good because it's not mine. It's not my flat. I'm looking after it for my friend Antonio. He's out of the country, shooting wildlife. Photographing it, I mean. That's what he does, mainly, that's his expertise. Black and whites of big cats hang on the walls in clipframes. There's a real one in the kitchen waiting for supper: Pancho. Pancho is the bona fide reason Antonio lets me stop here. He knows I like the cat. Or, to be accurate about it, the cat likes me, that's the way round it works with cats. Antonio's left him in the hands of cat-feeding agencies before, but it's never gone well, in fact it's gone badly. When he's returned, Pan-

cho (after the actor) has been sorely depressed, offhand and antisocial, the absolute last attributes you wish to find in your cat.

'Cats are for cuddling, aren't they, feline?'

When I speak to him in this direct, affectionate manner, he rubs round my ankles with his tail perpendicular and his back arched, doing that thing he does with his paw. He's a smoke-grey cat with enormous green eyes. A total babe, as they say.

'Ready for supper, then?'

My friend Rosie's bête noire is the fact that cats can't speak. It's not my bête noire. One-sided conversations are cool with me.

'Right, what's it gonna be? Liver and Heart? Rabbit Chow Mein?'

I'm a bit slack about cleaning his crockery, so his plate's speckled with brown bits. I don't think he minds, so long as it doesn't go on for more than a week. Rabbit Chow Mein's all we've got. Pancho settles on his haunches and eats, delicately, nibbling around the edge, purring. Human food supplies are even less promising than a tin of Rabbit Chow Mein. In the fridge there's a half-jar of horseradish sauce two months past sell-by, a half-jar of pickled onions in piquant vinegar, a half-jar of beetroot pickle, and two soused herrings in a jar, making that a half-jar too. In the bread urn there's one two-day-old granary bap in a paper bag. I can work with this, I suppose, just.

Feet up on the pine table (shoes off first, of course). I could run you through it, but why bother, enough to say it's not at all chichi in here, it's that relaxed good-taste thing – Antonio picks up his furnishings from a place called Evolution Because In The Third World It's All Limewashed Et Cetera. It's okay. The beetroot pickle, horseradish and soused herring bap sans butter and sans low-fat substitute, avec two piquant pickled onions on the side, isn't all that great, though I have tasted worse. I ease the snow goggles out of my pocket and set them beside my calf. I've placed a square of kitchen towel on my lap, performing the job of a napkin, raising the tone. Pancho lands on me, and begins bedding in, clawing; and this is the real reason why I employ the kitchen towel:

They may not fit, they may be less than ideal, they may give rise to feelings of unhappiness and dissatisfaction and misery, but even so, I don't want the thighs getting all frayed and churned into bobbly bits by the cat.

In the bathroom, I try on the goggles. Or rather I hold them to my face, because there's no strap or string or anything for keeping them attached, though there are very small holes at each side that you could use for the purpose. I watch the mirror for a while head-on, trying to work out why it is that obscuring the part around the eyes makes a person look so sinister. It's not just me either, it works for terrorists – I don't think they wear those balaclavas solely for disguise. Losing most of the nose is part of it. I lower the mask, raise it again. Lower/raise, lower/raise. Eyebrows are important, aren't they? Not having eyebrows is definitely significant. Holding the mask steady, leaning towards the reflection, I notice that the white of my left eye has a slight mark. I've never seen that before. Where did it come from, how do you get a mark on your eye? I turn my head to the right, to the left, switching profile, riding the goggles up and down the bridge ever so slightly, trying to find the best fit, and trying not to worry about the mark. Chin up. Mmm. They're not bad. Quite chic. Turning to the room to establish the effect on vision, I try them off, I try them on, I try them off, I try them on. Off/On Off/On Off/On. There's a peripheral loss in the On position, especially at the sides. I wonder if that's deliberate, or if people had different shaped heads in the Stone Age. I rest them on the cistern top and brush my teeth. The toothpaste-tang collision with the residual-herring-bap-tang is metallic. Nasty. Sloosh and spit and swash it out. Returning the goggles to my eyes I bring my face closer to the mirror, examining the cleaned teeth. Better. I run my tongue over the top row, producing a squeak. Clamping my jaw, baring my gums, the bone shield above reflects the skeletal relationship in a neat symmetry. I feel suddenly not uncheerful. Nobody else has got a pair like this, they're very exclusive. The goggles I mean. It's one thing but it's called a pair. Natalie & Me. We were one thing, but we could have been called a pair, a couple. Uncharacteristically, I slip the mask into my shirt top pocket.

I don't like to have anything in a shirt top pocket which will create a contour. A packet of fags, for instance, is out of the question. Credit cards, cards that get you through Security Systems, CashPoint cards, Reward cards or similar are okay. One at a time. It's a good place to try not to lose tickets for the dry-cleaners. The Natalie-and-me-mask won't be in here for long.

In the bedroom, head tipped back, lying on the bed, I stare at the ceiling. Over by the window, on the radiator, there's a new pair of trousers. They've been through the washing machine to soften them up; they're the kind that are too stiff when they're new. I turned them a few times while they were drying, so they're pretty much crease-free. They're in the ideal condition. Unworn. They seemed fine in the shop, but that means nothing. So far, I've had no disenchantment from those trousers whatsoever. Pancho joins me.

'Virgin trousers, Pancho. Nice.'

I was in new legwear when I first met Natalie. Monday nights I play five-a-side with Alan and some of his office mates, theBoys. They're all right, apart from being dickheads. What they like to talk about in the pub afterwards is who's driving what car, what car who's driving, who's going to be driving what car in the future, who's not going to be driving what car much longer; bhp, mpg, rpm, leather, alloys, front-end, rear-end, belt-line, hands-free 16-valve 12-disc motronic multi-changer, lowered suspension, headrest speakers, radials, immobilizer, residuals, et cetera et cetera. Et cetera. When all motoring possibilities are exhausted, there's conversation category 2: what bastard is going to be promoted, what bastard has already been promoted, what bastard thought he was going to be promoted but wasn't (haha), what bastard will never be promoted, not in a million years, and what they've heard the MD is thinking of in terms of a restructure. Quite a bastard, the MD, but not a bad guy. If something really exciting has happened, like someone they know has left one company and joined another, they talk about that instead. Here the two topics come together in perfect harmony: Yeah, they go, Fifteen Long Ones On Top minimum, 20 per cent, optional stake, and *serious* Annuals. It's only a Jap Turbo – a Mitsu? – they're well rated under the lid, but image . . . (a lot of head-shaking). It's a top-of Z3 at SD, though. Yeah? Yeah. Not bad Not bad. Not bad. Good move. The right decision. Definitely. Mike Cooper went in for it too. Not a happy boy. Hahaha. I heard the MD's a bit of a bastard.

What it is about this Lifestyle that I can't embrace with my whole heart isn't something I can put a name to. Or rather, I can put lots of names to it, but none of them quite covers it.

There are two pitches side by side, orange astroturf brushed with a fine green sand.

It was a January night, start of a new year, start of a new season (five-a-side seasons don't correspond to FIFA edicts, they're more random). I like the set-up. I like the way the floodlights break the night air and I like the odd colour of the surface underfoot, it feels . . . lunar. The pitches are separated from each other by a green-camouflage net curtain. In the time-slot corresponding to the one we have, a girls' team plays on the other pitch. TheBoys love that, they really do. There's no shortage of volunteers to retrieve the ball when it goes over. When I'm out of breath after a run sometimes I drop, head lowered, hands on knees, panting, and I watch the girls' match for a few seconds. They're good players. They work it in triangles, their passing's sharp. Give and Go, Give and Go. It's a normal shout in five-a-side, and it's one of their favourites. They play some sharp one-twos.

One of the dickheads is an ape who works in advertising. He never bothers with me much because he hasn't got anything to prove, I mean there's no work involvement. But between some of the other players, work carries over into the match. The ape has a running battle going with another one the same as him, a bear. Semi-fighting sometimes happens but the momentum for a proper scrap never quite gets rolling. The other Boys step in – chill out, cool it, they say, moving between them. I do like their Americo-Adspeak. Come on Guys. Relax. Break it Up.

No one ever says, It's only a game.

Which is right, because it isn't only a game. Because sometimes something like this happens:

ApeBoy and BearBoy were playing on the same side that night in January, which meant that opportunities for confrontation were reduced, though incidents *could* still break out when they wouldn't pass to each other, especially when that pass was the obvious obvious option. I was playing for the other side. I was running with the ball. I was wearing my new shorts – 1966 England Replicas. Très retro. And new white lycra cycle shorts underneath. I felt good. I was running up the wing beside the camouflage netting. ApeBoy and BearBoy both tackled me at once, one slid in from 2 o'clock, the other from 4. I jumped, but not enough. They crunched into each other and I was the side effect: their combined velocity slicing me under the netting in the semi-horizontal airborne position. My return to Earth took place on my left thigh on the arseside-side. It took place on the other pitch. I would've picked up a classic burngraze without the protection of the new white lycra cycle shorts, I got a pretty good one even with that protection. Natalie was coming down the wing in the opposite direction. I fouled Natalie. I scythed her down.

She was on to her feet first offering me a hand, which I took. It was cold and sweaty.

FuckSorry, I said to my feet as I rose.

I straightened and she looked at me, eyes shining blue.

'S'alright, mate . . .'

Shining blue.

' . . . I bin watchin you . . .'

Shining blue, smiling.

' . . . You're not a bad winger, are ya?'

I fell completely instantly completely in love.

Pancho's settled right in, doing that thing with his paw and purring.

'Do cats fall in love or do they just have a sexy?'

Pancho's a smart cat. He can't even be bothered opening an eye to a question as stupid as this.

2

What time is it? I'm falling asleep clothed too often. My eyes open filmy, my trousers are all creased, my shirt's worse – it looks like it's had a dry tie-dye. Sweating a bit. 06:33 the clock says. It's dark, but it's light, if you know what I mean. I didn't draw the curtains. I should still be asleep, but I'm not. I used to be. I could keep my head down till lunchtime, easy. There's something, isn't there? There's something I should remember. Mask. The mask, it's that, that's what it is. Is that why I'm sweating, did I dream about it? Better have a look at the Breakfast News. I might be on the fucking run.

I heard that when Breakfast TV started, it was going to be a serious thing. Politics-in-depth and all that. I hardly need say what's on the screen now. There's nothing about a stolen mask, but then, there hasn't been any news about anything. Radio might be better, it might be a more radio-style sort of crime, masktheft. But the bedside set's tuned to pirate soul – GropeFM, LoverMan – they don't have news there. *And* it's digital. If you try changing the station with the changing button, you just get rotating numbers for ever, except you *can* stop this by pressing two buttons at once. Then you get crackle. It's best to leave it, it really is.

What's that noise?

And where's Pancho? He normally wakes me up by drooling on my chin. It's his annoying habit.

Pancho's in the kitchen, rattling the mask round the floor. He must have pulled it out of my shirt top pocket while I was sleeping (he *is* a smart cat, I wasn't just saying it). I suppose he thinks he's found a prehistoric mouse-skeleton. I take it from him and rinse away the drool-stuff under the tap saying, Cats, in a loaded voice, heavy on the pathos. I shake the water at him. Most cats scarper if you do this, but Pancho just sits impassive, gives me the breakfast look. I don't like to serve the same variety for consecutive sittings, and anyway there isn't a full portion of Rabbit Chow Mein left. It'll have to be a trip out to see my friend Mr Well-stocked.

Double-lock the door and up the steps – it's cold. Double-unlock the door and pick up the Snowboard Puffa. It's the sort of thing you sometimes do without meaning to, buy a Snowboard Puffa, and then you find yourself wearing it. Good job I went back inside, I nearly left the mask behind. It'd be incontrovertible evidence, that. Up the steps again (did I say it was a basement flat before?), pulling a match along the wall, lighting-up behind a shielding hand, private-eye style, and on to the street. The beginning of my favourite film has that actor Elliott Gould playing Philip Marlowe. I like Elliott Gould, he's got a good miserable face. It's an update of The Long Goodbye, the film, set into 70s California. In the opening sequence, Marlowe's cat wakes him in the middle of the night. The cat's hungry but there's no cat food in the apartment (it's up on the 5th Floor), so Marlowe has to get up to go down the 24-Hour store for supplies. There's only one type his cat will eat, it's called Couri Brand. Gould/Marlowe lights the match for his cigarette on the wall next to the bed before he gets up. It's a trait of his, an epic tic. He's always smoking, and he's always lighting the match on the nearest surface. When he gets to the store, striking a match on the door-frame as he enters, he can't find any Couri brand. C-O-U-R-I. He has to spell it out to the shelf-filler in the shop, who tells him to get a life, buy any kind, cats'll eat anything. Yeah, right, he says. You haven't met my cat, he says. But he has to buy a different brand anyway, there's no choice. He hides it under his jacket as he returns to the flat, sneaks into the kitchen while he decants the contents into a Couri Brand tin, then shows the cat the tin, going: Look, Cat, it's Couri Brand, Man – Couri Brand, your favourite mmm nice. And then he serves it. The cat's not fooled. The cat turns its nose up. Pancho is exactly like that if he doesn't get his Felinix.

It's a long story, The Long Goodbye. Part of it's to do with Marlowe running his friend down to Mexico, part of it's to do with Marlowe's commission to find a blocked, drunken writer-guy (it's all interconnected, in a complex way, like private-eye films are). It's the writer's wife who offers the commission. When he finds the writer-guy (at a drying-out clinic) and introduces himself, the writer-guy deliberately mishears Marlowe's name, and because Marlowe's smoking, and because Marlowe's smoking Marlboro, he calls him Marlboro, and later Marlboro Man. When Marlowe returns to visit the writer-guy and his wife at their home a few days later (it's one of those desirable beach houses, with a heavy sliding picture-window door to the sea) the writer-guy calls out, Hey – here comes Marlboro Man.

Natalie called me Winger. Natalie *calls* me Winger. Because of how we met, mostly, but because of one of her favourite expressions too, I think: On a Wing and a Prayer. She whispered it, in the bath, in my ear, a truncated sound: Winganaprair. The way she used it would be as a full stop on a situation, like if I was trying to, say, explain something about global financial markets, or if she was trying to cook. Winganaprair.

'Winganaprair, Winger.'

That's one of the things about her, she does something like giving you a name and she carries on as though it's a simple fait accompli, and that's that, even though you might not like it you just have to accept that it's happened. No choice.

Marlowe was the kind of character who liked to think he

was the kind of character who didn't get involved. Dames? A shrug of the shoulder was the answer to and dispatch of the whole matter. Dames – It's cool with me. That's what he'd say. *It's cool with me.* It's his catch phrase. He mutters it when the writer-guy first calls him Marlboro Man: Marlboro Man? It's cool with me. It's cool with me. It's a line he uses most often when something bad or dodgy's up.

Anyway, that was how I felt about being called Winger. Shrug of the shoulder. It's cool with me.

When the football finished that night, I manoeuvred myself into a holding position which meant I'd segue in beside Natalie as the two pitches of players merged towards the double-doors, the double-doors to the changing rooms. I needed to be brave and to come up with a top line. This was it:

Are you alright? (I know, terrific. I know.)

Fine mate, she said. Are You?

Nothing that won't mend, I said. Listen, I said. D'ya fancy a drink. Sometime?

I took myself by surprise. Her mates were floating around after all. And theBoys weren't exactly out of earshot either. But sometimes. Sometimes you just have to say the words however embarrassing they are, otherwise you'll end up kerb-crawling her home or hanging about where she works or staying awake all night for weeks on end or something. Sometimes you've got to be Upfront, as theBoys say. You've got to be aware of what the Bottom Line is too. At The End of the Day.

We pulled up. Stopped. Her eyes became still, an opaque film arrived. A kind of defensive wall had been assembled. Her hair was dark redbrown, tied back – it was going to be about shoulder-length when it was let loose. I could tell that. It was stained with sweat where it met her brow. Her skin wasn't perfect, it was a bit open, like there would be freckles in the sun. Her jawline *was* perfect, assured and strong. She wore a black Adidas top, a sweatband on her left wrist and unlogoed midgrey sweatpants tucked into Tottenham football socks, the away pair. The outline of her shinpads ridged over her shins. We were still standing still.

Nice shorts, was what she replied, nodding at the 1966 Replicas.

A compliment on my legwear. A killer touch; *the* killer touch – she'd hit the spot first time.

Was that a Yes or a No then? It was harder to work out than it would have been because I was thrown right off by the shorts comp. It wasn't a Yes or a No. I had more to do. Why do they make you work like this? (I know, it's Darwin, isn't it?) Should I push it on the drink or switch to a compliment about *her* attire? Nat! Get a move on – what y'doin? one of her team-mates called out from half-way down the stairs towards the changing rooms. We were standing just outside the double-doors, causing an obstruction.

Be with ya in a minute, Nat shouted back. And mind your own business.

Are you a Spurs fan? I said, nodding at her socks.

Nah, she said. They're my boyfriend's.

Ah. It was my face that said it, not me.

S'alright, she said. We don't get on. Y'can still ask me for a drink. When?

In the showers, some of theBoys seemed to think I'd made an error by managing to get this date set up. They offered their views whilst indulging in the usual surreptitious tackle comparisons. Mine always went into hiding in their company. The mistakes I had made could be summarized as follows:

1] She was just a tart from the East End somewhere. D'ya

hear the way she talked? 'Mind yer own *bizniss*.'

2] Although girls playing football are quite respectable for a wanking fantasy, they're not suitable for the Long View to fiancée / wife.

3] I didn't have the details of her salary / pensionPlan.

4] Even thinking about getting on the pull out on The Park implied that my mind hadn't properly been on The Game.

As I sat drip-drying post-shower on the slatted wooden bench, I examined my burngraze with pride. It was a mottled purpling flash, like it had been laid on with a quick brush. I touched the broken surface while theBoys banged on. I concluded from their tone that:

5] They were jealous.

I went for the no-response response: refusing all eye contact and busying myself with a towel-drying so thorough that it included up and down between *all* my toes twice. What I'd seen of theGirls (theBoys' Girls, I mean) had led me to believe they had tight little mouths and were totally frigid even if they were well dressed. Which they weren't, they were expensively dressed, which is different. The closest theBoys would be getting to authentic sex would be corporate blow-jobs in multinational hotels a few years from now. Or even sooner. Inbetweentimes it was going to be soft-furnishings, Austrian blinds, fitted kitchens, Victorian baths with feet on them, bleached beech floors and colour-coded luggage for display on the luggage rack of this year's fully specced coupé. Even if I'm not well quoted on a lot of stuff, I'm pretty damn sure about this.

Your strides are always creased when you remove them from a sports bag, it doesn't matter how you've loaded them. There is a destructured style called Destructured that's meant to look like this. The ones I'd got weren't those. As I removed the bits of loose thread, lint, fluff and other foreign bodies that they always pick up from the sports bag, even if you wash it out before you begin packing, I ran an action replay through my mind.

She scored a goal, Natalie. I paid special attention to watching her play after I'd fallen in love with her, and just before the end of the match she chipped one into the far corner, a very tricky and delicate skill in five-a-side, with the crossbar of the goal being so low vis-à-vis the relative height of the goalkeeper. Her team-mates applauded, their claps cracking cold in the cold night air, and I applauded too, but only to myself, as I watched her track back and skip a couple of steps in celebration.

Felinix, MarlboroMan. Pancho won't give the time of day to any other brand. F-E-L-I-N-I-X. Felinix.

I can't say I appreciate the morning air round here; even when the weather's really cold it still hangs fuggy. One corner before the corner shop there's a tramp, bin-rummaging. His distinguishing feature is that he's wearing thick tortoiseshell-type spectacles with the arms heavily sellotaped. At a glance, for a second, the spectacle frames remind me of the mask, the shape of them as well as the finish. My friend Rosie says that if you hear a Barry Manilow song on the radio in the morning, one that you haven't heard for years, you'll hear it playing in a shop later in the afternoon and then you'll hear it again in a bar in the evening. And she's right. It's the same thing with those tramp specs and the mask. Funny moment in a nasty déjà-vu sort of way. And it means there are two more funny moments to come.

Mr Wellstocked's Modern Stores are of unwelcoming appearance. A few oldish-looking vegetables and sometimes some past sell-by fruit lie limp in a rack in one side of the front window; Mr Wellstocked sits on a stool in the other, his expression one of perfect glumness. The past sell-by fruit and veg is displayed in the position where sun damage is at its most likely. He seems to have no idea about shop-layout, and in fact he hasn't got much other stuff to sell. His method is to let everything run down to nothing, and only then to take the clapped-out low-specced shooting brake down to the cash and carry. One particular warm Thursday about nine months ago he had a dozen or so green pods lying in a small cardboard box in the window. They looked like over-size, wrinkled mange tout – they were new to me, I'd never seen them before. I asked him what they were and he told me they were special, from his brother-in-law, who'd sent them over from Lahore. Beyond this, he didn't have a name for them. Were they hot, I asked. (I don't like hot food, it burns my tongue.) No No, he said. Very mild. Very good. I bought two, and experimentally incorporated them into a Navarin of Lamb, a menu-staple of mine. You use green beans in a Navarin anyway, French beans. I got the lamb from that deluxe butcher in Holland Park Avenue, the one with all the game-in-feather hanging at the front. Only the best. I took the ingredients over to my ex-girlfriend's place, which was out towards Acton. Her kitchen wasn't bad for cooking in, which is unusual – a lot of kitchens you come across don't function at all as intended. These special-from-brother-in-law-in-Lahore beans had the heat of redhot red chilli peppers. The pair together were the strength of about fifteen. It's not often that I'm in serious error when I'm cooking (she didn't like hot food either), and I thought it meant something, this culinary fuck-up. Earlier in the relationship it would've been a laugh, but by then it wasn't. We stopped seeing each not long after.

When I was next in The Modern Stores following the Navarin incident, Mr Wellstocked asked me how I'd liked them, making a motion towards the remaining super-wrinkled few. The way he asked me, it really sounded like an innocent question, and his face gave nothing away. If he was going to play it straight, so was I. They were cool with me, I said.

This morning he's not here. It's his wife instead, who doesn't say much, she sits on his stool most of the time giving absolutely nothing away while wearing a look of veiled glumness very much like Mr Wellstocked's own, at the same time working on her PhD on her laptop – I know that's what she's doing, I asked her once. My luck's better than Marlowe's was anyway – Pancho's brand *is* a stock item *and* they have it in stock. Liver and Heart, our favourite label colour. It's the last tin of course. There isn't a copy of the paper I buy, skimmed milk only in the cooler (skimmed milk, honestly, it's not milk, is it?), and cigarette supplies are at an all-time low. In short, the usual.

I never took any of Mr Wellstocked's green things to Natalie's so at least I sometimes learn from my mistakes. Natalie had the use of an unusual kitchen-space in the specialized sense that it had a view, which *is* unusual in a kitchen. The kitchen *was* in the East End, so at least theBoys were geographically accurate in their original assessments, the only accuracy with which I was prepared to credit them.

We beckoned each other away from the double-doors to set the date up, so that everybody couldn't hear.

When she said When then? I said, Thursday?

When I said Thursday? she said, Fine. Time?

When I said 8.00? she said, Half-past'd be better, mate.

Sure, I said. Okay.

Place? she said.

Her eyes were shining blue again. The defensive wall had come down.

There was a bar we both knew on Old Street roundabout.

I only had to wait for three days.

It only seemed like three years.

3

I wondered what she'd be wearing. I had a lot of trouble deciding what to wear myself.

The Golden Rule on a firstDate is to select a pair with whom you are well familiar, whose faults you know and can live with. Although you might need to buy a new pair or two as part of advance preparations, Do Not wear them on the firstDate. They'll only cause anxiety, pain, distraction and discomfort all night long. And that'll just be the look of them.

I toyed at length with some deep blue Connections that had a nice grain and a green embroidered logo on the button-through flap where nobody could see it, a favourite detail. But the pocket-linings on these were marginally undergenerous, though they were at least appropriately constructed in the sense that they were the right colour. Some dark jeans come supplied with a white inner pocket, so a thin band of white material is displayed at the pocket-line. Unbelievable. Anyway, like I said, the pockets on the Connections were marginally undergenerous, and you never know when you might need to bury your hands deep in your pockets, even if only as a gesture against the rain. To tell you the truth, after only two and a half hours, I settled on a pretty standard pair of black Firetraps (with correct-depth black pockets). They were just on the edge of beginning to fade, which is almost ideal, and they featured double belt loops, which isn't a bad thing.

I didn't want to be the first one there, but I didn't want to miss anything or leave her standing about on her own either – I'm not happy if it happens to me, and Rosie told me once that girls really hate it. I stood leaning against a crash barrier with the bar we both knew in view across six lanes of traffic, smoking a Marlboro Man and savouring the pollution. At 8.35 a taxi pulled up on the other side of the lanes. She was wearing deep dark brown, which could have looked like black to an untrained eye at that distance. I was over the road and at the bar of the bar we both knew in time to pay for the drinks, which was good going, because the traffic was moving fast, it wasn't at a standstill. We selected high stools beside the window, which was good. If you go for an alcove you have a seating arrangement decision to make. Alongside can seem too forward, opposite too aloof. A table with low seats in the middle of the floor is a bit . . . exposed? Like being on a stage. Like when I was little, and suffered the trauma of being forced to play a shepherd in a nativity scene. It's not as bad as that on a table with low seats in the middle of the floor of course; I mean, for a start, you don't have to wear a frock over your trousers.

She put her bag on the granite ledge that ran along the window. We clinked glasses and took our first sips looking at each other over the rims. I liked the stool. Perfect height for me. You could put your feet up on the rail, or pivot yourself from the floor, flexing your back a bit. She sat knees together with her legs tucked back under, her heels hooked over the rail, her body language an S. Not a body language, just a body letter. I glanced at her feet. Chisel-toe suede. Sharp. Really very nice.

Footwear; to be honest, I don't even want to start talking about it.

So.

This is something, she said. Haven't been on a firstDate for a while.

Eyes shining blue; paying attention and not just getting drawn in was going to take maximum maximum concentration.

How about you? she said.

What! Did she think I was about to give up recent girlfriend history just like that? I made a face which was meant to look like I was considering a smart response.

'Eleven and a half months ago.' [Well done, son. Great resolve]

'What happened?'

We didn't get on, I said. Like you and your boyfriend. [Better]

You haven't been playing with that lot for long, have you? she said, meaning the football.

A straight evasion, couched in the way of being an inquiry. That's my tactic. Usually. So we smiled at each other, while we worked out strategies.

No. I haven't, I said. I've known theBoys for long enough, but I only started playing regularly about a month or so before Christmas.

'Mmm. I thought I never seen you till recently. I've been away a bit though.'

'Oh, where?'

'Spain.'

She had a very light dusting of tan, I could see that now. You often notice things once you've been told about them.

'On holiday?'

'Nah. Business, but I took a couple of days' holiday too.'

Bizniss was still the basic sound of it, but she was doing it softer. You do that when you're flirting, soften your voice. I was doing it myself, definitely.

'What sort of business?'

'Clothes. Rag trade, mate.'

Fuck me rigid. I took a drink of my drink. 'What d'you do then?'

'I'm a buyer.'

'You were buying clothes in Spain?' (A nightmare vision of bodyswerving matadorial strides danced in front of my eyes.)

'No, we've just opened a new shop in Bilbao. It was for that. It's not the time of year for buying.'

'Who's we?'

She named a fairly upmarket small multiple.

'Menswear or womenswear?' [$10,000 Question]

'Womenswear. Mostly.'

'Not menswear then?' [An obvious obvious double-checker, but I needed to be certain]

'No.' Slight pause. 'Wha'sUp? There *are* women menswear buyers, y'know. There are *even* women menswear designers.'

A demi-smile had arrived. She had her hair down, and on one side it flicked under her chin like it was also smiling.

Yeah man, Ally Capellino, I said.

Yeah man, Nicole Farhi, she replied.

A person of whom I have absolutely no recollection asked me for a light. I had a disposable with me and offered it over. I kept my matches, I prefer them. I stretched on the stool. Nat kept the smile on.

Same again? The first ones had certainly disappeared fast. At the bar I lit up, inhaling heavily. I still had some pre-match nerves here, even though the game had already actually kicked off. The alcohol was operating at the early stage, the stage at which it makes nerves slightly worse.

I came back with the refills, watching her via her reflection in the window. She turned from watching me via my reflection in the window saying, You shouldn't smoke, Winger, and she made a low exaggerated coughing noise. Not good for your speedy runs up the flanks. Or for your recovery rate.

You can't call me Winger, I said. I mean, I'm not calling you Midfield Maestro or The Big Centre Forward. Am I, Natalie? . . . Not that you're big or anything like that, I mean you're, well . . . a sort of ideal sort of size.

Early for a compliment, but once I'd made the blunder of using the word Big I had to compensate.

She took a cigarette for herself while I was saying this, concluding her lighting motion with the remark, I don't, hardly, inclining her chin towards it. She looked at me through the smoke.

She looked at me quite hard. She studied me. I don't like it, that, same as I didn't like being watched while being third shepherd from the left in the nativity. But I put up with it, I had to, being in love an' all.

'I think you are a Winger though. You haven't told me what you do yet.'

'What do you mean?'

'I mean a job or similar.'

'No. I mean you saying you think I'm a Winger.'

'You have to answer first.'

I knew she was going to say that.

I don't like the question. It's just a question I don't like. Even if I was something straight-out cool, like a poet, I wouldn't want to say it, because poets don't. They say something about something else when they're trying to say something, they don't talk about what they do. *Some speak of the future, my love she speaks softly, she knows there's no success like failure, and that failure's no success at all.* It's a Bob Dylan song, that. He's a poet. What's the title? I can't remember. I don't want anybody not understanding that there's no success like failure and that failure's no success at all. That's why I don't like the question.

Q. What do you do?

A. Well, mostly I watch football and worry about my trousers. I play football too. I shop, I like shopping, except shopping for trousers. Sometimes I go to a museum. More often I go to an art gallery. I like paintings, and I like cooking and sleeping. I like sleeping.

Even though I almost always *do* work, for money, I'm not into it, I'm really not. The idea of spending time in a way that defines you like that is just too . . . I don't know. Awful? And the obvious flaw in the whole scheme: work never gets you enough money to give you the possibility of not working.

'I work with food.'

Her expression remains a question.

'What's that mean? Are you a farmer?'

'Ha Ha. Try another.'

'A game, eh? Delicatessen at Sainsbury's?'

'I had to leave. I didn't suit the colour of the apron.'

'No, you wouldn't. Pizza delivery?'

'Kept falling off the moped. Warmer though. Try another.'

'Air Steward?'

'Air Steward? Warmer?'

'Well, it's food on the move, isn't it.'

'Do me a favour. Do I look like a [fucking] flight attendant?'

'Some of them *are* very attractive.' (Sharp. I liked that one. Except . . .)

'Most of them are gay.'

'Are you gonna give me an answer then?'

'I'm freelance.'

For some reason, that Freelance made her laugh. Everybody's at their best when they laugh, aren't they? When it's the first one you see from someone you already feel 110 per cent passionate about, it comes like the ball hitting the back of the net in the Cup Final while the Rothko hangs on the wall behind you in your own front room, while you eat a small zabaglione with a cherry on top while wearing the ultimately fitting pair of trousers (yeah, right) all at once. That was how that one came to me anyway.

The hours after her laugh are hard to remember properly. When I try to fit the bits together, it feels the way a Cubist might have felt when working: most of the sections seem to be available, but not necessarily in the right order. The staff changed the music to something that neither of us knew but which we both really liked. We mentioned it at the same time. She did a very slight dancy move with her shoulders and she sent me to the bar to ask them what this music was and my spine tingled. I think we got drunk quite quickly. Some of the time we talked about families. She actually *was* from Bethnal Green. She claimed not to believe in horoscopes so we didn't do that. She had one sister, older, and one brother, younger, so she was the neglected middle child, she said, and laughed, again, but differently. She used to be a tomboy, she played more with her brother and his mates after school than with anybody else. There was a long guessing session: she was twenty-five, I was twenty-six. Her favourite colour was brown, but only in suede. She didn't live with her family now but she saw them, and she saw her sister quite a bit. When I asked her did she talk about boyfriends with her sister, she did a snort laugh like I was an idiot. Her sister worked as a photographer's assistant. I told her about Antonio then, but she hadn't heard of him. He's on the up, but he's not famous yet. I talked about Pancho. She didn't have a pet, because of there being no garden. She shared a flat with another girl called Bernie, on the top floor of a converted old school off Commercial Road. They rented. We talked about football. Natalie. A girl who knows about football.

She got into the football through one of the other girls at work. It was casual, but two of the other girls in her team were Finnish, she told me, from Finland, and one of them played for the national team when she was at university. Neither of us had been to university. Natalie had started out on a Saturday job up West and moved on like that. I told her about Alan, about how I'd worked with him once, and about how he and theBoys were dickheads. She gave me another quite hard look then, and said, What d'you mean, dickheads, why d'you hang round with them, then? I said they were all right, in their way, just that they were, y'know, standard, with your standard male attitudes and that it bored me the way they never considered how stereotyped their behaviour was, that they just did what they thought they were supposed to – tying each other to lamp-posts at stag parties and weekends and all that. Mmm, she replied, but she didn't sound all that convinced or look it. To avoid receiving any further looks of unconvincement, I changed the subject. I asked her about her football career. There hadn't been a girls' football team at her school, but she played anyway – at breaks, in the playground. When I told her how I'd admired her chipped goal the other night she lowered her eyes and said it was a bit of a fluke. She asked me if she bruised me at our first meeting. You could say that, yeah.

She really was beautiful.

We'd been in the bar long enough, and when we were outside we didn't want it to be the end yet. We didn't want to eat, or go to a club. The weather was okay, a bit chilly, that was all, like it sometimes is when it's getting on in January. Usually it's February that's really cold. We got a taxi to take us to Hyde Park. We both laughed at the idea, we must have felt like we were tourists or something. Moving up Park Lane at night in the cab with the hotels lit up, I suddenly felt like I was somewhere else, I think we both felt the same; we went quiet together, anyway. You know that sensation you get when you've been up all night and you float out of yourself in the morning? I think we felt like that. We asked the driver to pull up at Lancaster Gate. We shared the fare and walked down the road towards the Serpentine, occasionally brushing shoulder/forearms accidentally-on-purpose.

We sat on a bench opposite the Lido. She pulled a thin silver tin from her jacket pocket and commenced joint-rolling.

Natalie! I said, shocked. I thought smoking was bad for you, I said, emulating her low exaggerated coughing-noise noise.

Winger, she replied, this is grass.

The information was delivered with a matter-of-fact certainty that dissuaded me from any follow-up. I was of course delighted to see the weed, although it doesn't suit me. It seemed the appropriate thing right then in the cushioned relative silence of the park with the moon glinting off the water. While she rolled I told her about how I'd come across a film crew a few nights ago, shooting some film, in a street round the back of Antonio's place. I'd been standing at the bedroom window, drawn by a blue light lighting up the air, just out of touching distance. It wasn't a natural light, so I walked out to see what it was. There were people and equipment and vans all over the place. Everybody had a clipboard. Everybody had a puffa jacket. I sat on a wall watching. I watched the lighting guys, who were the busiest and who were wearing heavily over-specified combats. They were moving hoisted halogen rigs on telescopic poles. They'd taped sheets of blue plastic film over the bulbs, that was how the blue light was made. Everybody's face was the wrong colour. Everybody's puffa jacket was the wrong colour (everybody's combats were the wrong colour in the first place, so you couldn't really tell what was happening there, colourwise). I turned to Natalie. I watched her tongue as it stroked the glued edge. I paused.

I never think about that when I see a film, she said. Y'know, that it's not the real colour.

After a half-second think she added, That it's not the real colour of life, just the colour of a film, and she laughed low, like this was a funny thought.

She finished making the joint and I offered the light, leaning to her with the match cupped in the shielding hand which she touched very lightly as the sulphur flared.

'What was the film about?' This through the first exhalation.

'I don't know. I didn't ask.'

'Weren't you interested?'

'Not really. I was interested in watching the, y'know,

mechanics of it. I stayed for a while, an hour or so.'

She passed the joint, smelling very sweet.

'Were there any stars?'

'I think it was cloudy.'

'No. Stars.'

'Oh, *stars*. Yeah.'

'Who?'

'Brad Pitt, Julia Roberts, the usual. Marlon Brando came and sat on the wall beside me.'

I passed the joint back.

'Do you tell a lot of lies, Winger?'

'No.'

'People do, don't they?'

'I don't know. Do they?'

'Yeah.'

'Is this in business, d'you mean?'

She exhaled. In bizniss, it's bad, but it happens plenty in real life too, she said.

Why d'you think they do it, I asked.

'It's for lots of reasons, isn't it, but mostly it's just because they're dishonest lying bastards. Men that is. Women at least usually lie for a reason, men just do it because they think it's normal. I mean. Truth . . . I don't know.'

She semi-shook her head. The joint had come back to me, and I hung my arm over the edge of the bench letting it burn. If she was going to have a conversation like this, I wanted to retain the ability to try to follow it.

'Did you lie to your boyfriend about where you are now?'

Not really, she said. I'm often out with Sam on a Thursday.

'Sam?' [Who the fuck's that? Another rival as well as Spurs?]

'My sis. Remember?'

'Did you tell me her name already?'

'Yes. Weren't you listening?'

'I was hanging on your every word, but er . . . you've got . . . er . . . beau . . . er . . .'

'Yes?'

'I might have just been looking at your eyes for a second exactly when you told me. They're very . . . Blue.'

'Mmm. I had noticed.'

'Well, you see them every day, don't you? In the mirror.'

'No. I noticed you looking at me like that.' [Really? I thought I was disguising it perfectly]

'Oh, well . . .'

'S'alright . . .'

'Well . . .'

'No, s'alright, it really is. Alright. Really . . .'

She leaned in to me. She rested her head on my shoulder. She tilted her face towards mine. She closed her blue eyes a quarter of a microsecond before I closed mine. There's no proper descriptive word that you can use to describe that kiss.

It was long.

Afterwards, in order to not quite acknowledge anything, I said, I'm not sure about these trousers I'm wearing. D'you think they're okay? (It was the grass. I'm hopeless on it, I'd *never* normally say a thing like that.)

'They might look better off.'

'Yeah, you're right, trousers, most of them'd look better off.'

'I'm wearing a skirt, Winger.'

'Oh, I didn't mean . . .'

I leaned my head back and looked at the sky. I was missing a sitter here and I knew it – a clear opportunity to talk about skirts coming off – but I was more concerned that she hadn't understood about me. That it had passed like an almost normal remark. We finished the joint in silence and then we kissed again.

After this kiss I said, Do you have to go to work in the morning?

'Well, sort of. The hours are flexi.'

'Flexitime. That's like the film not being the real colour of life, isn't it?'

'Y'what?'

'Like you could stretch time, make it longer than it really is.' The weed was kicking in properly for me now.

She rested right against me, she let her body-weight relax, and she put her arms around my chest, so that her fingers linked on my shoulder in a way that was sudden. The weed was kicking in for her too.

I nuzzled my face against her hair and traced her neck with the back of my hand.

It seems to happen when you fly, she said. When it's two hours later than it should be when you get there.

'That's more like losing it all together, isn't it?'

I suppose you pick it up on the way back, she said.

The rest of the night's conversation was like this. We shared the desire to talk in a stoned and semi-drunk way about absolutely nothing, about stuff we both sometimes thought about but never talked about with anyone else. About stuff that possibly wasn't even worth talking about anyway. We stayed on that bench for hours. Even a tramp bothered not to bother us. We watched the sun come up slow and red to our left. A gleaming round bald man emerged from nowhere to put in his early morning swim in the Lido. Watching him made us shiver and we held each other even closer. When the traffic began to start sounding like bona fide daytime noise, we had to admit that the night had ended. Our legs were creaky and we felt stiff as we walked towards Alexandra Gate, our arms around each other. She was wearing my jacket as well as hers by then to keep her warm in the cold morning. She was about to give it back as we looked for the cab. No, keep it, I said. I wanted her to have something of me.

When will I see you again? I asked.

When will we share precious moments? she replied.

We kissed and I said I was hungry – what about dinner tonight? She did hesitate a second, but the Spurs supporter was off on a boys' night out, and her eyes shone and she said okay. My eyes probably shone too.

When I said Shall I come to yours? she said, Yeah, what time?

When I said 8.00? she said, Half-past'd be better.

As a taxi pulled up I opened the door and she climbed on to the seat and turned round. She glanced down, nodded at my lower quarters and said, Actually, they're not a brilliant fit round the backside.

I watched the cab disappear and turned to walk west, feeling like you feel when you've been up all night and you float out of yourself in the morning. She was right about the trousers of course, but for once I almost didn't care. Almost.

4

At the newsagent's two corners further down from Mr Wellstocked's Modern Stores I pick up the Marlboros, the papers (local and national) and a pint of regular milk. It's minus the charm, the newsagent's two corners further down from Mr Wellstocked's Modern Stores, but a lot better stocked. Back at 42, I double-unlock the door, which means I'm locking it, for fuck's sake, because when I came back to get the Snowboard Puffa, I forgot to double-lock it. There's been a mail drop. Nothing horrible in a brown envelope from debt collectors or debt collectors' agents or debt collectors' debt collectors' agents, or any sub-agents operating on behalf of the aforementioned; just one postcard. Not bad. Good, even. Antonio writes from Venezuela, in his green pen:

Gringo –
Que pasa – Locked yourself out? Did you have to break in to read this? First day here (weather's lovely). Things are gonna run over – might be back a week or so later than planned – call me International Roaming. Check the e-mail (yeah right, I know you won't). Look after Pancho. And give him Kisses. How'd the Gunners get on?
Ant. X
PS All well with the passion grandissimo? All top biscuit?

You get a lot of hopeless stuff. He's living in a tent or something; he's given me five questions to which I'm unable to reply. International Roaming never works (e-mail's another planet, and anyway, the computer makes me sneeze). I've only locked myself out three times, *actually*. I'd like to stay on and look after Pancho, but I'm not sure I can. One–nil. I'm not up for giving an answer to the PS. There's a picture of an old washing machine on the front, from the 50s, and a slogan in Spanish (I think) which seems to mean: Labour Saving Device = Too Hip. I get busy with the tin-opener, which is rubbish, one of those you have to keep puncturing the lid with, the kind that won't roll round the rim properly; you have to finish the thing off with a fork. A new tin-opener would probably cost about 50p. It'd pay for itself with what you save on plasters and losing your cake in the first week.

'We should get a new tin-opener, Pancho. What d'you reckon?'

He's standing on his back legs wearing the huge expectant look. Here y'go. A kiss from your dad, and a brown-flecked plate of Liver and Heart from Mr Wellstocked.

This is the right way round to do it. Kissing a cat immediately after it's eaten isn't nice. Or possible.

It took me a while to work out how to work the ansaphone machine, but I got it in the end. You just press the button at the far left. Really. That's all you need to do. I hope it's not the police. Who I hope it'll be every time is Natalie, of course, but it never is. She didn't leave many messages, but the ones she did were good. Her voice bounced along like a song, and could switch to Formal Romantic for the sign-off: Love, in a breathy echo, which was kind of ironic and nice at the same time. Antonio heard the first message she left (I was out). He knew about her by then, it was after the second date. I use 42 as my official ansaphone address as well as my official postal address even when I'm not staying here, which almost never isn't the case. I rent a bedsit in Kensal Rise. I avoid it like the plague.

When I phoned in he played the message back down the line at full volume (not very loud) while making violin noises in the background.

She sounds alright, he said. Has she got a mate?

Yeah, I replied. She's got two five-a-side-fuls to start with, hasn't she? But you've got a girlfriend of your own, haven't you?

I'm only asking, he said.

I was calling from a telephone outside a Moss Bros, I was checking whether he needed a pair of those cheap cotton cuff-links. I was getting DJed for some photography dinner he'd got me a ticket for that night. I always cut these things fine, formalwear fittings are tense times for me, though formalwear itself isn't as dreadful an idea as it seems at first glance. I mean, it's almost impossible to look outstandingly bad in black and white. And there'll always be someone there whose trousers are a considerably worse fit than your own by a mile.

Anyway, it's Alan on Playback. He's got this to say:

Jenny says she wants to know if you'd like to come over for supper tonight. God knows why. He can look after himself, I said. She said you can bring a dessert. Call me at work, after 5. Bye.

He always hedges the generous offer with a rider, Alan. They're boring as hell their suppers anyway. (I don't know why they call dinner supper.) There's always some other Shirt there with his thin-lip girl, him talking about Investments – Net Opportunities in which we could all Fill Our Boots if we only get in there quick, and, of course, the old old old old old old favourite, Property Prices – thin-lip gazing at Shirt like he spends his days conquering Everest or something. That's how it was last time when I went over, only last Friday actually. At the peak of boredom, I usually drop in a question to piss everybody off in the style of: Have you been to see the X Retrospective at the ICA? It can throw them, but it's only a microsecond before they're Back On Track. Painting-by-numbers is their thing. They know about the last big cheque that was paid for a canvas at Sotheby's, the World Record price for a Picasso, and how many people attended the Blockbuster Monet. Extraordinary moneyspinner. Oh, and you get a couple of framed good-taste posters on the wall, to match the good-taste decor. All right, it's plusher than Kensal Rise, a lot plusher, but I still don't like it.

Jenny's okay in certain ways; she likes spending Alan's money, for instance. She spends a lot of it on Labour Saving Devices. She has a kitchen-arrangement that's very well equipped, but not for what you'd accurately call cooking. It's that thwack, clunk, ping thing as the food-material makes its way from freezer to plate via microwave. As soon as we've finished (it doesn't taste of anything, I'm sorry to say), the very nice china is racked carefully and the comforting shoosh thing begins. The dishwasher darling – so essential, I don't know where we'd be without it. I could do her an A1 blow-up of Antonio's postcard and present it nicely framed for her birthday. I like those photocopy blow-ups where you lose all the focus. Maybe that's what it is I don't like about the decor thing down there – it's too sharp, not scuzzy enough. I don't know. Kensal Rise is scuzzy enough all right – but that doesn't work for me either. I don't know.

Jenny initiates conversations over the (and I don't understand why they buy this) Ecologically Sound coffee (I mean it doesn't taste very good, I mean you can buy much better, and it doesn't suit their kitchen). Jenny-initiated conversations are most usually of the type in which she gets on my case. It's good of her to bother, I know that, but I can't say it gives me pleasure. Last time:

'Did you speak to Lindsay then?'

'Yes.'

'And?'

'I arranged to see him next week.'

'Well, you should. It's an excellent opportunity. He's a great friend of James you know – super guy.'

James is one of theBoys. Anyone who knows anyone else in their circle is a greatFriend and each of them one by one is a superGuy.

'Right.'

'You should mention James. At the interview.'

'Mmm. Sure. I will.'

Actually, I didn't speak to Lindsay. Lindsay owns a Wine Merchant's (not an off-licence), and Jenny's trying to get me fixed up there, as an assistant manager (not a trainee). She says there's a future in the Wine Trade, that it's a growth area. I thought it'd always been all right, that drinking wine had always been popular. No, she said when I mentioned this. Wine is really opening up as an investment area now.

Ah, I see.

I had a go at imagining standing behind the counter all day, doing nothing for hours on end, sometimes selling a bottle of licoricey Burgundy at a price that exceeded my weekly income by a factor of fifty-five, and decided I couldn't be bothered.

And Tissy got in touch with you? she pressed on, the question in her voice unnecessary as she knew Tissy had. She slipped out of shoes which had bracelets across them, tucking her feet to the side.

'Yes.'

'And?'

'Well, I went down there, and I had a sort of chat. She was a bit busy, on the phone a lot. Then we went out and did a job somewhere in Clapham.'

And how did you get on, she asked, tucking her legs even tighter under herself.

'Kind of okay . . . It might not be just dead right for me, Jenny.'

'Well it won't be all excitement at first, will it? You'll have to bear with until . . .'

She means well (probably), but she was looking at me a bit like my Great Auntie used to if she discovered I hadn't been to Sunday School. She wears clothes of the type Princess Di made popular during her awkward pre-personality period. It's a style that's always been about, isn't it? Rosie met her once, at a birthday party in a canteen bar. After we'd done the pleasantries and Jenny'd moved on, Rosie whispered her first impression: She's the kind of woman who irons her knickers. I've pressed boxer shorts myself, in my boxer-shorts days, but I knew what she meant.

Tissy was a friend of a friend of Jenny's. One of those women who are In Control. She chainsmoked Gitanes so she had very nicotined teeth and very unruly hair and builder's hands but she was still quite handsome in a terrifying way. She wore those bizarre cavalry-twill pants which women like that sometimes wear. She looked less than bothered about perfectly laundered underwear, though, I could say that for her. I guessed she was about forty. She'd got a fairly big small workshop full of slaves who adored her down in Streatham. It took me an hour and a half to drive there; bad news for a four-mile run. The slaves had fabric spread out all over the place; on wide square trestle tables, over the floor, hanging on the wall – on every available surface. The fabric was being converted into curtains, deluxe deluxe curtains – interlined, crosslined, backlined, the works. Hideous patterns. I didn't mention it.

They slid or glid, however it is that you describe the movement of curtains, on super-expensive track. The track came in a variety of finishes (pewter, chrome, brass, gold – none of the normal white plastic), and there were any number of ways of making the curtains open and close – motorized, computerized, remote controlled, et cetera. The proposal was that I could become one of Tissy's freelance-

Boys, a fitter of these curtains on-site. Apparently there was very good money in it. On-site meant in terraces in Clapham and Wandsworth, and sometimes in Kensington and Chelsea. And if it all went according to the masterPlan, eventually in Belgravia and Mayfair. I was meant to look impressed by this. We drove to the address where my experimental hang was to take place. Tissy's driving was mad-neurotic, she called everyone who crossed her a fuckingPrat, and she called many people who didn't cross her a fuckingPrat too. The car was an estate, very distressed. In between swearing she banged on in a way she may have thought of as conversational about government schemes which meant certain tax breaks were available to make employing the slaves virtually cost-free. It wasn't the sort of talk I liked, it was dull, and it was in the wrong money-per-hour region for my taste. I was intending charging for my services. I was intending to Top-Her-Up-Heavy. (I sometimes think in theBoysSpeak, despite myself, though I don't talk in it, not if I can help it, anyway.) I had a pair of aluminium steps and a tool kit. I was my own man, well equipped. I was an independent. Freelance.

We pulled up in one of those tree-lined side-streets. She had a jailer's bunch of keys which were the source of a lot more swearing before she found the three which got us in. We surveyed the site, took some measurements and I set about fixing the track in the downstairs front bay window. The view through the window was of houses the same as the one we were in framed by the trees. City trees are better at lining roads than framing houses. Tissy kept giving me advice about how to do things, which was a pain because it wasn't complicated. Except . . . you know how the wall's always rotten above the window? Well, this one was no different. I hated the house, it had brass dimmer switches. It was nothing like my Great Auntie's used to be but it had a similar smell, it had the smell of old people, though young people must have lived there, you could tell by the CD titles on the sideboard. The sideboard itself, in old dark wood, made me think that they'd be old young people. Anyway, after a fairly epic bout of swearing (mine) I got the thing up. Then I helped Tissy hook the curtains, which were surprisingly heavy with all that inter, cross and back lining. I stepped away to admire them. They were yellow and green and featured a filthy floral pattern. I had another looking-impressed struggle. I watched a while as Tissy 'dressed the curtains', which certainly was a new one on me – she spent half an hour making the pleats just-so on each side. Meanwhile I fixed up the hooks for the tie-backs on the opposite side, and I fiddled about doing the fuckingPrat pelmet fucking thing. Tissy kept stepping out for a Gitane because these clients were fucking non-fucking-smoking fucking-Prats. On one of these fag breaks I had a look at the bill which she'd left on the sideboard. It came as news to discover that you could pay a decent four-figure sum for a pair of curtains. It came as distasteful news. I mean I didn't like it. I was wearing blue overalls, which were not too awful as a fit – quite loose all round, they were consistent like that, I didn't mind them that much. They were a heavy cotton variety of sub-denim material. I bought them specially for the job, from a surplus shop just off the Mile End Road. They had a long thin narrow pocket on the outside of the right leg; I guess tradesmen would use it for keeping a folding metal rule in or some decorating scissors. Seeing that bill – I don't know how this came about really – but the way it made me feel, I was impelled to do something about it. Which turned out to be something stupid. Which was that I stole a letter-knife from the sideboard – the first kind of semi-valuable object that came to hand. I dropped it into the special pocket. A very strange act. Not like me. It was the first time I'd ever ever stolen anything. It was a week and two days ago, this. A Wednesday? Is that right?

Pancho watches me as I count on my fingers. Half-point-four times round. Nine days, yeah, that's right. The Eskimo mask was the second thing I stole. Yesterday. I can't go to supper tonight, and not just because the letter-knife story might've broken. I've got other things to do.

We sat in silence while Jenny topped the coffee and stirred the sugar crystals and drizzled the cream. If Alan wants a cigarette he has to go out the back, and it's the same for me.

So how did you leave it with her then, she asked.

I sipped the coffee. 'I left my number.'

'She'll be in touch?'

I sipped the coffee. 'I guess.'

She'd had enough of this and changed tack. I expected it: 'And how's it going with Natalie?'

I didn't want to say anything at all about anything, but Jenny played with her ear which meant she was going to pursue it.

I stopped sipping the coffee. 'Not to plan.'

I joined Alan out the back.

Actually Tissy won't be in touch, because it was a made-up number I left her with, not the real one. It's absolutely possible she's been in touch with Jenny though by now, she's got Jenny's proper number all right. I can just hear it – Listen, darling, that boy you sent, has he any previous form . . .? I couldn't detect anything in Alan's voice on Playback, and there wasn't any hint of anything last night at the snooker, though thinking he *might've* heard something was making me extra-edgy and making my snooker even worse. So if she does know, she can't have mentioned it to him.

'Innocent until proved guilty, eh, Pancho?'

He's moved over to his basket, arranging himself in his favourite head-lolling-over-the-side-pre-1st-slumber-of-the-day dribbling spot. A post-coital sort of position. Food's the only thing cats really love, isn't it?

After the firstDate all-nighter in the park, I had a slumber myself. I walked all the way back to Antonio's and I smoked a few more cigarettes and then I just crashed out. I had a wake-up call arranged with the operator (you can't rely on alarm clocks alone) for well before half-eight. For 3.30 p.m. to be accurate. Because I knew I'd got another problem coming. Viz:

The difficult secondDate trouser decision.
Which is understating it somewhat.

Antonio's mirror in the bedroom is squeezed between a chest of drawers and the laundry basket. It's a mirror like those like you get in fairly upmarket small multiples. It's full-length and tilts near the base. It sits on hefty feet. For getting a really good look at yourself it's more or less perfect. Which is a bad thing if you suffer from the problems I do. Sometimes I think my legs are too short, other times I think they're too long. There's something definitely not right anyway, that's for sure, and footwear doesn't help. After I'd woken and showered, put on some music and the TV (children's programmes, I won't watch afternoon telly – that's one of my signifiers for knowing I'm dead), I lay back down on the bed wrapped tight in two towels, doing what my stepdad used to call his perspirations. You can make the shower run very hot in here, if you make it run quite slow. I could see myself in the mirror and we had a serious conversation:

Right, the absolute non-starters for the secondDate are as follows: anything remotely summery (let's at least get the season right), those cord-pulls from two years ago (they should be at Oxfam by now), those cords actual from two years ago (they are at Oxfam now), any cords at all (I have funny turns in trouser shops sometimes), those exquisite charcoal-grey Industrias I blew £200 quid on (they were never even anywhere near a fit, though they *are* made of a very exclusive wool blend), all the black ones (I wore black last night), the white pair (I have no recollection of buying them, I discard them), all the checked ones (I have funny turns in trouser shops sometimes); any that are too tight round the balls, that are too short, that don't have big enough pockets or have pockets that are too big or the wrong colour. Any with turn-ups. All the cargo pants. All those featuring flare zips. All those with dye problems.

I tallied these as I went along, counting on my fingers. I went right round one-and-a-half-point-four times. That was nineteen pairs.

Any that are out of date. Half-point-two of a time. Another seven pairs.

Good. The editing was going well.

[And don't forget, son – you're looking for something that's any improvement on a not-brilliant fit on your backside]

Three hours later, the bedroom the usual scene of devastation, I was double-locking the front door wearing one of Antonio's suits.

5

On wearing other people's clothes: They're always a better fit than your own. The grass is greener on the other side, et cetera.

I stood at the far side of the green waiting for a bus. I read a graffiti poem someone had done in black marker on the perspex over the advertising.

Somewhere between the pale
And beyond it
Somewhere between the moon
And over it
Somewhere between the shit
And the fan
I am.
DMH 99

I liked it that it was signed. The signature was tagged, graffiti-style. It was also dedicated: to the Dutch girl. Not a bad poem. I copied it down around the edges of my newspaper, wondering about the Dutch girl, trying to picture Dutch girls. Vermeer's one, the Girl with the Pearl Earring, was the only one I could think of.

6

I arrived at the block off Commercial Road at 8.25. Early: not good style, Marlboro Man. I walked round the block until 8.35, then I reapproached the intercom and this time I pressed the button. A female voice which wasn't Natalie's answered.

'Hello.'

'Er, is Natalie there?'

'She's going to be a little late back from work. Is that Winger?'

'Yeah.' I was known. That *was* cool with me.

'I'm to allow you up.'

Provided your host has the decency to open their own front door, then their unique flat-smell leads you the right way. This was the last one at the top anyway, so it was easy. The door which was half-open was numbered 24 in brass. The meaning of life in reverse (if 42's right in the first place). The space inside was open-plan with roof lights, and an arched end-window which looked out in the direction of the river. This window was a backdrop to the kitchen, which was separated off by the worktop pier. Bernie (I supposed) was standing behind it, semi-turned to the fridge. She straightened to face me head on, holding out a cold bottle.

'She said I was to offer you a drink. Beer?'

'Thanks. You're very obedient.' (I've got better confidence-façade opening-lines with people I don't fall in love with at first sight.)

'Only if I care to be. Shall we sit down?'

She led me to the seating area. She was lean, so she seemed tall, even though we were probably the same height. There were two ethnic-pattern sofas split by a coffee-table in rough wood. It was fairly plush. Bernie sat on one sofa and I sat opposite. The obvious arrangement. You don't sit beside your new girlfriend's [?] flatmate the first time you meet her when your new girlfriend isn't there. Definitely not. I didn't need Rosie to tell me that.

'Bernie? Isn't it?'

'I'm sorry. I should've said.'

She leaned across and we shook hands. She had red bright hair, cut into a sharp bob. Her skin was milky, not like skimmed or full-fat, like semi-skimmed. She was wearing a too-big jumper over ski-pants, one of those casual at-home outfits that girls have.

'Did she say how late she'd be?'

'She said as soon as she could. Probably about another half-hour. It's the time difference, she's waiting for some faxes of some samples from –'

She was shaking her head like she couldn't quite remember where the samples were coming from. It sounded thoroughly plausible, but the irrational feeling that Natalie had to see the Spurs supporter for half an hour somewhere infiltrated my mind. It was a stupid thought, not one that I'd normally have. It was a jealous thought in fact. Uncool.

'– she arrived at work rather late, I believe, because she was out rather late last night, I believe.'

Her delivery was nice. Completely flat.

'Oh. Did she say where she'd been or anything?'

'I don't believe I can remember any more about it. I think she had a nice time, the way she sounded.'

It was very good of her to say that. It was a way of being friendly. Girls have lots of stipulations about passing any information under this sort of circumstance. Rosie'd told me; and I knew anyway.

The walls of the flat were stripped back to the basics. I held the beer cold in my hands, and I started marking hexagonal shapes through the brick courses beyond Bernie, over her shoulder. Just visually, in an abstract way, in my head. It's something I do if I'm feeling like I'm being interviewed or assessed, trace the nearest pattern. It was our relative positions that made me feel this way, and not just the physical stationing. Her knowledge of lots of things about Natalie, and my lack of same.

Do you play football, I asked.

'Never much cared for it. I believe you're not bad yourself, albeit a little clumsy.'

Some details of what she'd heard would be allowed through, then. Well well.

I've got a natural left foot, I said. It's a sort of mixed blessing. Do you play any other sport?

'I run. Do you call that playing?'

'I call it torture. I do it to myself sometimes as a punishment.'

'For what?'

'Excess drinking. Et cetera.'

'Mmm. I do my thinking when I run. One transcends the pain in that way.'

Did she mishear me, think I'd said excess thinking? There was something about her use of language, the code she was in. It sounded genuine enough and I didn't mind it. 'One' – it's the most removed way of saying 'I', isn't it?

What do you think about when you run, I asked.

'Who I'm running from. HaHa. Sometimes.'

She drew her knees up and pulled the jumper over them. She passed her hands through her hair. Are those your running shoes, I asked. I nodded at her foot. She was wearing trainers which were like Adidas but weren't, they were like cheap market-stall copies. No socks. She'd crossed one leg over the other under the jumper – the Adidas copy was bouncing lightly up and down. It looked an uncomfortable position. I wondered if she did yoga or something.

'No. Though these are my fast shoes.'

'How d'ya mean, fast shoes?'

'I feel when I'm wearing them that it's possible to make a

quick escape. If necessary. I wear them most of the time. HaHa.'

Second funny laugh. I hoped I wasn't unnerving her. [I wasn't]

'Does that mean you have slow shoes too?'

'No. Listen, Winger, I don't mean to be rude, but I need to shower. Help yourself from the fridge if you want more to drink. Put some music on. Okay?'

Sure, I said.

She stood up and stretched.

Are you going out then, I asked.

'Yes. I'm meeting some friends for supper.'

'Supper?'

'Yes.'

'Where?' [I was checking how empty it was going to be in here tonight. *So* obvious]

'Islington.'

She was half-way across the floor. She stopped and turned.

'Any more questions?'

'No.' [She knows I've asked the *so* obvious question. Idiot]

'I'm going for supper in Islington. First I'm having a shower.'

Yeah, I've got it, I said.

Bit sharp, her tone, but my fault – provoked by me. I might've gone in for a similar line if it was all the other way round, I might let the intruder know that I'd got them sussed. It was fair enough for her to call this meal supper. I worked the times out, thinking it'd be 10 minimum before she got there. That was giving her half an hour for her shower and her après shower, half an hour travelling time and a half-hour drink before. 10 would be the earliest. And she could easily be a more-than-half-hour-and-après shower girl.

She turned again just before disappearing to the bathroom and said, By the way, nice suit.

Ah, Nice cop / nasty cop routine. Though her remark was aimed clean at the right spot, she wasn't my type and I wasn't hers. We could tell. I wasn't going to be doing an instantly-completely thing twice in a week. Thank God. And anyway – the suit was Antonio's, so it really wasn't my compliment to take. Actually, I'd got my newspaper sticking out the pocket. What sort of behaviour is that?

On wearing other people's clothes 2: It's like driving a hire car. Your normal rules are subject to change and revision. I wouldn't be buggering up the lines on a suit of my own. If I had one.

Why I haven't got a suit of my own: Trouser crisis, squared to the power of n.

I removed the newspaper and left it on the coffee table. I'm un-brilliant at working someone else's CD; but after several long minutes of gentle under-my-breath swearing, while simultaneously making a million personal and cultural assessments based on the available selection available, I got it going. Somebody who lived here knew their soul. I chose Aretha.

The moment I wake up before I put on my make-up . . .

' . . . I say a little prayer for you.'

Natalie was standing at the top of the two stairs, the two stairs that dropped down to where I was standing holding the CD case, trying to get the little booklet out of the front flap, which I can never do, I think it's impossible. I stopped in the futile attempt straight off.

Hey, I said. I didn't know you sang.

'Lots you don't know, Winger.' And she moved over to me and put her arms around my shoulders and kissed me short and hard and fierce.

Did you have a good day, I asked.

'Lovely, thank you, darling. Bit tired. You?'

'Fine. Did you get any sleep?'

'Couple of hours. Went in at lunchtime. Bernie bin looking after you?'

I was beginning to work out the way she spoke. Mostly she straightened her accent out and just occasionally deliberately dropped something like 'bin' in. Like when she did the line, 'I thought I never seen you till recently' on the first-Date, which I did notice. I didn't think it was like she was camping it or anything when this happened; I thought it was like she was keeping in touch with something. Because although she fitted this environment, style-wise, and although it was close to where she'd been brought up, location-wise, she'd made some sort of social move. Maybe her intonation was like her anchor. Maybe it was that.

'What?' [Forgotten the question]

'Bernie? Bin looking after you?'

'Mmm. She gave me a beer. Would you like one?'

'Are you offering me one of my beers?'

'Sure.'

'Well thank you, I don't mind if I do.'

D'you work late often, I asked.

'Mmm.' She took a slug and I watched her neck as she swallowed. She placed the bottle on the fridge and I watched the pulse in her wrist.

'Listen, I'm gonna shower and change. See ya in a minute.'

'Bernie's in the shower.'

'I know.'

Of course. Debriefing number one. It's cool with me.

They emerged together half an hour later (quick, almost speedy), dressed and perfumed and delegation-like.

We've got a fiver on the suit, Natalie said. My money's on Kenzo, she continued. Whereas I believe it's a DKNY, said Bernie.

'It's an Antonio.'

That's not true, they said together.

They made me show them the label. Natalie pocketed the winnings. Excellent. An illustration of her authority vis-à-vis her work. And cool for me that she could think she'd put some money on a winner.

The three of us left together. They lowered the lights so the flat was lit like the fall before stage-up. We waited on the pavement with Bernie until her taxi, and when it arrived she and Natalie kissed goodbye. Bernie shook my hand saying, It was nice to meet you, and I said, You too. Natalie linked my arm and guided me into the back streets.

I'll show you a pub I know, she said.

'Okay.'

But first we kissed long, leaning against the wall, and as we separated we looked into each other's eyes for a time. We started walking.

'What does she do, Bernie?' Though I dislike the question myself, it doesn't mean it's one I'm unwilling to ask of other people.

'Craft. She's got a studio.'

'What d'you mean, craft?'

'She's freelance.'

'Ha. [Touché] Does she make a lot of money?'

'Why?'

'Just wondered. I mean, well, d'you make a lot of money? Nice flat sort of thing.'

'I do all right. The flat's pretty expensive. I told you I knew Bernie at school – she could've been sent private really. Her dad's rich. But y'know, 60s and that – against their principles. I don't pay the full bundle. It's a nice squeeze.'

'What's that mean?

'What?'

'Nice squeeze.'

'Bit O luck.'

'Ah.'

'Do *you* make a lot of money, Winger?'

'Are Spurs playing at home tomorrow?' [I knew the answer to this]

'No way. You're not answering a question with a question.'

'Not bundles.'

'Enough?'

'I can buy you a drink if that's what you mean.'

We were at the entrance doors. The Green Man.

Wide-boys, locals, builders still in their overalls, old people, very old people, and pre-clubbers; it was a catholic mix inside The Green Man. There were a few Suits too (not me, it's a completely different kind of suit). Natalie knew one of the girls who worked behind the bar by name, and a couple of the old people from the other side called Hello Love as we ordered, asked how her mum was, said to send her their best. I followed Nat's lead on how to behave. We were evidently together. I mean we'd entered together. The version of together body language we were doing was 'but it could be business'. We sat in a corner, side by side, tucked in snug beneath a framed print of Bobby Moore being held aloft with the World Cup. Très retro, but not, if you know what I mean. Appropriate.

So.

This is something, she said. Haven't been on a second-Date for ages. Spurs are away tomorrow, but you know that already, don't you?

'What?'

'You'll've checked. I'll be disappointed in you if you haven't.'

Aston Villa, I said.

'Exactly.'

We touched glasses. Pints.

Last night, she said. I really liked it.

'Mmm. You could say that for me too. [Squared to the

power of whatever it is that's more than n]

We lit cigarettes, even though she'd said she didn't hardly, her rate was on the up now. I thought it was a good sign.

Will you see anyone from work in here, I asked.

'Doubt it. No. Why?'

'Well, you know, me being with you, Spurs and all that. What's his name anyway?'

'You don't need to know.'

[That was true] What about these other people? I nodded around.

'What d'you mean?'

'I mean you're semi-famous in here. A celebrity, almost.'

'They wouldn't be into the private lives of semi-famous celebs, this lot.'

I glanced up to see how many of this lot weren't into the private life of a semi-famous celeb. Enough of them were.

'D'ya tell a lot of lies, Natalie?'

'That wasn't a lie. Chill out. Another drink?'

She went to the bar. We weren't going to be at peak match fitness for Monday's football, that was for sure. I don't know why I was being edgy, apart from not being on my own ground and being in love. Love, that makes you edgy, doesn't it?

She came back and we tucked in closer and our talk switched to clothes-talk, which was great for me, I could learn a lot while still being informed enough to contribute intelligently. Ideal, as Rosie would say. D'you know that some designer-wear women's trousers incorporate light-weight stretch lycra? (It'd never work for boys, that.) Or did you know there's a whole range of urban clothing called Directional Casualwear? Or that this season it's going to be a wool story? That's what the reps say, anyway, when they're trying to sell the range, It's going to be a wool story. It changes season by season; first it's a black story, next it's a white story, then it's a wool story. I loved it, listening to the clothes-talk. She told me how the job had been a bit of bother when she first started, dealing with nonces and ponces at trade shows and all that, everybody with attitude and angle and making out like they were your friend when really they just wanted something out of you. But things shook down, and it was a good outfit to work for and she dealt with people she liked as much as she could and the company looked after her. It all sounded pretty well sorted. She sounded pretty well sorted.

I don't know what happened to the time, because suddenly, after what seemed a very short stay, they were putting the towels up. And dinner, what happened to that?

Outside it had become a cold night. There was a van across the street on a corner, steam drifting from the funnel, 'Crêpes' written in a gilded arc over the serving hatch. Mmm, I said. D'you fancy a crêpe? I wonder how they're serving them.

'You know how to show a girl a good time.'

I looked at her. Eyes shining blue. It was okay.

There was no queue. One of the crêpemen was burly and one was slight.

What fillings are you doing? I asked through the hatch.

Whad'ya mean? It was the burly one who did the talking. I didn't think I'd asked a trick question.

'For the crêpes.'

'Whad'ya mean, crêpes?'

There was evidently some sort of something in operation here that I didn't understand. I tilted my head up to the sign – 'Crêpes, y'know, pancakes.'

The burly one looked to the thin one, who leaned out and twisted his neck to read. He twisted back in and said to the burly one, He means the writin'.

'Oh, that. Nah, mate. We just bought the van second 'and. It's burgers we're doin'. Oranotdog.'

I turned to ask Natalie whether she'd like a burger or

anotdog, but she was walking away, turning up her collar. I ran three steps to catch her. There was no point asking whether she wanted a burger or anotdog or not because there were tears of laughter rolling down her face.

Winger, she said as she recovered, that was good.

'How did you know it wouldn't be crêpes then?'

'I only live round here, mate.'

That was true. I glanced back. I'd made a terrible faux pas, I could see the burly one shaking his head and laughing with the people who'd turned up behind us to buy burgers or otdogs.

But are you hungry, I asked.

I could eat, she said.

'Do you have food at the flat? Are there ingredients there?'

'Basics n'that. Some.'

'Would it be okay for me to come back and cook?'

'Might be. Are you any good?'

'Well, it's always tricky when you're playing away, y'know, but . . .'

It took her under an eighth of a microsecond to cut in with: We'll *both* be playing away, Winger.

She'd be at home actually, but I knew what she meant.

7

I remove the mask from the Snowboard Puffa pocket, turning it in my hand, watching Pancho fall into sleep, purrsnoring gently. His head lolls over the basket edge in a way that looks thoroughly uncomfortable, his whiskers touch the floor. I read through the papers thinking the thought of going back to sleep. I used to lie in. I could keep my head down till lunchtime, easy. But I could never actually return to sleep. There was none of this fuckingPrat waking at 06:33 though, that was the difference. Right now, I feel like I could feel like sleeping for a whole day. But I won't. I've got other things to do. There's nothing in the papers about the mask, and the radio's still saying nothing either.

I'll ring Rosie.

'Hi, Rosie. Where are you?'

'I'm at work for goodness sake. Where d'ya think?'

Rosie works in a florist's. She's chief florist, or head florist, however they say it. We met at a wedding, she was doing the flowers. She's good.

'Call me back on the land line. It'll be cheaper.'

She worries about the condition of my finances. She's often out doing deliveries, not because she has to, but because she likes to. She's a sort of freelance, or at least she has a freelance's mentality anyway. The mobile *is* the obvious first call – she doesn't *have* to be in the shop, for goodness sake. Re-dial@Petals-Я-Us (it's not really called that – I don't think I should name the real place).

'Hello?'

'Hello, could I speak to Rosie please.'

'Very droll. Where've you been hiding?'

'Here and there. Listen, have you heard anything on the news about a stolen mask?'

'What?'

'A mask stolen from a museum.'

'What museum?'

'Can't say.'

'Can't say, eh? What's it to you then?'

'What's making that crinkling noise?'

'I'm wrapping, as you well know. What's with this slipperiness? Why d'you care about masktheft? What's up?'

'You haven't heard anything then?'

Are we going to have one of these kind of conversations, she says.

'What d'you mean?'

'One of the ones where you answer questions with questions until we get to the point.'

'Do we have a lot of conversations like that?'

'What do you think?'

'*You're* doing it now.'

Listen, she says. What's up? she says.

'Nothing.'

Nothing, she says. Just interested in masktheft all of a sudden, then, yeah?

'Sort of.'

'Sort of? Why?'

'So you haven't heard anything about it then?'

'Listen. I've got a bit of a rush on. I'll catch you later.'

'Can we do lunch?' [As theBoys' girls say]

'Do you think –'

'Rosie. I *have* to talk to you. Seriously.'

'Alright. Meet me here. One. Don't be late.'

She was going to say, Do you think I've got the time for lunch??? She always says that but she has got the time, if you get your interruption in early and it's serious. There's a posh crêpe place we go to, Astravoid, near the King's Road, where they definitely don't sell no burgers or otdogs.

8

When you're playing away in someone else's kitchen, the likeliest problem is going to be knives. I take my own knives to be sharpened about every nine months or so. The man (I think he's Czech, he wears the sort of trousers that haven't been washed for thirty years) who does the sharpening in an arch behind the market picks the least sharp, and, running his thumb down the blade, always says the same thing – Kerablinka! You could ride all the way to Catford on this one, my boy.

I get my knives sharpened. This is the point. Most people don't.

'What are your knives like?'

Natalie gave me a semi-blank look as we turned the corner. 'What?'

'Are they sharp? Just one sharp one would do.'

'Not sure. They're alright, I think.'

That told me all I needed to know. The knives would be blunt and probably sub-standard in the first place. I can't work with that sort of implement. I started to think of recipes you could do without needing a knife. Scrambled eggs avec toast?

'D'you think you'll have any smoked salmon at your place?'

'Nah.'

If you're going to do scrambled eggs for supper (it *is* supper after the pubs have shut), you've really got to go deluxe and serve it with smoked salmon. Smoked salmon is easily sliced with a blunt knife – do this just before you're ready to serve (you don't want the salmon getting cooked – that makes it nasty – you just want it slightly warm). Take the pan off the heat and stir the salmon gently in. The egg will finish cooking in the residual heat. You can add a little splash of Lea & Perrins, but it's completely unnecessary. It's really rather good, as they say, but a non-menu item ce soir sadly, madam.

I'm ahead of myself anyway. Will there be eggs at her place?

'Will there be eggs at your place?'

'Most probably have a few.'

Omelette? Doing an omelette's a nice move. Women respond to a man who can fry.

'D'you like omelette?'

'Nah. Makes me feel sick.'

[Fuck it]

What else? Pasta? Nah, pasta ain't sexy (boiled bread, very overrated). And anyway, this fridge doesn't sound like it's one that's going to contain fresh Parmesan. I could maybe do a basic Croque Monsieur.

'Got any ham?'

'Doubt it. Bernie's vegetarian. She does most of the food shopping.'

'There'll be cheese then?'

'Definitely.'

'How about bread?'

'Hmm? Might be Ryvita.'

Not even looking good for Welsh Rarebit – also not sexy (soggy, got beer in it, doesn't even taste that good) but as a last resort . . .

Natalie turns the key in the lock and I trace her fingers. The door opens with a creak and inside it's the same as it was, like the fall before stage-up. She sees to the music while I go through the cupboards. Not brilliant. Really not. A lot of useless stuff like silver cake boards and mini brioche moulds. Very bad knives indeed. Bread, when they've got it, must arrive sliced. I glance over as she lights a candle. Even though her face in the flaring wick is lit like Titian's Venus, or, to be absolutely accurate, that Vermeer's

Girl with a Pearl Earring, she could none the less be the sort of person who just hacks 'slices' off in lumps using a blunt knife and a two-handed lumberjack action.

Anyway. How about ingredients? Not promising. The fridge reveals two half-bottles of white wine, both stoppered with rubber corks (aesthetically unappealing), half a carton of low-fat substitute (aesthetically unappealing and not good for frying with), and dead salad and vegetable matter at the bottom (aesthetically très unappealing and not good for anything). There's one egg, one and a half pints of milk, many cheese remnants, and an unopened packet of TVP on the middle shelf. I refuse to recognize TVP as edible material.

Diana Ross starts singing, *Am I really hard to please, perhaps I have such special needs . . .* Unexpected, but nice.

Natalie joins in, sashaying over.

Do you eat out mostly then, I ask.

'Course. You were taking me for dinner tonight, remember?'

'Yeah. Sorry. Is there any flour?' [It's a long shot, this]

'Should be. Bernie sometimes buys pastry, and you have to have flour to roll it out with.'

Quite (as they say). There was a just-under-half small bag. Enough.

'How about a frying pan?'

The frying pan was beyond and behind a load of plastic supermarket carriers under the sink. Never been used as far as I could tell. Not ideal, but better than one that's absolutely warped and knackered.

'A whisk?'

She kissed me then like this was going to be fun. Bernie's mum had supplied a few things like whisks and all that. There was a potato masher, a fish steamer and a melon-baller. I've never seen anybody use a melon baller, except on TV.

'Is there anything we could mix stuff in?'

We tipped the fruit out of the fruit bowl. We were in business.

'What's it gonna be then, Winger?' She sat on the worktop pouring wine into very chic glasses, the drinking end round here considerably better provided for than the cooking end.

D'you fancy anotdog, I ask.

'Can you make otdogs out of that?'

I give her a quick sidelong, and I think she isn't joking. She has such Special Needs in Cookery Class anyway. Which couldn't be better. I can hardly fail to look the part whatever I do.

'Well, no. Not really, 'cos I'd kind of require sausages. And onions that make me cry when I cut them rather than when I look at them would be handy too.'

'What fillings have you got with your crêpes then?'

She hasn't worked it out by assessing the ingredients, don't think that. She definitely knows nothing about cooking. I'm not wrong about this. It's banter what she's good at, mate.

Even if there was an apron in sight I wouldn't wear it. But I do need to protect Antonio's suit-trousers.

I've already taken the jacket off and draped it over the sofa. Natalie hung it on a hanger. I liked that on two counts:

1] her instinctive professionalism,

2] the feeling of belonging I felt, not a usual feeling for me to feel.

Tea towels are normally found in a drawer near the sink and this kitchen complies. What I really want is a plain white glass cloth with blue double-embroidery tramlines down the long edges. But there isn't one. The best I can do is a Woolworths check. Could be worse. I could be wearing it on my head as third shepherd from the left in the nativity for a start.

On improvised chef-wear: Fold along the long edge to give a hem about one inch deep. Tuck it into the waistband of your trousers and it works pretty well as a wrap, provided your waistband is properly calibrated. You don't look too much of a fuckingPrat. You look as though you have intent. You look sharp. Almost.

The first pancake is guaranteed to not work, particularly in a new pan. I talked Natalie through this, explaining that it would happen.

'Why's that then?'

'It's kind of . . . a ritual thing with new pans, the first one makes the pan, well, sort of ready, y'know . . .' [I'm bluffing. I don't have a clue, I don't know what the real answer is]

I scraped the first pancake into the bin, loosened my shirt, heated the fat (premier cru extra virgin olive oil, which was to be found sitting on the marble top looking pretty and very much like a gift) to really hot and poured the batter direct from the fruit bowl into the pan (Bernie's mum had neglected to supply a ladle). I freed the edges with a fish slice (Bernie's mum had neglected to supply a spatula) and shook the pan till it loosened and I could skid it round the base. To toss or not to toss? That is the question.

'Can you toss?'

Natalie was still sitting beside me (in contravention of Health and Safety regulations) on the worktop. She'd kicked off her shoes and had her left leg stretched out horizontal like a springboard. She was leaning forward pulling gently on her toes with her hand, her chin low down to her knee, stretching her hamstring. She was wearing opaques. I didn't know if they were tights or hold-ups, though I was trying to see.

My thought was standard-issue-boy-competitive: If she's going to casually do a warm-up exercise like that, I'm going to have to do a toss. Very dangerous, but I'd got no choice.

It's all in the wrist action. It's a non-vintage toss, but it comes down flat and roundish and right-side-up, slightly lapping over one side of the pan, but that's okay, no one would notice, you can pretend it was deliberate.

'Winger – [ ]'

She says it just like that, slow and soft. You see, women *do* respond to a man who can fry. Tossing's a bonus feature.

I made four. We had them rolled with sugar and lemon. There were lemons on the coffee table where we'd emptied the fruit bowl. They're for G&Ts, really, she said. There wasn't a lemon squeezer, so I quartered them bluntly and squeezed the juice from the palm of my hand, which I would've done anyway. I know what's cool and sexy. And *that* is cool and sexy.

Half-way through eating, we begin feeding each other. I can't remember which of us starts it.

Her bedroom was minimal for a football fashion girl. No posters.

They weren't hold-ups. Good.

9

We wake to knocking on the door.

'Fuck.'

It's still dark, isn't it? Yes, it's still dark. It was too dark.

'Fuck.'

I know what she means. This could be Spurs.

Where are my trousers?

'Winger!!!'

Where the fuck are they?

Only one thing to do. I'll hide in Bernie's room. It's too dark there too. Fuck. There's a shape in the bed. Fuck. Bernie. Fuck. I never heard her come back. 'Nat said it'd be okay . . . shush,' is the best I'm going to be able to come up with. If she wakes. She looks like a sound sleeper. Like you can tell. I hope she is anyway because . . .

My trousers are on the bedroom floor.
I left them on the fucking floor.
I left them on the fucking floor in Natalie's room.

I mean I haven't got any trousers on.

Fuck. Unless Natalie's very fast or it isn't Spurs, there's going to be a lot of evidence lying about. However very fast Natalie is, she's bound to leave at least a sock out. At least. Fuck.

It's not cool with me, this.

It's uncool with me.

'S'alright, we don't get on.' She said that, didn't she? That was what she said.

Everybody needs physical warmth, I suppose. Is that why you keep going out with them, the people you don't get on with? It is, isn't it? Or the fear of being alone. Is that it? It is, isn't it? It must be. Is it? I don't know. I know something though. I know I don't need Darwin to tell me a territorial dispute is upon us. I know I'm on Spurs's manor. There'll be a fight. Probably. Definitely. But the thing is this: I didn't decide to fall in love with her, and I can't undecide it either. And another thing is this (just in case you're thinking): this isn't like anything else before. It isn't. It's not like ended-eight-and-a-half-months-ago-after-a-bad-Navarin-of-Lamb-episode. It's different.

It goes without saying that I'm carrying a hangover (of the upbeat variety – we'd taken the wine to bed with us), and that it's way too early for me. It always helps set off a train of thought, this combination: too early waking + hangover + an approaching boyfriend + me hiding in the room of someone I don't hardly know + me not having any trousers on, mate + me not having any other clothes on either. Mate.

It's the sort of hassle you don't need, as theBoys would say. Plenty more fanny about, they'd say.

That's where me and them differ.

Muffled sounds, and the front door closes gently. Is this a good or a bad sign? Nat pushes Bernie's door open, on to me, where I'm hiding behind it. She's whispering my name. It must've been a good sign. I lean out and she offers me her hand and draws me to the threshold. She's wearing a silk kimono-style gown and holds another one out to me.

'Who was it?'

'Plumber.'

What the fuck is a plumber doing here at this time on a Saturday? (Charging double, that's what, as if I didn't know. I've come across a couple of plumbers.)

'How'd he get to the door then? What about the intercom?'

'He's got a pass key.'

'Where is he? Has he gone?'

'Yeah. I sent 'im off.' [Bloody right, a red-card offence. Early bath]

'What did you say?'

'I said I wasn't up yet. He's coming back later. Sorry.'

'Sorry for what?'

'All this lark. Fuss n'that. We could do without it. Couldn't we?'

Well, yeah, maybe. But there's an implication in there to clear up right away:

'Didn't you like it? Last night?'

'It was lovely . . . I didn't mean . . . and the pancakes too . . . just . . . Dodgy moment. That's all.'

'And there's a We, is there?'

Her expression played the sweeper system, which can be hard to read. Don't ask me that, is what I reckoned it said. I carried through though, pushing round the back.

'I could just go, it'd be easier now than later – I mean in a few weeks or months or whatever – when it'll be worse. For us both. Probably. For me, for sure, anyway.'

'Entertaining and heartwarming though this is, for me, for sure, anyway, I'd prefer it if you both left now.'

Shit. She wakes up like a razor, that Bernie.

We backed out with grace and bowing and in the corridor we did the joint leaning-against-the-wall-semi-bent-over-muffled laugh of relief. We straightened up with the joint-heavy sigh.

'Shall I? Go?' [I don't mean this, I obviously don't mean this, obviously]

'I've got a better idea. It's a while before that plumber's back – we'll share an early bath.'

[Early bath] [!] [Shared]

Eyes shining blue as she said it. She could have thought for ever and not've come up with a better idea. Could I have been in any more love than this?

10

After breakfast and before the plumber returned to overcharge for fixing the thermostat, I left. I had to leave because we all had things to do, and I had to leave because it was a point where we had to leave each other anyway, I knew that. I walked towards the tube station, marvelling not only at the trousers but at everything else sartorially on display in the windows round and about. There's a lot of Asian wholesaler clothes outlets nearby and the gear they sell is totally wild, as they say. In one window they'd got a pair of multi-logoed gold combats with a zip-round-the-knee feature so you could take the bottom part off and wear what remained as shorts. Hellish. I studied them for ages (I never thought of buying them, don't think that). It was good weather for standing around studying things, one of those brilliant blue mornings when the sky was clean and sharp and a just-warm wind was blowing, like you were on a beach at the end of the day. It helped the de-hangover process. I was feeling better anyway after the bath, but I don't much like wearing the same suit in the morning as I wore the night before; of course, I hadn't been planning on staying over, so I hadn't taken an overnight bag or washbag or even a change of pants or anything at all.

I was sporting a new jewellery feature – one of Natalie's hair tie-backs, of the elasticated fat-band style – round my wrist. It was turquoise. It's not the sort of thing I normally do, adorn myself in this way. It made me feel most bohemian, not the sort of way I usually feel. I usually feel uptight. But I don't know, maybe bohemian is the logical extension of that. Maybe bohemianism is just uptightness disguised. Perhaps I *am* bohemian. It's more that I wouldn't dress like that, y'know. Hippy Strides are high on my list of atrocity, obviously; but maybe the reason that loon pants and flares are all the wrong shape, colour, pattern, and made out of the wrong material (thereby conveying the idea of general psychic looseness) is because they're really a cover for the wearer's uptightness. And maybe uptightness is simply bohemiansim waiting to happen. Could be. It's almost a theory, nearly.

I kept the hairband round my wrist, turning it like worry beads as I walked away from the hellish combats wondering about all this.

The Whitechapel Art Gallery, which was just down the road, was open. Inside they had an exhibition of small paintings that were done by a Belgian person under the influence of mescaline. In the free catalogue, the artist claimed that he wasn't really the drug-taking type, that he was more the water-drinking type, that it was fatigue that was his true drug of choice. I could relate to this, feeling as I did suddenly light-headed, so I sat down. The paintings were of the squiggly abstract variety, they were okay but there wasn't quite enough of something in them – colour, I think – to really detain me. A curator came in through the end doors and walked slowly across the floor with her assistant while they talked, loudly enough to hear, about arranging a lecture about the show. I've been to one of those, but I didn't like it. Art should speak for itself. The curator was fantastically beautiful (it's often the human exhibits I like best when I visit a gallery – only the Rothko room at the Tate doesn't comply, and that's *not* because the human exhibits aren't any good). Her hair was cut short shaggy chic and she was wearing very cool clothes; her trousers were 50s screen icon, wide all the way down, in a silk-mix. I had a conversation with Fisky, the person who cuts my hair at the Shovelhead Hair Salon about that sort of trouser not so long ago. Conversations about trousers with girls are the kinds of conversation I often initiate – the grass *must* be greener on the other side et cetera, except

I've discovered it isn't – that girls have a surprising range of gender-specific legwear problems of their own (a good fit on hips, but the waist too big is by far the commonest). Anyway, Fisky (she's one of those people who only have one name) told me she'd been wearing a pair of these 50s screen icons to a wedding herself, and that they do give certain specific problems: if you wear slingbacks with that sort of trouser, she said, then the hem can catch between your own sole, the sole of your foot that is, and the inner sole of the shoe, which more or less trips you up. It can be very embarrassing at a wedding, this, or anywhere, in fact. When I was speaking to Rosie about it on the phone a few days after the haircut – I hate people seeing me just after a haircut, when it's still got static in it, so I normally stay in, same as on a bad trouser day – she said that she had that problem too. What can you do about it, I asked. You can turn them up, she said. Get them out of the danger zone. What! I said. Like turn-ups!? (I couldn't *believe* she was suggesting this.) Yeah, you've got it, genius, she said (she lists 'being a bit sarcastic sometimes' as her unappealing habit). But it is a fashion disaster to do that, she continued. Damn right, I thought. I hate turn-ups. Fluff traps is what they are. The reason why girls get into this problem with wide 50s trousers is that they *do* look good with slingbacks, they make an ideal combination. The curator was wearing low-heeled soft leather loafers with hers, which worked – looked sharp and appeared to do away with the sling-backs-catching syndrome. Maybe being around art a lot helps in solving aesthetic dilemmas. Or maybe it's talking about it that does it, the conversation I was listening in on was very good quality, better than the lecture that would be a result of it, you could be sure of that. I made a note about the loafers on the free catalogue, so I'd remember to tell Rosie later on, and Fisky too, the next time I got my hair cut. At any other time during the past eight and a half months, I might've felt and behaved like a standard-issue boy and hence I'd have been very interested in the fantastically beautiful curator and followed her from a discreet distance. But that morning it was all I could do to stifle a yawn as I half-heartedly moved about, semi-checking the prints (there were prints as well as paintings), while being distracted by her only in the specific sense of noting the icon-trouser/low-heeled loafer combination. Soon I just lost interest in everything in front of me and went for a coffee.

I sat sipping, thinking about the size of the trouble I was in. Or the volume of it really. E=MC squared as the scientists say, or L.O.V.E. Lurv LoverMan as the soul singers sing. Big trouble cubed and orchestrated: Ain't no mountain high enough, Ain't no valley low enough and all that. It was far too soon for me to start getting het up about Spurs, none of my business, and jealousy is a feeling I refuse to recognize on a normal day. We hadn't had a proper conversation about anything in this arena yet, Natalie giving it a deft sidestepping bodyswerve if and when it came up. We didn't talk about it in the bath, when I suppose we could've done, seeing as it was the result of a Spurs-panic we'd come to be rising so early and having the early bath in the first place. It didn't seem appropriate. I didn't want to talk about it anyway. When you're having your first shared bath, you don't want to instigate a cross-questioning scenario, it'd completely bugger up the ambience. What we talked about in the bath was nothing. We washed each other instead. I could still feel the soap in her hands on my back and I could still feel the soap in my hands on her back. The only thing I was sorry about was that her smell was being washed away from me, but that was the price I had to pay, and I didn't mind. Another one of the things about her is that she pours oil and bubbles into the bath and lights candles around it even though it's first thing in the morning. That's why I didn't mind. I could still hear her whispering, Winganaprair, Winganaprair, singing it almost, soft and low. I thought it was weird – it was the first time she'd made the sound – but I didn't say anything. Listening to her voice in the flickering light was enough.

I left the coffee shop and the curator and the mescaline paintings. Before I sorted out a route home, I couldn't help but look into a big, bizarre-looking outlet called Super Sport's Shoe Factory. The apostrophe in Sport's troubled me. Somebody called Sport? An Australian? I doubted it, even though as it turned out the staff had that Antipodean grace. I needed some new football socks for Monday. My old ones, I thought, might be on the point of going all bobbly bits. Amongst the available selection, they'd got some England Italia 90s (that was the kind of shop it was, way out of date). I thought they'd be good with the 66 shorts, these socks, that wearing them together would be a sharp juxtaposition, a joke almost. (It goes without saying that attire is no laughing matter, but there are certain games like this that can be played. Only on the Park though, not in real life.) I bought them. The assistant didn't bother with eye contact as he took the money, that was the sort of clothes shop person he was, right offhand, not that I mind that sort of thing sometimes. There's more to life than Nicole Farhi. Does she *do* football socks, I wonder? I walked away not unhappy with the purchase (it's hard to go wrong with [sports] socks), but pretty unhappy with the Super Sport's Shoe Factory carrier bag in which I carried it.

Nat hadn't got to the point of being day-dressed as we kissed goodbye. She'd put on football-length socks (*not* the Spurs ones) with the kimono gown, to keep her feet warm, post-bath. She was wearing them pushed down, extra-time-in-the-Cup-Final style. She certainly knew how to leave me with a residual image. We'd parted saying we'd see each other again Monday night at the game. That was the way it had to be really, because Spurs would be showing up later in the day, or at least on Sunday I guessed. I didn't ask, I was pretending that I was cool, and that everything was still cool with *me*.

I arrived back at number 42 in the afternoon and sat on the bath-edge listening to the radio (there's a transistor hanging from a hook beside the mirror, all it can receive is the sports station, and you mustn't touch the dial or it doesn't work at all). I took an unusual interest in the state of play at Villa Park, and was very disappointed at the end of the day that it finished goalless. I was hoping for Tottenham to take an eight- or nine-goal stuffing and to have the manager dismissed and to end up playing with seven men and to have their goalie score an own goal and for them to be knocked out of the cup even though it wasn't a cup match. The only pleasure I could find in a scoreless draw was in being able to impute to Spurs himself the characteristic of his team (impotent at the front and mean-spirited at the back), preferring not to dwell on their so-called glamour image or their so-called reputation for playing the game with so-called flair and so-called style.

In the evening I went to meet Antonio. I'd changed out of his suit by then – naturally I'd removed the bits of fluff I'd picked up with the Sellotape-rolled-round-the-hand method (I've thoroughly tested all techniques, I can guarantee this is the most effective) – and restored it to its rightful place third from the end in his wardrobe.

I walked out wearing combats, though of course I don't like fatigues, they're not my trouser of choice. They were comfortable-ish, if only about 90 per cent satisfactory general-fit wise. I felt totally off-duty after the night before, which helped. It goes without saying that I wasn't expecting to see Natalie out and about round our way, or I would never've put them on. Additionally, I didn't even have to begin to begin thinking about thinking about pulling, which was more than cool with me. I hate the word pulling, actually, it's just an example of me inadvertently thinking in theBoys' speak. Not that the alternative words are much better. One of the good things about how me and Natalie got together was that it was just an accident, so no pulling or copping off or scoring was involved (there was actual goal-scoring, of course, but that's different, obviously.) Scoring's as bad a word as pulling, it sounds like a porn mag title. I suppose it probably is a porn mag title. Anyway, the whole of this ill-named activity was a chore from which I'd been totally released, and I was glad about it, even if it was a Saturday night. Which it was, I noted, as I looked around, taking in a vast variety of ill-fitting new trousers and other odd schmutter, most notably a glut of silly head-wear like you always get in the aftermath of Christmas. The Rule of Hats is that after thinking very very carefully about wearing one, you should decide against.

I met Antonio in one of those bars they have all over Shepherd's Bush now, the ones that like to think they're groovy – but can bars in Shepherd's Bush ever be groovy? I've hung around the area for a while now, and I'm pretty sure that, however you look at it, the answer has to be No. Antonio was coming over from his girlfriend's, Kate, who has a flat near Barnes and works in insurance but really she wants to be a writer. *I* think about being a writer sometimes, but I've never met anyone who makes a living from it, or even gets published, so it hardly seems a clever move. Also, personally, I never write anything, there's that too.

Aside from Pancho, the other reason I get to stay round Antonio's on a virtual rent-free long-term contract is that I'm the human burglar alarm – you know, because Antonio's always somewhere else, my presence makes the place look occupied. He was already at the bar when I arrived, drinking beer from the bottle and eating nuts. He eats more nuts than anyone I know, and he works out a lot, though he's still only about my size. He's not musclebound, but he does look unnecessarily fit. He's that type. To be honest, he wears his trousers just a touch too loose, but he's more than okay, and he definitely helps me out more than he needs to.

'How's it going then? You haven't been seen around much.'

Shrapnels of nut splay as he says it. It's his annoying habit. Sit well back.

'I've been kinda busy.'

'Zat so? Not work?'

[There's no need for that, is there? But . . .] 'No, not work.'

'What's her name then?'

I have to hand it to him, he's in there quick, though I suppose it is the only other likely option. And for a private-eye-friendly detection detail, her hairband is still on my wrist.

'She is called The Goddess of the East with Eyes of Shining Blue and a Far-Post Chip of Exquisite Delicacy.'

'Not a Far-Post Chip Butty?'

'No. And Antonio, you must be serious because I am completely in love and in big trouble because she already has a boyfriend as well as me. He is a bastard called Spurs.'

This helped Antonio to hate him too, as I knew it would, him being Arsenal (nominally) – he never actually goes to the matches.

'You'd better get them in then, hadn't you, while you run me through it.'

Sure, I said. Can you lend me a score till Monday?

Sure, he said, handing it over. That's three thousand four hundred and seventy pounds you owe me now then, yeah?

It's a lot of money to owe, isn't it? Antonio got left an endowment from a trust fund or something like that from his uncle in Buenos Aires, and he's well weighed-up in his work, so he *is* able to help me out, and we've known each other a long time and we get on like brothers, but all the same it does bother me, this debt. I stood at the bar mentally ticking off all the things I could try that would never make enough money to enable repayment. Even when I'm not thinking about this, it's always there, forming a background concern to my other concerns.

I returned to the table with the cold bottles and my concerns and ran him through my new concern. And at the end of this, he said, Well, you don't *know* her all that well, do you? Are you sure it *is* love?

Had I missed something out? Or is it just not a thing that's possible to convey to your fellow man in words, is it like pain – it has to be physically physically felt for the other guy to have any chance of getting an authentic grip on it? I leaned back, lit one of his cigarettes and squinted.

What to say to help him out? Ah, I've got it:

'Are you in love with Kate?'

'Well, she's my girlfriend, isn't she?'

'Come on, you can do better than that.'

'We've been together quite a long time now, must be, well, it's more than a year, isn't it?'

'Yes . . .'

'We're used to each other, and we get on, we like the same films and music and . . .'

'Yes . . .'

'We're compatible: horoscopes, Chinese Year of the Cat, and . . .'

It's the moment to interrupt properly: 'If you could only have one of them, who would it be – Kate or Pancho?'

'C'mon, that's not a fair question. I could ask the same of you – Goddess of the East Chip Butty or Pancho?'

'Antonio, I have to tell you, Natalie is the answer.'

He leaned back, lit one of my cigarettes and returned my squint. Zat right, he asked. Zat is right, I replied.

'Are you still the safe person to leave looking after my cat?'

'Yes. Absolutely.'

He went very thoughtful, I could almost see cats and girls rolling around his eyes like a fruit machine, chinking down to rest, cats in the left, cats in the right, and all the money falling out of his mouth.

Well, he said, Well, well.

I like Kate, I read one of her stories called The Secret Lives of Cars. It was a children's story, about cars that turned into animals at night, about a boy Jaguar which really *was* a big cat, and how the Jaguar was trying to get it together with a girl Puma. She'd done illustrations too. It made me laugh. I feel responsible now. I think this drink was the moment when Antonio started thinking about his relationship with her in a different way, i.e. as being potentially over, or not worth continuing with. To be honest we'd not had a conversation about love before, even though he is a deep thinker (he's not one of theBoys, obviously). Why we hadn't, I don't know, and even this effort was short-lived. We moved on, caught up with things, made arrangements for work (I help him out on shoots sometimes), and although we returned to the subject, it was really only to the details – the colour of Nat's duvet, that sort of stuff – after the main telling. Maybe it's because we're not expert in the field, maybe that's why it is that we didn't get any further with it, or maybe once you've told your mate you love someone, there's nothing much more to say. We moved on to car-talk. He's not one of theBoys in that way either, he talks about cars c/f environmental damage and what a load of superannuated penis extensions they are. It's partly because his is always breaking down, and that really he'd rather be in the desert riding a camel anyway.

I don't know. Maybe this conversation had nothing to do with anything that happened very shortly after, when he and Kate started their trial separation. Maybe conversations never do, so maybe I had nothing to do with it either.

Maybe even Pancho had nothing to do with it. Maybe him and Kate were going where they were going anyway – like people do, they always split up in the end, don't they, even when one writes a story for the other.

11

It's still only half-ten as I leave the flat for the second time. Back down the steps and double-lock the door. I've put Pancho a couple of extra helpings down for when he wakes up. I'm going to be out for a while.

I'll be much too early for lunch with Rosie if I take transport, but I've got to get out, and even though I don't much like walking in the middle of a weekday, I think I will. I don't much like walking in the middle of a weekday because of how it makes you feel: like you should have something else to do. And you have to see the people sleeping in the doorways, in the glare of daylight, and I don't like that, not at all. I read Down and Out in Paris and London when I was younger, and I remember little about it except two things. The first is that Orwell, in his undercover life as a tramp, worked in the easiest places to find casual work – cafés and restaurants. He worked across the range, from greasy spoons to five-star hotels. He discovered that the food was considerably less germ-laden in a greasy spoon than in a five-star. This was because it went through so few pairs of hands in the greasy spoon, whereas it went through so many pairs of hands in the hotel. It was a vivid image for me, the description of the journey of the meal from the first chef to the second chef to the service-lift operator to the first room service waiter to the second room-service waiter until eventually it arrived at the client in the hotel room. All those hands carry germs, and in addition, when the food fell on to the floor in the five-star it was dusted off and returned to the plate – this could happen any number of times between kitchen and room service – then you had lift operators removing bits of carpet from the butter-pats and waiters cleaning toast on the seat of their pants. (You should never use the seat of your pants for cleaning anything. It's not made for that.)

The difference in a greasy spoon is that the kitchens are exposed to the diner so that he or she can see what goes on, and mostly only one other person touches it, that's why the food's more hygienic. The kitchens in the Ha Nazdaroveeyeh restaurant, the one we went to on the third date, were set out like that. Part of the reason why I had to do more than my usual amount of talking on that date was in order to keep Natalie from watching other boys cook. (The chefs were at least ninety-five years old, to be accurate, but I still didn't like the idea.)

The other thing I remember about Down and Out was the feeling that the worst aspect for everyone in there, for all the tramps and the dispossessed and everyone, was having nothing to do all day. It was that that really demoralized them. I think Orwell said they were mostly not a bad lot, some were even a good lot, they just hadn't got anything to do in the daytime. It's the flip-side of being defined by work, isn't it, being defined by not work.

Plenty of people don't seem to mind though, about this, the work-definition thing. I mean, Rosie makes an ideal life for herself with her flowers and Natalie's right into her clothes. Antonio? He's fine, he loves what he does some of the time, and he's professional about it even when he's just doing it for the money. And theBoys – work gives them something to talk about, in fact it gives them everything to talk about, and something to live for. That Tissy I met, she'd probably die without her work. It's the sweatshop miles from anywhere, the slaves, the Gitanes, the fuckingPrat clients, the filthy-pattern fabrics and everything that keeps her alive, you can see that at a glance. And there's that expression I remember from a book at school, from English Lit: It's a hard life if you don't weaken. I think that's supposed to mean if you keep your nose to the grindstone, you'll be okay, you'll survive; I think it even implies that work will keep you sane.

It's knowing all this and seeing the people sleeping in the doorways that's making me not enjoy walking down to SW10 in the middle of the day. Or at least it's the thinking about it that's doing it.

I check the inside breast pocket of my Snowboard Puffa, fingering the mask. It's safely there, as is the letter-knife. I bought the Puffa from a Snowboard Coolwear shop, where the staff are chilled and have a nice vibe. Nick, who owns the place (I don't know him well, but we talk sometimes), assured me that a Snowboard Puffa is a staple item, and that the one I'm wearing now would turn out to be a classic. It's normal for these clothesBoys to say stuff like that, it doesn't mean a thing (he said a fleece was a wardrobe staple too), but I bought it anyway. I suppose the redeeming feature of the Snowboard Puffa is that the breast pocket is already puffed up (and it's on the inside), so at least the shirt top pocket rule doesn't have to be applied. I check the mask again. The label stitched on to the breast pocket says: Unique Brand/Unique Product. I don't know about that. It's not like I've never seen anybody else wearing one. But the mask is unique. Even if the Stone Age Eskimos mass-produced them, each one must've been different, made from a different piece of bone. Ivory. Like art – there is only one of it; it is Unique Brand/Unique Product. The letter-knife though, with its embossing and engraving and shininess, is masquerading as something individual when really it's naff crap. I don't want it. I didn't want it in the first place. And I haven't got any letters to open. I'll buy a proper knife. And as I dispose of it in a bus-stop wastebin, a stanza of writing in a familiar hand in black marker on the perspex over the advertising catches my eye. DMH 99. It's another one of those poems. It's another one of Rosie's moments. That's two already today, which is two too many for my liking. And they're disconnected as well, which seems somehow worse. I mean, I've had one tramp-spectacles/mask déjà-vu, and one bus stop poem déjà-vu – it's in a different league to a pair of Barry Manilows this, for sure. I'll speak to her at Astravoid, see what's to be made of it. She knows about runes and tarots and all those things. She can be a mystic and a sayer when the occasion demands it.

12

Whereas theBoys have the ability to be whatever the opposite of mystical sayers are on any occasion, demanded or otherwise. During the pre-match kick-about the game-after-meeting-Natalie, once they'd given each other the usual what-a-blinding-weekend they'd had (really belting – totally out of it: Scary Skunk, couple of Es, Charlie Marching, the works; even had a bit of grub), they turned their attention to me and demonstrated their anti-mystical talents using their un-unique brand of lingos.

Was she the bizniss then? said SwiftyBoy.

Did you get her on the treatment table? said ApeBoy.

What's she like in the box, is she a good dribbler? said TommyBoy.

She looks a useful header, said BearBoy.

HoHoHo. Yeah, I thought that too. Does she score many with her head then? said LardyBoy.

In response to this I played keepy-uppy on my own with my back (10) to them, watching the ball spin, playing it with plenty of slice, feeling like I could do it for ever. It was a way of sulking and of showing off at the same time, and of ignoring all that crap. You mustn't rise to the taunting, you must shut them up with your performance on the park, my son. Alan managed to almost raise a smile (from me I mean; for the rest, making each other laugh was a piece of cake, what with their easy wit and charm) by pitching his contribution at a different level:

'Have you, in fact, made a deposit? What was the opening rate of interest? What's the projected dividend? And the risk factors? Is your investment safe, matey?'

He can be rhetorical if he fancies. But he's talking about her as a commodity just the same, so, driven to a verbal response, let's get the words pinned down right:

'D'you mean 'av I shagged it?' [This is the only question that matters, isn't it?]

'It's possible to speculate that a merger may have taken place, yes.'

He admires himself for this one with a very smug smirk while skanking a mispass off the outside of his boot.

'Alan, it's not really me you should be concerning yourself about in that area, is it?'

'You what?'

'Your shorts, Alan – are they not a bit tight? Your sperms will be getting all overheated and will be dying by the billion down there. You do know that, don't you, Matey?'

The focus of the banter turned to Alan's Umbros, the size of his arse, and shorts/sperm permutations took over the agenda. Cool with me, switching attention away from things I don't want to talk about or to be talked about. [The boy done good] If they couldn't all mind their own bizniss, then they could at least mind each other's and not bother with mine. After all, I needed to get my head into a cut-clean space. I needed to get myself sorted, because this was going to be a tricky fixture. Three things in particular:

1] Natalie hasn't even turned out yet and I haven't even seen her for two-point-five days. [A certain amount of tension out there, Trevor? Absolutely John, the number ten's keyed up for this one, and no mistake]

2] When she does turn out, will theBoys behave? What will I do if there's any leeriness from them? I mustn't let it affect my concentration, I must appear unperturbed. And I mustn't spend time gazing moonfully over at her or anything like that, because:

3] I need to play the game of my life tonight. Nothing less than the game of my life will do on my full debut in front of my new girlfriend. [ ]

When Natalie did emerge I did the standard-issue boy

thing despite myself and pretended not to notice her, commencing my hamstring stretches instead. You won't believe what she did. She came across our pitch (normally they go round the fence and in through the gate at their side) and walked right up to me and whispered in my ear and pinched my bum for goodness' sake! TheBoys couldn't see the small print of the manoeuvre, she did it in one discreet indiscreet action, but tout de même . . .

As she jogged off and the heads turned my way, I said the first thing that came to me, which was that she'd offered us out for a match, y'know – Girls v. Boys.

In a couple of weeks or so, I said she'd said.

Any time, said the BearBoy.

Yeah, any time, said the ApeBoy.

It was a first for them, finding a subject on which to agree.

They were looking after Natalie with semi-disbelief.

'Is she sure?'

'We'll murder 'em.'

I knew how they meant this. Useful-looking players though they were, they were girls after all. Mind you, they hadn't actually made such an offer.

'Are we gonna get started or what?' Alan kicked off in his normal way, booting it high from his hands, and we spread across the ground, heads tipped back to heaven like we might be waiting for a UFO to land.

13

It's an unlucky number, isn't it?
Even the Apollo mission fucked up.

14

What she'd actually whispered to me was that I was to get rid of my Boys and not go drinking, that she would do the same with her Girls, and that she would meet me at the Ha Nazdaroveeyeh restaurant at, let's say, about nine-thirty? I wasn't about to argue with any of that. In the changing rooms after the match I said to theBoys I couldn't do the pub, I'd got . . . other arrangements. Not doing the pub after the match is an offence. Amongst the team head-shaking at this appalling faux pas, BearBoy said that he supposed I'd be putting in some heading practice, hoho – he's the kind of guy that doesn't like to give up on a pearly one-liner until he's wrung every last drop of humour from it. Yeah, right, I said, Nice jeans, mate, I said, nodding at his red chinos. Very dashing. Are they new?

I had my head tipped back to heaven once more as I limped away in the direction of the restaurant. I was tracing the outline of the moon – it was only just lit, like the edge of a coin. I was thinking about spacemen in their moonsuits, about how heavy moonsuits must be to walk in, even if there isn't any gravity. They're quite decent to look at, though. I mean moonsuit design isn't too terrible. Which is pretty good going, considering that lunar wear must fall into the garment category, Outward Bound, and that Outward Bound legwear is absolutely nearly the worst available on earth.

One cast-iron piece of advice about trouser-purchasing: If and when, for some insane reason, you find yourself moving about in the outlet that sells the one-man igloo tents and the silver vacuum flasks, don't buy the trousers. However seductive they might appear at the time, and however alluring the labels might be to read, with their superb technical descriptions apropos the extraordinary properties of the fabric – the lowest weight, the highest performance, and a construction value to see you all the way across the universe and back – they're not hip. I've handled a pair which came with a lifetime guarantee and claimed to be bomb-proof. Though they featured seven standard pockets plus another five secret ones with a patented double-zipped security system, and any number of Velcro tags whose functions were not clear, they still weren't hip. You can buy as many pairs as you like; I promise you'll never ever wear them again once you've got them home. Don't bother. It's a total waste of time, it's a total waste of a lifetime guarantee, and it's a total waste of bomb-proofing.

The reason why I was limping was because my left leg felt numb and heavy even if it wasn't inside a moonsuit. I'd been dead-legged by MarkyBoy, one of the quieter, more civilized of the team, one of the ones who'd refrained from pre-match innuendo – he's an accountant, I think. In fact, I know he is. He didn't mean it, or rather, he did mean it, I know that too now. I'd been accidentally roughed up more than necessary during the game, which was down to me putting myself about more than usual, making the extra effort. I'd even got a burngraze down the left side of my face, along my jaw, from where I'd gone flying in the goalmouth.

Marlowe takes a kicking in The Long Goodbye, in the police cells where he's being held as a suspect. He'd driven his friend down to Mexico in the middle of the night, his friend (I can't remember the guy's name) had brutally killed his own wife but Marlowe didn't know that, Marlowe didn't even ask him what was up when he turned up, middle of the night or not. He was an old friend in some kind of trouble, and that was all he needed to know. It's like that between Antonio and me. Well, he helps me out of the shit, anyway. So they released Marlowe without charging him, the LAPDBoys, because the friend had been reported dead in Mexico, which meant that was that, case closed. He was pissed off, battered and smoking as he emerged from the cells in a black suit with a white shirt, one of those white shirts with the long 70s collars, nice, a cool get-up, and the best impression I could hope for for myself, I thought, as I lit up behind the shielding hand.

It was the first time I'd ever been to the Ha Nazdaroveeyeh. I peered through the smeary window, and though I could see Natalie wasn't there I couldn't be bothered with the killing-time-walking-for-late-coolness-round-the-block routine because I ached all over too much. The prospect of sitting down and ordering two beers was pulling like a charm, and anyway if I had round-the-blocked I might've bumped into her, which would have had the effect of totally decooling the operation, or at least making me seem as though I was lost when in fact I prefer to be known as someone who knows his way around. I stood finishing off my peering and wondering if it was impolite to enter before Natalie had arrived when somebody pinched my bum. Somebody wearing my brown suede jacket.

'Hello, Winger.'

'Hello.'

'What can you see through there then?'

A few empty seats where we could sit down, I replied. What can you see?

'An injury.' She put the back of her hand to my cheek. 'You pick 'em up, don't you?'

'You can't score a hat trick without getting a few knocks, y'know.'

'You scored a hat trick!?'

[You didn't notice!?] 'Yeah.'

'Did you win?'

'SwiftyBoy had to leave early, so the numbers were unbalanced, so I scored two then I switched sides before I scored the other one.'

'Who d'ya score two for?'

'The side that lost.'

There was a pause.

'So you scored one for the side that won.'

'Yeah.'

'So you won and lost then.'

I paused. I suppose you could look at it like that, I said. How did you get on?

'Scored one. We won.'

'I know. You had a brilliant game. Shall we go in?'

I opened the door for her like a gent, and she thanked me saying, You're a gent, you are.

We talked the weekend round the block while we decided what to order, sitting at the long table beside the four old men who were clanking their glasses and doing their vodka-toasting. I wanted to tell her I'd been missing her ever since we last parted. I don't know why it is that I don't say the things that I want to say when I easily could, but I know that I don't.

Listen, she said as bread arrived, Bernie says this is fucking stupid. Me seeing you. She says what's up with me, why d'you want two boyfriends? She says, Isn't one enough trouble?

Shit. Shit, shit, shit. Shit. Is she wearing my jacket to give it back to me?

'She says that, does she?'

'Yeah.'

'Well . . .'

'She says I don't even know anything about you, what you do or where you live or nuffink. I mean, what *do* you do, Winger?'

'Doesn't she like me?'

'That's not the point . . . She thought you . . .'

' . . . Yeah?'

' . . . she thought you were fine.'

[Only fine?] 'Maybe it's Spurs she doesn't like.'

'It's not any of that. It's *me* she's talking about. I mean, I know it's only just started but . . . it can't go on, this. It'll be too much, and . . .'

Hey, hold on, I said.

Although I was expecting an episode of seriousness, I wasn't ready for it right then. Or rather, I wasn't expecting it right then. I thought perhaps we could be like teenagers and have a few more dates before we admitted to being anywhere near where we were, or where I was anyway. I'd already run some practice conversations through my head in readiness though. The kind of conversations where you come up with all the right lines and all the cool answers because of the huge amount of thinking time you're allowed.

It was you that invited me out to dinner, I said. You can't . . . (Chuck, dump, drop – which one will it be? All the words for this end of the transaction are horrible too, aren't they – and transaction's not all that nice either) . . . you can't chuck me already. It's too soon.

'But it's like you were saying on Saturday morning – it'll be easier now, won't it?'

'I didn't mean it. What I was saying on Saturday morning.'

'What did you mean then?'

'I meant I was offering you an escape which I didn't want you to take.'

'Why?'

'It's . . . Well . . . It's kind of pre-emptive face-saving for me for a start. Protection.'

'What against?'

'Against rejection. Especially after . . . y'know, the night before.'

'What!?'

'It's like an insurance policy sort of remark. For if you hadn't liked, you know . . . in bed – my smell or anything or something.'

'You didn't mean it then?'

'No. No. And . . . well, it's more tricky than . . .' (I was going to say, More tricky than usual, but that's not what I meant.)

'Usual?'

'No. No. I mean, you having a boyfriend already. I mean . . .'

What do I mean? One of the things I mean is that I like the idea of a scrap with the other guy. God knows why because I'm absolutely completely crap at it and always end up with a split lip and a broken nose if fighting ever breaks out, even randomly, in the street or something. The thing is, there's more often than not another boy hanging around when you first get together with someone, isn't there, even if he's only at the edge of the frame. You have to see him off by stealth, if you can, and never get yourself in a position where you meet him – that way at least you spare your lip and nose. I definitely mustn't mention anything about this though, because it's a shameful admission, and makes my motive sound territorial. Which it isn't, not at all, at all, at all, it really isn't. But it must be a part of the Big Picture. Talking of which [it *must* be worth going for a subject change here] –

'D'you know Rothko?'

'Plays for Arsenal?'

'No. Painter.'

'Pictures, y'mean?'

'Yeah.'

'What sort of pictures?'

'Abstracts. Enormous abstracts. Really big, mostly rectangles, mostly in just two colours, mostly called things like Orange on Red.'

'Mmm. I'm not sure. They sound like colour swatches . . .' She looked thoughtful. 'I always used to paint abstracts at school,' she said.

'Did you? That means you're deeply expressive and sensitive.'

'I know.'

'D'you paint anything now?'

Only the bathroom walls and my nails, she said. D'you?

'I've done bathroom walls, but not my nails, though I did buff them once.'

'Buff them?'

'Yeah, I thought it might help. They go numb and white at moments of stress.'

They weren't like that then, at that moment, though they should've been. I carried on, to get off the subject of numbness of nails. I did art at school, I said, but I remember it more as a lesson for looking out of the window and daydreaming than actually getting anything done.'

'What did you dream about? What *do* you dream about?'

'I can't even remember my dreams from last night, never mind from back then. I *day*dreamed about my bike mostly.'

'Alright, what did you dream about your bike then?'

'Improvements, modifications.'

'Like what?'

'Taping the handlebars. Chroming the chromework. Respraying the paintwork. Ultimate methods of wedging lollipop sticks through the forks, y'know, so you could play a tune on the spokes and give it a speedway-style kick-start.'

She started smiling. 'Kevin Sprake used to do that.'

'Who's he?'

'My first boyfriend.'

'I hate him. When was that?'

'Mmm . . . when I was in Mrs Lord's class. When I was eleven. And Fatty Stokes, he used to do it too.'

'Your second boyfriend?'

'Yeah.'

'You went out with a lardyBoy?'

'We all make mistakes.'

'That's true. I hate him too, as well, anyway.'

'You're right to, he was nothing to look at and he chucked me for Fat Suzy Bull.'

'Sounds like they were well suited.'

'They were . . . Actually, all the boyfriends I had at school used to do it, that lollipop thing.'

'Well, I guess it must've been all the rage when we were kids then, lollipop-spoking: perhaps that's the kind of boy you should be searching for now, the lollipop-spoker kind.'

The way I pulled my body back and upright as I said this made it mean: Is Spurs that kind of boy? We both knew it. Some people might have described the look with which she replied as noncommittal, but to me it was an indefinite, No, he ain't – it's just not his sort of thing.

The food arrived. I'm not kidding, it was mash and eels. The old men drank a toast to it as it was passed over their heads. And they drank a toast to us. And they drank a toast to our good health, and to their good health. And to our appetites, and to their appetites. And to women, especially beautiful women . . .

'I like it here Natalie.'

'So do I, Winger.'

'Will we come again, d'you think?'

Her reply was another noncommittal look. My interpretation of this noncommittal look was that it said: Winger, I'd really love to.

What about him, anyway? she said.

'Who?'

'Your Rothko.'

'Oh. I wondered if you'd like to go and see some paintings.'

15

Antonio has a video called The World's 100 Greatest Goals. There's a sequence where Pelé (satin blue shorts are not normally a good idea, but where they really come off is as part of the Brazil kit) runs on to a long pass during the Mexico World Cup. The keeper rushes out. It's a 50/50 ball on the edge of the box. Pelé plays the most divine dummy; it doesn't matter how many times you watch it, you can never quite work out how it's done. With a treble-feint of his body he throws the goalie completely off balance. The effect this has is that Pelé appears to pass the ball to himself without touching it. He picks it up a few yards further to his right. Desperate-looking defenders are sliding back to cover the line, the keeper's still on his backside, without a winganaprayer. Pelé triggers the shot. The ball skims just wide of the far post. It *isn't* a goal. But it's on a video called The World's 100 Greatest Goals.

I explained the sequence to Natalie using the salt as Pelé and the pepper as the goalie and beer bottles as defenders and her placemat as the penalty area and a screwed-up napkin as the ball while she held her hands as the goal posts.

That's how good these paintings are, I said. Well, they're not exactly like this, obviously. But they're this good. Would you come to see them?

Winger, she said, what do you do for a living?

16

You can only get away with avoiding entering into the well-trammelled-conversation-convention thing for so long, I suppose. I think the reason I'd managed to get half-way through a third date without actually talking about what I do is because of the enormous amount of practice I've had. I imagine that the kind of child I was was the kind of child who would respond to the question, What are you doing? with the answer, Nothing. Nothing would be the reply even when Nothing was the truth, I mean even when I wasn't trying to cover up whatever it was I was doing that I shouldn't've been. Mind your own bizniss, as Nat would say.

I didn't want to tell anything about anything workwise because . . . What? Because of the danger of appearing . . . I think limited is the right word. Yes, limited. The fear one has in saying one's only one thing is that one'll bugger up the idea that it's possible for one to be something else as well. One. Yeah, it's definitely the most removed way of saying I. The idea of being defined and thereby confined, it frightens me, it does. If for instance I was a truck driver, then I wouldn't be able to say, I'm a Private Investigator as well, by the way, would I? Because someone like Alan's Jenny would start a well-trammelled-conversation-convention, raising serious doubts that you could be or do two things simultaneously – that it can only be possible for one person to focus in just one area of specialization – and would no doubt begin to helpfully suggest skills retraining and an access course et cetera as the way forward.

An image of rows of people sitting down in colleges and universities floated in front of me; halls full of desks all the same, turned-over examination papers all the same too, an invigilator, a clock, walls made of bricks through which I'd be tracing shapes and marking patterns (if it were me doing the exam, I mean). That would be when I wasn't staring at the back of the people's heads, despairing, because they must be the kind of people (and if I was there, and I could be, I would be that kind of person too) believing in the certificate, the passport that allows you through the gate to the global air traffic of life: arrival 8 a.m. / departure 6 p.m., destination job, the only deviations being measured in fractions of feet higher or lower – upgrades, downgrades, MD, SD, PA et cetera. Like there's something worthwhile about it all, like it provides some kind of guarantee. I watched a programme on TV some time back about a man who ran an anti-head-hunting business. Companies hired him to lure people away from them – difficult employees – so the companies didn't have to pay severance money or fight an unfair-dismissal case. He was good at it, the anti-head-hunter, he succeeded in making the people involved feel flattered and desirable, made them feel head-hunted, in fact, rather than the opposite. That's the sort of thing that really happens when you're in that system, when you've got the passport. You get to enter your classic Alice in Wonderland world, complete with your anti-head-hunter. So the whole business thing depends on matters outside your control, or factors even more random than that – somebody's mood, what somebody had for breakfast, the way somebody feels constricted inside their grey flannel trousers.

I circled the cruet between us in a holding pattern, the salt shifting gently like sand in a shell. A few grains scattered as Pelé made a safe landing and taxied to a halt at Natalie's elbow, which was pivoted on the table, her head resting in her hand.

Well? she said.

'Natalie, I had a sandwich-bar venture.'

'And . . .'

'And now I freelance for a company that produces articles for magazines and stuff.'

'What happened to the sandwich-bar venture?

'I don't want to really talk about it.'

'Come on. Where was it, for a start?'

'Acton, but I don't really –'

'Acton! That's no place for a san'wich bar, Winger. 'S miles out.'

She was absolutely right about that. Yeah, I said. Location was a bit of a problem.

'Why d'you have it there then?'

'I think we thought west was the way forward, whereas in fact it turned out to be east.'

'Facing in the wrong direction, weren't ya?'

'Yeah.'

'Did you lose a lot of money?'

She was leaning forward with a forkful of eels held square to her face, a position she'd been maintaining for the last three questions. I was anxious to see this mouthful disappear.

'Quite a bit, yeah.'

This answer did it. She leaned back and ate a bit more.

'Are you a failed entrepreneur then?'

'I'm a never-wanted-to-be-an-entrepreneur-in-the-first-place entrepreneur.'

I must've been looking miserable about it, and she must've realized that I really really didn't want to talk about this, as she drank from her drink quite slowly and changed tack.

'What about these articles then?'

'What articles?'

'Winger . . .'

'I sort out photo sessions.'

'What kind of photo sessions.'

'Food article photography for magazines.'

'What sort of magazines?'

'Lifestyle.'

'What, like Wallpaper*.'

'Exactly like that, there's a new one coming out called Carpet* too. They're not so bad to work for, those titles. We do the men's market too.'

'What, porn?'

'No. Middle-shelf stuff.'

Oh. Not porn, then, she said, in a tone that we both understood and appreciated. What is it you do exactly, she asked.

'Production, direction. That sort of thing.'

'You produce and direct photographs of food?'

'Yeah.'

She seemed to find this amusing. Eyes shining blue smiling.

Doesn't sound that bad, she said. [It isn't] Sounds funky enough, she said. [I'm not sure 'funky' is the mot juste]

I gave out a huge sigh.

'What's up, Winger?'

[I'm finding this talking stressful, that's what] I attended to my thigh, pretending I'd pulled a muscle. She ignored this plea for sympathy and carried on.

So, she said. Is the money in it alright then? Are you making your losses back?

'Nat. One thing at a time, eh?'

She looked at me. My tone was off. The pressure of the interrogation had made me forget that I was only answering at all in order to avoid getting my jacket back. Sorry, I said.

You'll talk about anything except what you do, she said. The rest of it's nice though, your talking I mean.

'It is?'

'Yeah. It is.'

'Oh. Good.'

'S'alright. Not all blokes talk, y'know.'

'Don't they?'

'No.'

I went quiet while I thought about this and began to develop a new line of concern: do I talk too much? I didn't really have time to get properly stuck into that, thankfully, because Natalie kept going.

Is that why you're good at cooking then, she asked. D'you have to do the food for the photos?

'No. We use chefs, if there's proper cooking involved. I have it prepared in restaurant kitchens and then we spray it just before the shoot and then Antonio does his stuff with the lenses and the gels and it all comes out looking hip and sexy. Not looking much like food, but looking a lot like a magazine picture.'

'So you just set it all up, yeah.'

'Sort of.'

'And what *did* happen to the sandwich bar, then?'

'Ahh, Natalie . . .'

Ahh, Winger, she said, mockingly.

She mopped her juice up with her bread. That had the appearance of real food all right. She looked up. You can have a rest now, she said. I don't want to put a spoke in things. [That means there are things. And that those things are things she doesn't want to put a spoke in. Good.]

Rather than a lollipop stick, I replied.

Exactly, she said, smiling.

She'd worked the conversation round the tangent. Made a pattern out of it. I liked that.

The eels and mash all gone, the waiter took the plates away and the old men toasted the passing of a good meal. Natalie rose.

'Where y'going?'

'Toilet.'

She was wearing strides with no back pockets so the contour of her bottom was completely uninterrupted. I've heard people call the pocketless ones Slacks. It's not accurate, that. Slacks are what Americans wear – those evil things with pleats at the top and sharp creases down the leg.

There was nothing slack about the ones she was wearing, nothing at all. As she crossed the room, the ninety-five-year-old chefs all stopped paying attention to their work simultaneously – they were professionals, so it was only for a second – and the comrades paused in their toasting. I couldn't blame them.

I returned to worrying about how this whole conversation had begun. Pelé, I said to the salt, you're an expert at feinting and executing the elaborate dummy, what now? We went through a few alternative lines while we ran rings round the pepper:

1] What about your sister? Is she with Bernie on this? Does she think it's fucking stupid too? [Definitely definitely not. The answer to this could easily be, Yes]

2] I think we should give it a little more time. Get to know each other better. [No, no, no. Agony-Aunt/UncleSpeak]

3] I love you. [ ]

4] D'you fancy a match? Girls against boys? [In a way I'm already committed here. This could be it]

The comrade who was the winner of the how-much-of-your-dinner-can-you-leave-in-your-beard competition leaned my way. Rothko, he said, is not bad. Modern, yes, but not bad in his way. For myself, I'd take her to see Vermeer – Vermeer is a poet, and he understands women too. He semi-closed one eye in a half-wink, like he was passing on a very decent tip. The Dutch School, he said. The runner-up in the food-in-beard comp. spoke to the winner. Georgie, he said, are you forgetting Rubens? Ahh, Rubens, said my friend the winner, Rubens, of course. His eyes began rolling as he rubbed his hands together. When his eyes stopped rolling, they began to circle instead, like Saturn's rings. Rubens absolutely was the man, no doubt about it. As Nat returned, the runner-up winked at me, saying in a low growl, Rubens. Rubens. She looked from him to me and back to him as she lowered herself, saying to the man, I hope he hasn't been bothering you, inclining her head my way. Which made him laugh and had him and his mates raising their glasses again.

What've you two bin on about then, she asked as she sat down.

'Nothing. Art. D'you fancy pudding?'

'I wonder if they've got crêpes?'

'You wouldn't eat a crêpe that wasn't cooked by me, would you?'

The apple pie's best here, she replied.

'Oyy!' [It's me and Pelé who are the main men at feinting and evading, not you]

'Oyy what?'

'Oyy nothing. Did you tell your sister about it, us, what does she think?' [Moron. You really are a Moron]

'Yes.'

'And . . .'

'Well, she asked me about you and everything and . . .'

'Apple pie?' The waiter had come across. He addressed the inquiry to Natalie.

'Two.'

'Custard?'

'Yes please.'

She looked at me and I nodded, Yes please.

'So custard for you both?'

'Yes. Both with custard. Thanks.'

The waiter seemed happy with this.

'And . . .?'

'As a matter of fact, she didn't mind. I told her Bernie had been a bit down on it, so –'

'So she wanted to be more positive?'

'Yeah, a bit.'

'Don't they get on, Bernie and her?'

'Not always. Sam thinks, well, Bernie's got it easy, y'know, with her family money and that.'

'You don't think so then?'

'I don't think anybody has it that easy, really, one way or another, do they, and a good friend's a good friend. Like you and your Antonio. I don't suppose you two agree on everything, do you?'

'No.'

'There you are then.'

'So what did you tell her – Sam?'

'How d'you mean, what did I tell her? About you? Are you fishing, Winger?'

'No, Natalie, I'm not, no.'

'Yes, Winger, you are, yes.'

'No, no, no, I didn't mean –'

Yes, yes, yes you did mean, more like, she said. Actually, I told her you were sweet.

Sweet? What is that supposed to mean? Sweet is like a baby brother, isn't it? Sweet is a puppy, or a kitten. Or zabaglione. Is Marlowe sweet? I think not. Is Pelé sweet? No. The first man on the moon, is he sweet? Negative, ground control, an astronaut is not sweet. Rothko, Vermeer, Rubens, the Belgian mescaline artist, are they sweet? No, artists are not sweet, they are hard, getting away, as they do, with looking cool in their distressed paint-spattered jeans. Are my trousers making me look sweet?

The legwear I've selected for this evening in hope and anticipation of a third date is new, designed in Japan, made in Italy, and expensive. Casual but sharp, sharp but casual. Marlowesque, you might say. Even my footwear – which I never mention – is working well in combination (I never name-drop either, but these shoes are Patrick Cox, also new). Additionally, as I'm in love, I've barely been eating, so I'm looking particularly lean and lithe. There's nothing sweet about them, me, or anything, and that's the way it should be. Sweet, I ask you.

The pudding arrived.

Some people call 'pudding' sweet, I said.

'Or dessert. Some people call it that.'

Indeed (as they say), I said. What d'ya call it round yours, the pudding course?

'At home at mum's we call it an afters. At the flat, we normally call it a spliff.' She loaded a mouthful and she studied the bowl for a while, like the contents might hold the answer to something.

We could go back to the flat for some sort of afters, she said.

I liked that, and I stopped being cross about being called sweet. 'We're not splitting up then?'

'I'll talk to you about it later.'

17

Walking back to her flat, the six wide lanes on one side, the neon shop fronts on the other, us between them, me carrying both kit bags (You're a gent, you are, mate. Yeah, sweet, I am, that's me: I hadn't totally stopped being cross. in fact I was holding a grudgette – it's my unappealing habit), Natalie started saying how she'd have to be going away for a week [OhNo] in a couple of weeks' time to 'Buy Fall'.

'What d'you mean, Buy Fall?'

What she meant was that in your clothing bizniss, your buyer does her buying well ahead, so what you have in the shops now, your buyer was out sourcing a while back, almost a year ago, in fact.

Sourcing? Is that what you call it then, I asked.

'Yeah.'

I thought that was good, I have to say. Sourcing clothes made the process sound primitive and sleuthful, an appeal to the old hunter/gatherer instinct (I went through an earnest period. Reading Darwin and Orwell and everybody like that was part of it, that's how I know these things).

'So can you buy other seasons as well as Fall?'

Yeah, you can buy Winter too, she said.

'What about Summer, can you buy that?'

'Yeah.'

'And Spring?'

'Spring as well.'

I thought this was really something, the idea that you could somehow own the seasons in advance. It sounded like a version of theBoys' Arbitrage, which is one of those $6 million words that they have for things that happen at work. MarkyBoy tried to explain it to me once, arbitrage.

It's about speculating on the likelihood of something before it happens, I think. I didn't understand it properly to be honest. The way I picked it up, it sounded like risking what you hadn't got in order to buy nothing. All subject to Market Forces, as they say, which makes them sound like deliberate acts. Mass panic would seem a more accurate description, when you watch them on the news when they're having a busy day. All subject to mass panic. He is a nice guy, MarkyBoy, because I was clearly looking blank after his first description of the arbitrage transaction, so he tried to re-explain by tearing a beer mat, peeling the label off the top, and drawing wiggly lines on the exposed surface like a graph, lines that, now I remember, looked a lot like the markings of the Belgian artist's mescaline prints. Pen lines always bleed on torn beer mat, that's the way in which the lines he made were similar. After he'd gone to all that effort, I made out like I was following him, the same thing I used to do with my maths teachers.

You buy Spring and Summer together, she said. We do that in September.

'So you buy Fall with Winter?'

That's right, she said. For instance, she said, those trousers are new, aren't they?

Replies I had to bite down: What d'you mean, Trousers? D'you like them? Are they alright? The legs are too long, aren't they? What about the arse, it's bad, isn't it? They don't really fit at all, that's the truth, isn't it?

The best thing to do, I decided, as I bit these replies down, was to just answer the question.

Yes, I said, with all the disinterested insouciance I could muster.

'Flat fronts are coming through the designers now. They'll be all over the high street by Autumn. It's just trends.'

Can you tell when I bought everything I'm wearing then, I asked.

'Not necessarily. I can tell *where* you did though, and I can tell you where you didn't. You didn't get none of it down Whitechapel Market for £5.99, darling, did ya? HaHa.'

Too right I didn't, I said.

You can get bargains down the market, she said. That's where I picked up this top.

She undid the jacket and pulled it open like she was about to display a load of knocked-off watches. She fully revealed the flower-patterned sleeveless vest that had been semi-visible throughout dinner. Rubbish it was. Girls and their tops, honestly. It's a completely totally imbalanced situation. A boy can never pick up a shirt for a fiver from a market that looks anything other than a shirt for a fiver from a market when he's wearing it, and that's that. A girl can pick up some spangly thing that occupies no more space in a drawer than a handkerchief, which originally cost £1.99 but was knocked down to a quid, and look absolutely stunning in it, and that's that too. This sleeveless vest with flower pattern was one of these.

It's lovely. It's a lovely top, I said.

'Mmm. It's only clothes though, Winger.'

[Only?] 'What d'you mean, only?'

'It's what's inside that counts.'

I don't like homespun truths. Especially not that one.

At this moment I hadn't read the piece in Modern Painters which I later picked up from Antonio's studio – an article about a touring exhibition of American Abstractionism – or I might've been able to run her (and me) through some ideas inherent in the surface/depth model. I'm still getting to grips with all that, though, and I hadn't even read the article then of course, so instead I said, But packaging is important, isn't it?

It is for presents, she said.

Actually, I'd got one with me. I was going to give it to her at the Ha Nazdaroveeyeh but I wasn't sure it was the right moment back there. I thought it was now. We stopped while I took it from the end-pocket of my bag.

Her unwrapping style was over-excited five-year-old. It was a hair scrunchy, deep blue velvet, in a silver cardboard box, a sort of replacement for the turquoise one. She took it out and she pulled her hair through it and admired the result in a shop window. In the shop window that contained the hellish combat pants, in fact.

Look at those hellish combats there, I said. You know, clothes *are* important. I mean, you wouldn't wear *those*, would you?

'Do me a favour. Some kid'll really love 'em though . . .'

Yeah, that's alright, they might be alright for kids (although if you ask me it's at the risk of deep psychological scars in later life), but you'll get adults wearing them too, I said. I've seen them. (Deranged people, however happy enough they seem.)

'That's true. But you have to go through those things. Like when I first started out working as a Saturday Girl up West. I spent all my time – in my lunch break and after work – shopping, browsing shops, buying clothes – ended up wearing some right dodgy stuff. I even had an Aceeed headscarf with a Smiley, but you steady, don't you, you work yourself out, you sort out your own style. Everything becomes more normal, doesn't it.'

Not for me.

So, I said, you wouldn't buy strides like that, then, in your job I mean, when you're out buying Winter and Fall and so on?

She answered with her snort laugh.

Exactly, I said. I mean, if everybody in the world wore stuff like that, the world'd look rubbish.

'Yeah but . . .'

'Yeah but nothing. You see, part of how the world looks is because of you, and in some way the packaging says something about what's inside. About the content.' (I thought I wasn't doing that badly here, considering I hadn't even read the article yet.)

'Well, yeah, you've got a point, in a way. But only a tiny part of how the world looks is down to me. And only a tiny part of that. Just a tiny part of a tiny part. I don't buy everything that everybody wears, do I?'

'Only a tiny part of how the world looks is important though, isn't it? You've just admitted that, really, by snorting at those combats.'

'I do not snort.'

'You do.'

'I don't.'

'You make a noise of derision.'

Well, she said. And she played with the scrunchy, rolling it round her wrists, then she pulled her hair back through it. I can make a noise if I want to, she said.

We walked on. I watched her reflection in the shop fronts, admiring the way that my (now hers, that was a present too, I just hadn't told her yet) jacket together with the flowery top from off the Whitechapel Market and the pants that weren't slacks combined with the new hair scrunchy. More than cool with me. It was an outfit. I retained the image as we turned off the main drag.

It was becoming clear how it all worked. Clothes, I said, are the new art.

'Ha ha. Like blue was the new black, after grey was, and brown was, that is. Does that make me an artist then?'

'Yes.'

'And d'you want to be an artist, Winger?'

'No, Natalie, I don't.'

We were at the door of her block.

'What do you want to be then?'

'Can we talk about this inside?'

She hesitated before unlocking the door. We were addressing issues of both form and content now. I mean, for her to let me in again was bad form (from Bernie's point of view at least). And if she didn't, I'd be dis-content. (Ha ha, not funny, I know – my other un-appealing habit, making an un-funny joke at a difficult moment. It wasn't that bad, on this occasion, as I didn't say it out loud.)

Nothing has to happen, I said, as I followed her up the stairs. We can just, y'know, Be, for a while, can't we? Won't hurt anybody. We kissed on the half-landing. She pulled out of it saying, I'm really knackered and tired and I ache. How about you?

Same, I replied.

'Let's just go and get some sleep then, shall we?'

That'd be cool with me.

In her bedroom in the middle of the night we both woke up and went to the bathroom for water. You know that kind of waking, when it seems like you haven't been to sleep at all. The light was on low in the bedroom as she returned from her water-getting, and in order to divert attention from the impending difficult conversation I could somehow feel coming, I began arranging our clothes on the bed cover, which was white, ideal. I talked her through the dish I was beginning to produce and direct as I went. First I used my trousers as a bed of black squid-ink pasta.

Black pasta. My trousers? What's happening? Trousers aren't for this. This isn't what trousers are for.

But I carried on. Scallops are the classic accompaniment to black pasta, and for this I dressed my trousers with her underwear. I tossed a side salad from the flowery top and her green football socks which she'd discarded in the corner (she hadn't been wearing the Spurs away socks that night, a very good sign). Marine sponges from under the window-sill I used as bread rolls on the side. Two make-up pots for salt and pepper.

Are your Rothkos like that, she asked, surveying the masterpiece.

No, they're not, not at all. This is more like a Damien

Hirst. It's a concept piece, baby.

I stood up on the bed, wobbling.

It's called, The Physical Impossibility of the Idea of Love in the Mind of Someone Who Isn't in It.

Always get your first use of the Love word in in a neutral(ish) way. Not that I've ever done it before. Mentioned Love first. Or even at all. It just seems safest. She tried looking at me hard then, but it was tricky for her, because she was standing and wobbling too. And I wasn't returning her gaze anyway because I was concentrating down at the bed, thinking.

Thinking: this isn't what trousers are for. Trousers aren't for this. Or are they? What's going on?

She bent to rearrange a bra-strap on the pasta. She was wearing the scrunchy on her wrist, like I had before with her old hairband. It was all she was wearing. She stood, even more awkwardly off balance, trampolined herself steady. Her intervention had added some symmetry.

'Is this like your freelance work, then, Winger?'

'No Natalie, this isn't like my freelance work. No.'

'What then? Winger, what? And while we're at it, what are you doing with your life? You can't go on fucking around like you are.'

Wow. And she doesn't know the half of it.

'I've got no [fucking] idea.'

'You must have.'

'No, I really haven't. Natalie. I really want . . . [What? Really want what? What?] I really want to play a dummy like Pelé, and paint a painting like Rothko.'

'But that won't be enough though, will it? It's already bin done.'

'You're right. You're absolutely right.'

'So?'

'I want to buy the seasons in advance.'

[I want to buy the seasons in advance?] Fuck. I'm out of my trousers and in my own concept piece with the girl I love. Fuck. Maybe trousers are for this. For getting rid of – once you've got them off, you can really think.

'You what?'
'I want to buy the seasons in advance.'
'You're full of shit, Winger.'
'No I'm not.'
'Yes you are.'
'Not.'
'Are.'
'Not.'
'Are.'
'Not not not.'
'Are are are.'
We were horizontal now. We were fighting. The argument had been subverted from the realm of the metaphorical to the realm of the visceral (I've read that article now). The clothes art was getting knocked all over the place. It was okay – a concept piece doesn't need to last, it's just the concept that does. It was cool with me.

18

A friend of Antonio's once told me that he'd slept in a disused tram carriage, somewhere in the north of Italy. I think it was the north, I think it's colder there. He was in bad shape at the time, this friend, from what he was saying. He said he'd been on the road for a while, and had developed the appearance of the type of guy you'd definitely prefer not to speak to on the street, the type that if he approached you it would be good news if all he was after was a cigarette. Anyway, he'd been walking aimlessly for too long and it was getting near to dawn, and he came across this tram carriage abandoned beside a cemetery wall. They must have things like that in Italy, I've never been. Even though it was abandoned, it was still locked, so he had to break in. He said this was a trouble he hadn't needed to go to, because he found that later, when he left the tram, the driver's door had already been forced. And in fact there was a mattress made of cardboard up there too, behind the driver's seat. He said that he slept like a log in that tram, though the cemetery wall bordered a six-lane highway on which the traffic was just revving up for the morning. Everybody knows how dramatic Italian drivers are with their horns, even people who haven't been there. He said he slept well, though. In fact, he said, that episode of sleep was the beginning of some sort of recovery for him. I don't know what had been wrong, I thought maybe he'd had a nervous breakdown or something – but I didn't find out because I don't ask questions like that. You don't always need to ask, though, do you, sometimes you can just tell.

Later, when I was thinking about him, I wondered if it was perhaps because he was inside and under cover when he awoke that he felt better, or I wondered maybe if it was because he'd found the other bed as well; that he'd been able to imagine there'd been someone like him before. It might've helped him feel, not that he had a home, but that he lived somewhere, that he was in some sort of continuum, like a family, even. Who knows?

Anyway, it's the sleeping conditions I encounter on the walk down to SW10 that remind me of him; his tram carriage would've been a five-star in comparison. How do you sleep like that, curled into the doorway of an office entrance, in the shadows of a million TO LET boards, when it's late in the morning and the sun's out and the traffic's there? I mean, even if you've got a horrible horrible hangover, it doesn't seem possible. *I'd* never be able to sleep in these circumstances. Sleeping's not a public activity. It's a private matter. I once saw an artist in the window of a gallery in the West End sleeping in chocolate. She wasn't naked or anything, she had her pyjamas on, which is probably why there wasn't much of a crowd. I didn't like it. She didn't *belong* to where she was sleeping, it was inappropriate, that was what I didn't like about it. And that's what I don't like about these people on the streets. That's what I mean about Antonio's friend; at least he belonged to that tram during the time he had the good sleep.

I keep checking my inside pocket, fingering the mask. It must be normal to do that, when you've got a stolen treasure on you. A couple in linked arms bounce across the road to my right. He's wearing bronze flares textured and patterned like fish scales, and she's wearing yellow hipsters decorated with purple stars. They often come in pairs, strides like that. I could drop into one of the shops down near Rosie's – I might pick up something myself. I've got time to kill yet, and I'm not sure that, leg-wise, I'm dead right for what I've got in mind. In fact, I'm pretty sure that, leg-wise, I'm not dead right for what I've got in mind. The Snowboard Puffa though – the Snowboard Puffa is spot on.

I may not be well quoted on a lot of stuff, but I'm right about this.

I keep checking my inside pocket. It's hard and cold and fine in my hand. You can wedge your little finger into the eye-hole and your little finger gets caught sharp, like if you put it into your mouth and nip it.

'Are you alright, mate?'

The guy looks like a tramp. He's one of the sleepers, woken up.

All right?

Yeah, I'm all right. But I need a pen, it's a pen I need, to copy the poem down, the second bus stop poem. I think I've been standing here, haven't I, standing here a while, probably. I wonder if he's got a pen on him.

'Have you got a pen on you?'

'Never without one. Mightier than the sword, aye, reight enough. You would nae hae a cigarette on yoursel at all, would you?'

It's a fair swap, a MarlboroMan for a biro. I haven't got anything to write on. There are hundreds of flyers skating about the pavement, but they're not ideal, you always lose flyers. Anyway, I want somewhere clean. I want *something* clean. I can copy it on the jacket lining. It's an orange lining. It's nice. I can write it under the authentic label.

Somewhere before the border
Or beyond it
In the shadow of the hill
Or over it
Somewhere my heart stood still
Didn't it?
DMH 99

It's got a title, this one, it's called Appropriate (For You).

The sleeper man reads it with me, reads it out loud, and does a good job of the reading like drunks often can, as I write it down. It takes a while, I have to go over some of the letters twice. It looks good, transcribed there. Authentic. And the pen doesn't bleed like it did on the beer mat, so the lines are clean. I don't normally write on my clothes. He takes his pen back, and another fag. And he stares at me, like he's looking for something.

'You've got a mark on your eye, son, d'y'know?'

'Yeah. I noticed it last night. It's new, I think. It's alright, it doesn't hurt or anything.'

New? he says.

'Yeah. I think so.'

It's a sign, he says.

Sure. A sign, that's what it'll be.

Mind how you go, he says.

'I will.'

'Mind how you go now, son.'

'You too.'

'It's a sign.'

Yeah, right. A sign. Quarter past eleven. I could do with some coffee, and some shops. Appropriate Strides (For Me), that's what I need. Like there is such a thing. A sign. Do me a favour. Fuck.

19

That morning with Nat, when we woke in the debris of the clothes art, my strides were utterly inappropriate for me because:

1] They were crumpled.

2] They were clothes art.

3] They were all that was left of last night. They were the recoverable leftovers of redolent meaning.

4] They were really, seriously seriously crumpled.

I pulled on the silk kimono to start with, pretending I wasn't bothered about the situation. Hard, but if you go through these things, you'll be a man, my son, in the words of that verse everybody likes. It was like a usual Tuesday for Nat (except I was there). She set about getting ready for work, singing I Say a Little Prayer. I wondered if it was becoming our tune. I don't normally like a cheerfully singing person in the morning, but this one I could accept without a qualm. I moved to the kitchen area and found a coffee grinder, a manual one, and coffee beans in a foil packet. It didn't work very well, the manual grinder, but you could get grounds out of it, albeit over-large ones, if you persevered. I was stuck trying to find a filter or an Italian espresso machine or any other obvious coffee-making device, but I worked it out. I've seen this sort of set-up before. I found the brown plastic cone, the thin packet of filter bags, a jug, and I stood pouring the boiled water a little at a time, holding the filter bag gingerly by the lip to avoid it collapsing in on itself, listening to the liquid as it trickled through at an abjectly slow rate. Luckily I had a productive arrangement with Antonio that day. It wasn't till the afternoon, but at least I could feel like I was going to be working too, like I belonged, if only in the most tangential way, to the working-lifeThing that Nat was buzzing towards. It was just a straight studio shoot we were going to be doing, for a new men's magazine, a feature about biscuits, which would almost certainly be a copy of the same feature from one of the other men's magazines. No doubt about it, that's how it works with commissioning editors. This is the kind of crap I don't want to be doing with my life, that's for sure; however, some sort of form has to be shown towards assuaging my Antonio MassiveDebtConcern, although I don't actually pick up any money from the work. He just knocks my fee off what I owe him and then lends me fifty quid.

Bernie appeared and padded about in moccasins.

Even though I don't *ever* want to start talking about footwear, I can't let this go without some comment. I hate moccasins. They remind me of bungalows or something else equally horrible. Scones? Pyjamas? Sort of both of those, but really more like muffins. Yeah, that's it, muffins; they're not cakes, they're not bread, they're just stodge, and they stick to the roof of your mouth. And they're of indeterminate colour, just like moccasins. Moccasins, I ask you.

Bernie gave me a funny look and a GoodMorning in her flat delivery, which I liked less now. I was concerned that she'd be giving Nat a funny look too, in the bathroom-hall or wherever, some part of the flat where I wouldn't see it. I know what girls can be like. After what Nat'd said about how Bernie stood vis-à-vis the two of us, my being back there wouldn't be going down a storm. But then I thought that maybe it wasn't a funny look she was giving me, because her face stayed like that. Maybe that was just her normal expression in the morning. And anyway it was a bit early for a funny look, early in the day, and early in the whole relationship itself as well. I poured the girls coffee; they had nice mugs, of course, with spots on them, like a Damien Hirst spot painting, spookily enough (I mean, considering the clothes-art title that had come to me). Bernie's funny look changed slightly to the good, but if she was happy, she was happy only at the effort I'd made, because she concocted herself a cup of herb tea instead and shoofled across to the table (shoofling is the only way of 'walking' in moccasins).

Are you going out like that then, Natalie asked me.

I tightened the belt on the kimono, which is virtually impossible to do as it just slithers and comes loose again straight away. You couldn't call it a design.

My trousers are all creased, I said.

'D'you want an iron?'

She clearly hadn't had a good look at them because they were covered in duvet bobbly bits as well as creased. They were in the sort of condition where they needed cleaning before ironing before wearing as far as I was concerned. Not to mention their artistic redolence.

'Er . . .'

'I've got a pair that'd probably fit you.'

She went away and she came back. Charcoal-grey herringbone. They were good quality, at least. She held them up against me. Yeah, they'll fit, she said, smiling. She knew a great deal less about the way trousers fit than she should, given her job description, that was for sure. I had no option but to take them from her, she was being helpful, and as far as she was concerned I could always iron last night's Italians anyway. She prepared to leave. She looked demure in a pale blue cotton shirt, Comme des Garçons (it's *not* name-dropping to identify someone else's label), and brown suede jacket, mine. She was wearing hipsters which fitted as closely as the so-called slacks, and featured an embroidered pattern at the semi-flared leg-ends (it works for certain people), and a pair of flat clog-type shoes the tops of which were made from a synthetic material which had the appearance of a suede/velvet hybrid. Only girls can get away with wearing those, though they do sell them to boys too. Her hair was twisted back into the deep blue velvet hair scrunchy.

She bade me farewell with a kiss and a, Be neat, whatever that was supposed to mean, and she left muttering Winganaprair, Winganaprair.

I turned to Bernie and we both stifled a sigh. She was looking at me funny again. I had the trousers held miserably in front of me, and I began to wonder whose they were. Spurs's??? No, that can't be true. Natalie wouldn't do that. There was no way I was wearing them, anyway. Bernie was looking at the trousers too now.

She said, D'you think they'll suit you?

It's not really the first question you raise when it comes to trousers, I replied.

'What d'you mean?'

'Oh nothing. Whose are they?'

'I'm pretty sure they came from her dad. She picked a few things up from her mum's not so long ago. She's developing an interest in vintage clothing.'

She's never mentioned it to me, I said.

'You've probably got other things to talk about, haven't you?'

She rose from her tea-drinking. It was the kind of question that didn't require a reply, so I didn't give one. She picked up an apple from the fruit bowl, saying, What have you got on today then, Winger?

'A job.'

'Oh. What job's that?'

'A photo shoot, down off Rosebery Avenue somewhere.'

'You're a photographer?'

'No, I'm a director. I sort of sort everything out. Sort of thing.'

'Oh.'

I could see her absorb this, and it was evidently not unwelcome news. If it wasn't improving my standing with her, it wasn't making it any worse. There are duller-sounding ways to spend time, after all.

Are you walking? she said.

'Yeah.'

'We'll be going the same way. Give me ten minutes – you could keep me company?'

'Sure.'

Outside it was wet but not raining. Bernie was more or less exactly my height – I was grateful that she was wearing her fast shoes. She would've been higher in heels, and I've got the standard-issue male problem about walking alongside women who are taller than me. Her ankles showed an inch between the fast shoes and the frayed hem of her jeans. I like fray-hemmed jeans a lot, believe me, but I can't wear them myself. I've tried it a thousand times in a million combinations. They just don't work. Maybe it's my hair. Possibly my shoes, I don't know. But I know one thing – in the rain frayed jeans conduct water up your leg faster than anything. At least I don't get that.

I pulled my collar up. Harrington, nice collar. Where exactly are you headed, I asked.

'Studio.'

'Where's that?'

'The way you're going, I'll show you.'

It's a bit military, actually, her delivery. But I think she's being okay. I think she's still being nice, in her Bernie way.

'What d'you do there, in your studio?'

'I make pots.'

I glanced down at her wrists. They looked muscled, strong. Noticing details once I've been told about them, again.

'Do you have a potter's wheel? Do you throw the pots?' (I've always fancied a go at that.)

'Some I throw, some I build up, the ones which are too big to throw.'

'Build them up?

Yes, she said, one layer on to another.

'Like a sculpture?'

'Yes. Something like that.'

I tried trying to imagine doing it.

'Is the pot under the window one of yours?' (It's on the other side of the kitchen area at the flat. It's big with a kind of dripping glaze running down it. I flicked some ash into it while I was waiting for them to do their shower bizniss the first night.)

'Yes.'

'It's symmetrical, isn't it? Is it a built-up or a thrown?'

'A built-up.'

'How do you get it so even?'

'Experience and practice and doing it every day.'

'Do you work every day then?'

'Yes.'

'Self-discipline must be important for an . . . do you call yourself an artist?'

'That's a difficult question, Winger. I don't know. There are very few ceramists or ceramicists that are properly called Artists, but on the other hand one doesn't like to think of it as Craft. I mean, one doesn't necessarily care for the connotations implicit in that word.'

Fuck me. She was using words for talking in that I only use for thinking in. I mean, I only speak them out loud if I'm deliberately trying to piss theBoys off. TheBoys dislike long or unusual words. They prefer abbreviations, mpg, NYC, bhp, ftse, et cetera.

What about your stuff? she went on. Is that Art?

'No. It definitely isn't.'

'How *do* you describe it?'

'Commerce. I suppose.'

'You're only in it for the money?'

[If there was any] 'Mmph. Yeah.'

'What *do* you want to do with your life then?'

What *is* going on? That's twice in six hours I've been asked this one.

'What does anyone want to do with their life?' And I flashed her my best smile – the one I specifically developed in my infancy to please my Great Auntie – to carry the question back and to take the weight off me.

Get married and have babies, she said.

I wondered if Bernie also listed 'being a bit sarcastic sometimes' amongst her unappealing habits. Well, I can't tell her I haven't a [fucking] clue. It won't help. So I try :

'Have you got an agent, and a gallery and all that?'

'No. Not yet.'

'Have you always wanted to pot?'

'Well, I was lucky, I guess. I grew up surrounded by beautiful things. I wanted to make some of my own. When I first put my hands into clay, I just knew I was . . . well, this is going to sound a bit shit, Winger, but I felt like I was home, y'know?'

'Home. Really? When was that?'

'An art summer school. I was twelve.'

'It must be very primitive. Is it? Dealing with clay? Like mud, the Earth?'

This was the moment for her to have a good look at me.

'Yees. Yes . . . It is a very instinctive process, actually. I lose myself completely. Hours pass and I don't know where they've gone.'

Sounds wonderful, I said.

She gave me the once-over once more. She'd've seen that the trousers didn't suit me all that badly, in fact, that they were quite sharp. Or rather, they would have been quite sharp if it wasn't for the eleven major and seventeen minor fit-related complaints. They were original 50s. Although I *do* wear other people's clothes, it's a different matter when you have them forced upon you. But you have to meet with triumph and disaster and treat the two impostors both the same et cetera. I was being as brave as I could about it. And the clothes art really *was* unwearable.

The sky was giving the appearance of rain. We walked fast, her fast shoes were good for it, my PatrickC's not so, the soles still shiny and prone to skidding. New leather soles are awful for that. We didn't say anything for a while and then she picked up where we'd left off, like people do.

'Yes. Sometimes it is wonderful.'

She said it almost to herself. And then she opened up and turned to me and said, I wish Natalie would sort herself out and realize her potential. She's wasted buying and selling, she should be designing, you know. She's talented.

She is, I said, half in affirmation, half in question, allowing Bernie to answer.

'Yes. She's a very creative person. She should develop. She has a great soul.'

That's articulated that one for me then. That's what I think every time I look into in her eyes. Soul blue is the colour of them. And soul blue is the distance of them. That's their thing.

We'd arrived at the studio. It was part of one of those yards with units.

Would you like a look round, she asked.

Thanks. Yeah. I would.

20

In the afternoon, while Antonio was setting up in a warehouse space he shares, I was unloading my bag and unadmiring the magazine boys' attire. I mean, for my money, retro and pastiche as they may be, viscose 70s slacks only really work their retro and pastiche magic if you're lead-singing in a retropastiching pop group. Just about. Otherwise I wouldn't bother. In this company, my own trousers, Natalie's dad's trousers, were looking class. That they didn't fit by a mile was bothering me considerably less than it should've been, though it was possible that the collection of body pains I'd begun to feel were distracting my focus. My back was aching like a bugger, and my right leg was hurting badly. I started sorting the props and thinking about last night – had there been some incident on the pitch I couldn't even remember? I didn't pick it up in the bedroom, did I? An art injury? I just couldn't remember.

The biscuit feature was a feature about how sexy each particular brand had been discovered to be. The magazine boys had been havin' it large down the office, testin' biscuits for foreplay-dunkability and so on: Marianne Faithfull, Mars Bars – you've got the idea, you've got the picture, you've got the whole piece. They made use of a blow-up doll for practical demonstrations. They brought it with them. They were throwing Jammy Dodgers about, givin' it tampon innuendo. That's pronounced, in-your-end-ohh! Which was pretty subtle for them. Normally it's: The good thing about Trace is she lets me have a poke when she's on – toffee apples or what! I don't know what that is, toffee apples. And I'd like to think they don't have real girlfriends, that they make it all up. I mean, the job they do is uncool in every sense; worse than sleeping in public in your pyjamas in a window, worse, way worse, than moccasins or muffins – about as cool as tattooing your girlfriend's name on your dick to show how much you love her. These boys *are* the boys who *are* the bona fide dumbers-down of everything you could ever talk about; even if they did art it'd be, Jackson Pollock – Well Hung Or What!? Giving the Punters What They Wants, is the way they describe matters. *And* in addition, they are the wearers of very, very bad clothes. But all the same, they do have girlfriends – I've seen them – and I don't know what to make of that.

What was the winning biscuit then, Antonio asks.

Viscose Slacks 1: Obvious innit. Chocolate Fingers. In bunches of fives! V'you got 'em, mate?

The inquiry is addressed to me. I picked up Jaffa Cakes, plain and dark chocolate Hob Nobs, and, oh, everything. Everything you can think of. Plus five different selection boxes, just to be on the safe side. And half a dozen packets of chocolate covered Snack Squares, though I'm not sure Snack Squares are officially biscuits. I bought them at a version of Mr Wellstocked's on the walk over, together with doilies and paper plates and other minor accessories. It was a version of Mr Wellstocked's that actually *was* very well stocked, a version that practically seemed to specialize on the biscuit side. I displayed the goods.

Viscose Slacks 2: Nice one, bro'. (He's white. They all are.)

Viscose Slacks 1: We thought y'might, y'know, do something with Caprice here. He picks up the blow-up doll, kisses her, nothing more than a peck, and hands it to me.

Viscose Slacks 2 adds: Nothin too hardcore though. Summink tasteful. Y'know.

Well, I say, I think we ought to deflate her first. Soft wrinkled plastic has limitless possibilities, doesn't it? It's like melted wax, or, in a different light, volcanic lava, no?

Viscose Slacks 2: Yeah, man. (Give them the obvious, you can't go wrong.)

It could be a duvet or a body, or a duvet and a body all rolled together, I continue, the possibilities coming thick and fast. A beach even, if Antonio softens the lens, he could make it look like that. He's a skilled man.

Viscose Slacks 1: Deflate Caprice? Let her down? 'R you sure? Be better if it were like she were like a real bird, wouldn't it? Innit?

Winger: Might be too hardcore?

Viscose Slacks 2 to Viscose Slacks 1: No worries. The real babe's on the cover for this anyway. Breakfast telly, the one with the monster thruppneys. She's gonna have a couple of Digestives coverin' 'er nipples – they only just about do it, y'know.

All-round impressedness at this. Respec' to the areola (one unusual word theBoys *do* know).

Vicose Slacks 1: Strapline goes: Melinda Frock – One Dunk Or Two? I think it's that anyway. Does it sound right?

Sounds good to me, says Antonio. Sounds top, he drawls in his dry-as-a-bone drawl. It's only having him here that gets me through it. Offering the viscoseBoys some of the Snack Squares, I'm informed they're both on a diet.

21

Clay makes air smell sweet and damp. As Bernie walked me round her workshop through the sweet damp air, the thing I noticed most about her was that she was the same as she was before, not two people, one mask for work and another different one for home, as is often the case. Now I think about it, Antonio's like that. He has technical matters to deal with when he's photographing which distract him, but he doesn't change much, apart from donning the veneer of dryness at the appropriate moment.

Bernie had thick brown slabs of clay rolled out like pastry rectangles.

What's going on with this clay, I asked.

'It's drying. It has to dry a little before I can work it into bigger pieces – it's to do with structure.'

I didn't know you needed to do that with clay, let it dry. And I didn't know there were so many types. There were heavy plastic bags of it on the floor, different colours, and they produced different weights of pre-dust residue, pre-dust residue which I was trying to keep off Natalie's dad's trousers. Dust residue will become dust actual, and when you see it in this embryonic state, you realize why dust comes in many forms and colours, just check the turn-ups of your trousers for a sample cross-section – if you're unwise enough to wear trousers with turn-ups, that is.

There was even more dust sparkling in smaller bags. Bernie said they were pigments for glazes.

The powders of the pigments were spilling on to the surfaces of the bare wood shelves. I ran my finger through the colours. I'd like to say I didn't do the really obvious obvious thing and draw a heart containing two initials pierced by an arrow in the red iron-oxide residue (my favourite of the pre-dust colour selection) but that would be a lie. I stood well away from the shelf as I did it, of course.

The kiln was in the corner. I expected it to be rustic and made of bricks, but in fact it was electric and didn't look all that much different to a regular commercial oven, just bigger and more basic.

While Bernie stepped into her overalls, still wearing her fast shoes – you can put your feet through your trousers all right that way, but taking them off with your shoes still on is not really worth trying – I picked up a finished pot from a long bench. There were pots arranged in files of descending size, like ranks of unpacked Russian dolls. They were all alike too, like Russian dolls, turned in a classic urn shape. They were in a natural finish.

It's unglazed, isn't it, I said.

Well, yes, apart from the rim, she replied.

There was a narrow band of colour shining around the lip at the top, like a collar. The feel of the unglazed part shivered through me and made me grind my teeth, like certain kinds of carpet do on bare feet, or if the open end of a cigarette filter ever catches on my tongue.

Are these the kind you throw on a wheel, I asked.

Yes they are, she said. I call them my pot boilers, those. HaHa.

'Do you shape them completely by hand then?'

'No, I use these too.'

She handed me a template from a selection she kept in a shortbread tin. They were hard plastic shapes and she described how you held them against the clay as it turned in order to cut the pattern of the foot/plinth part at the base. They were like guitar plectrums only bigger and unsymmetrical. I handled another one. Under the clay-powder residue, the surface was embossed by type and figures. Can you buy these then, I asked, imagining there must be a potter's supply shop somewhere which sold specialist pot-making tools. She laughed. No, Winger. I cut them myself. Look properly, you'll see they're made from old credit cards. I looked properly. It was true. Now that *is* nice, to actually make money out of them instead of the other way around. I picked the pot up once more, trying to overcome my teeth-grinding thing.

'This colour at the rim – do you have to fire it twice then, once before and once after?'

Yes, she said. You fire it first, then you apply glaze – we call the first firing the biscuit stage.

Really? (What's going on, is it national biscuit day or something?) *Can* you fire pottery more than twice, I asked.

'Yes. You're very inquisitive, Winger.'

'Oh, well, y'know. I'm not normally in a potter's studio.'

This was okay. She put the kettle on. I walked about touching surfaces. Dusty surfaces. Everything was dusty. I had to avoid bumping my trousers into everything, and there was no chance of a sit-down.

Yes, you can fire more than twice, she said. There's a potter whose work I admire who uses that technique. She makes pieces that look as though they're melting.

'So you can do it as many times as you want?'

'Well, no, ultimately it will shatter. It depends on the strength of the original material and the firing temperature and the glaze.'

I returned the pot to its place in the rank, being very careful not to rub it against any other of the pots. I hadn't overcome my teeth-grinding thing, not at all.

They're nice overalls those, I said. Where d'you get them?

They're the best I've found, she replied. They're a good strong cotton. I go to a surplus shop off Mile End Road. Do you photo-directors require overalls then?

'No. It's just . . . Well, listen, Bernie, I'll tell you something, but don't repeat this anywhere else, okay?'

'I'll try not to.'

'I sometimes think about wearing dungarees –'

She interrupted by sucking through her teeth like a

plumber quoting a job: That *is* bad, Winger.

'– not seriously, of course, because it's the fashion faux pas par excellence, of course. I never stop to handle a pair or anything like that. But I do *think* about wearing them. And work overalls are the only way you can get away with it, if you're a man, I mean, aren't they?'

'You're having me on.'

I could see how she could think that. No I'm not, I said. I'm serious. The thing is, it would get you out of the problem of what trousers to wear.

'Is that a problem? Generally? I'm quite able to see how you might feel a little odd today, not being in your own pair, but . . .'

'Do they look stupid, these?'

'They look alright. They're rather good, actually. A tiny bit loose round the bottom maybe, but I think you'll survive. Do you worry about your trousers looking stupid then?'

'No.'

'Are you sure?'

'No.'

'You're not sure?'

'Er . . .'

I tugged at the thigh material. I stuck my hands deep into the pockets. At least they had deep pockets. I was on the edge of panic, I was trying to contain it but I could feel my fingernails going numb.

'You do worry about it, don't you?'

'Yes. Actually, I do.'

'Hmmm. That's called KecksComplaint, isn't it?'

'What!? Is it? Has it got a name?'

'You're really not having me on, are you?'

I lit a cigarette. I pulled the match across the wall. It didn't help, it just made me think of the word Flares, but I had to try *something* to reconfer my cool. I inhaled enormously. I clenched my fists to hide my white nails and burnt my hand on the dying match head, for fuck's sake. Bernie, I said, I don't know why I'm telling you this, but worrying about the fit of my trousers and other associated trouser aspects occupies much much more of my waking time than it should. And sometimes my dreaming time too. I let out the balance of the enormous inhalation and coughed. Don't mention this to Natalie. Please.

'Isn't there something rather more important that you should be spending your sleeping and waking time worrying about?

'What? What's that?'

'Well, I've seen you and Nat together for a combined total of about three-quarters of an hour, but it's been enough.'

'What?'

'Being in love with someone else's girlfriend should be of slightly more concern than the size of your trouser waistband relative to your own actual girth, shouldn't it?'

'What d'you mean, In Love?'

'Come on, Winger, don't play the disingenuous. I've just said: I've seen you two together for three-quarters of an hour.'

'Has Natalie spoken to you about this?'

She only looked at me in answer, and the look said, You know better than that; girlfriends don't pass information of this nature, not under no circumstances.

I knew that already, of course. I hitched up the trousers. Slack. They were too fucking slack. The waistband, by the way, I said, is merely *one* aspect of the whole situation. And I don't have girth.

She pulled some clay out of a bag and whacked it on to the bench. She repeated the action. Everybody has girth, she said. She took one last handful of clay out and began melding, like kneading dough, and as she did she turned her head sideways and asked sweetly, Are you displacing your worries about love and life into your trousers, d'you think?

'No. I've always been like this.'

'Have you? Has your whole life been such a displacement?'

'I don't think it's as simple as that.'

'You think it's more complicated than that?'

There was no point giving her my whole take on the world and everything in it. Bloody potters.

Would you like it to change, your life, she asked, still melding.

'I don't know. I'm used to it. Yes. I would like it to change. As a matter of fact I think it might be happening already actually.' [I mean last night I used my trousers for clothes art, and I did that *in front of* Natalie]

'Ever been in love before, Winger?'

'Listen, I didn't say anything about being in love, did I?'

'You'll deny it, will you?'

I tightened my belt beyond the last hole. I need an extra hole in this belt to hold these trousers up, I said.

'Evasion, Winger.'

'Bernie, I can't tell you if I haven't told her yet, can I?'

She accepted that this wasn't far off an answer. She passed me my herb tea. It smelt like Ribena substitute. I wouldn't be drinking that.

Give it to me, she said, indicating that she meant the belt. I unslid it. Hold it on the bench, she said. She took a hammer and a steel-punch from a drawer underneath. The punch-handle was engraved with that spiral diagonal pattern. It reminded me of metalwork at school. And so did the stance I'd had to adopt – my groin pressed against the bench to hold the trousers up. I always had problems with my school trousers like that, problems to do with belt holes not being in the right position, problems that were exacerbated by those hook-and-eye fasteners on the inside of the waistband - the illest designed trouser fastener ever – problems which were somehow made worse when having to wear the metalwork apron. The thought made me wince.

The punch hovered over the belt in her hand.

'Where do you need it?'

'Twelve mm after the last one.'

'That's very precise, Winger.'

'Details are important, Bernie.'

She pressed the tip of the steel against the leather and brought the hammer down on it. It didn't pierce the first time. It took three attempts.

'There.'

'Thanks.'

Bernie, I said as I rethreaded it, I mean there must be something up, mustn't there? Between her and him. Or why would she bother? With me.

I'm saying nothing, she said.

She'd returned to her clay very deliberately, pressing down with her palm, spreading the material to some determined diameter. A practised action.

'Don't think I'm taking this lightly or anything, Bernie. I've never felt like . . .'

I paused. I tightened the belt. Better, although of course surplus waistband material gathered at the top now. She turned her head and finished the sentence for me, in measured syllables: Never felt like this about anyone before?

She made the words sound ironic. Bernie, I said, just because it's a cliché, it doesn't mean it isn't true.

'You've never felt like this about anyone before?'

I think I stood there looking dumb.

'Go on. Try to say it.'

Yes, I did stand there looking dumb.

'Go on, you can do it.'

I've never felt like this about anyone before. I said it out loud.

She looked at me. I looked at her. Well done, Winger, she said.

'Thanks, Bernie. Thanks.'

'I think you've just taken a step forward.'

I think she was right.

For your reward, she said, I'll let you off drinking that tea.

22

My eye was watering as I walked away from Bernie's studio that morning. I've only just remembered. Maybe a little shard of something flew off the bench as she punched the belt and I never even felt it at the time. It can happen, that. Maybe that's where the mark began. The woken sleeper keeps calling after me as I move away, A mark on your eye, son, it's a sign. Drunks – they get a fix on an idea and never stop talking about it.

It doesn't matter where you go – Bond Street flagship emporium, Kensington department store, High Street, Mall, Chico Casuals in Tulse Hill (don't bother), the Hip-Mart at World's End. The choice is yours, it makes no difference – the most common mood of the retail shop assistant is bored, bored, bored. I enter a small multiple, not the one Nat works for. Once in a while I have considered working in a clothes shop myself, so that I too could assimilate myself to being so entirely at ease with all manner of attire (including, specifically, of course, legwear) that, over time, I would be left filled with feelings of nothing other than total and complete ennui and tedium, bordering almost on derision, at the sight of garments.

There is of course the other worse kind of clothes shop assistant, the kind you hide from, the Enthusiast, the type who'll talk to you over your shoulder even after you've been scrupulous about avoiding eye contact, forcing you to say, No, I don't want any help thanks, I'm just browsing.

Honestly, in what other context would you ever be forced into the use of the word browsing? I know, on the Internet. (Exactly.)

I try five pairs, which fail for the following reasons:

Pair 1 Ridiculous fit. Nobody in the world's that shape.

Pair 2 Ridiculous fit. Nobody in the world's that shape either.

Pair 3 Five miles of unnecessary leg length.

Pair 4 Supposed to be my size but no chance of fastening at waist. Faulty.

Pair 5 Designed by someone without a bottom, for someone without a bottom.

The assistant here is straight out of the Infants, of the very very bored, bored, bored ilk, and is wearing silver body-cut Capri-pants with cuffs and buttons at the hem, a style that might be described as urban spaceBoy, ideal for if the moon was a warm and fashion-conscious place. You wouldn't catch me in them even if I was in pantomime. As if you could trust this person to sell you trousers.

There are other shops on the way (let's face it, I know where they all are), but there's a fat chance of finding anything appropriate. You really need to set two days aside for trouser shopping, it's not something you can do speculatively like this. Killing time is all I'm doing, just killing time.

I sigh and leave and walk, and hear sudden fast footsteps behind me and somebody call out:

'Hey. You dropped this.'

It's urban spaceBoy. He hands me the mask.

'Fuck [Fuck] Fuck [Fuck] Fuck . . . [Fuck] Thanks.'

"T's okay. It's always happening. You'd be surprised what we find in the changing rooms.'

'Really? Right. Thanks.'

'I found a snorkel once.'

'Did you?'

Yes. What is it anyway, he asks, leaning in to me, suddenly unaware of the concept of personal space, a concept with which he'd had no problem while being bored and dangling his legs from the shop-counter and pretending to read CD box info-labels half a minute ago.

'It's a family heirloom.'

Oh, he says. That's interesting. What is it?

'It's a mask.'

I thought it was, he says. It's *so* unusual. What's it for?

'It's for keeping snow out of your eyes.'

Oh, smart, he says. Cool, he says. I just love accessories, he says. And he walks away. Take it easy, he calls, as he walks.

Take it easy? That's Rosie's catch phrase. Can I count this as the third déjà-vu of the day? It's not even *lunch*time yet, for goodness' sake (as my Great Auntie used to say if untoward events happened in the a.m.). Fuck. I must be more careful, I could get arrested like this. I need a safe place for it – a bag with a lockable pocket. I need to buy a bag anyway.

23

After the photo shoot with the viscoseBoys, I picked up the fifty quid from Antonio, sorted a couple of arrangements, and walked West chewing a Fig Roll, which didn't really fill the gap, so I stopped off at a sandwich bar. I try to avoid them as they make me sad, but sometimes I really need a sandwich. The cramped West End booths where you get old-fashioned fillings served by old-fashioned Italian men are the ones I go for, they're the kind of sandwich outlets which are the least like ours was, out in Acton. Ours was hip and unsuccessful. Avant-garde we were, which is not another word for shite, as I read John Lennon once said. It's another word for empty. Post-sandwich-purchase I sat on a wall, half-way through my honey and banana on white, when a man at the wheel of a car parked at the kerbside in front of me came to my attention. I'd sucked my carton of juice down to the stage where I was making slurping noises and it was decompressing like a collapsed lung. I don't like to mess about doing that for too long so I stepped up to drop it into a wastebin. That was how the man came to my attention. The bin was just in front of the car, and my movement to stand gave me an oblique view across the windscreen where the man was leaning forward, slumped, with his arms cradling the steering wheel. He looked like he might be ill or like he might even be dead, and I walked around to the other side, the roadside-side, to see if he was okay. I didn't know what I was going to do if he wasn't okay, I've never done St John's Ambulance, Duke of Edinburgh's, Mountain Rescue or anything. I crouched a little to see through his window and he must have caught this movement because he glanced sideways a second and I could see that his eyes were red, he was crying; it was MarkyBoy. I stood back sharp and assessed the situation.

BMW, big black one. I crouched again. He had his head back down, but it definitely was MarkyBoy. I wasn't sure if he'd recognized me or not, and I was less than clear about what to do now, because I knew him but I didn't know him all that well. You have to know someone really well to comfort their crying; or not at all.

I went and sat back on the wall, holding the other half of my sandwich in its paper bag and keeping my eye on him. I'd heard about this sort of thing, from theBoys. It's the sort of thing they take the piss out of, a guy Losing It. Losing It can get you disowned, it's a very uncool thing to be doing, even more uncool than lacking commercial ambition or not being able to handle your drugs. A couple of years ago, when I was working with Alan, one of our colleagues, Rufus, failed to return from his lunch. He'd gone to a pub and started drinking and he'd stayed there until he decided that the thing to do would be to cut his wrists, which he did by breaking his glass on the counter and using that for the job. In the middle of the afternoon, the story started filtering in – someone had gone out for cakes and had seen the ambulance and had spoken to the medics and picked up the details. We were younger then and even Alan was a bit shocked, though you could see the gleam in his eye, you could see how he was working out the chain of promotion, where the gap lay, who'd get to fill it, how much better off this could leave him. And though I despised him for his response – it's wasn't even standard-issue-boy response, it was advanced – he wasn't exactly wrong to be thinking that way, because that was the way it would go. That's the way it goes. We'd never seen a suicide attempt before, but he was right to be thinking that trying to kill yourself would be a bad career move, falling as it does into the category Losing It.

There's a sequence in The Long Goodbye where the villain and his posse of sidekicks apprehend Marlowe as he arrives at his apartment in the middle of the night. Because Marlowe's friend, the one he took down to Mexico, has gone dead with the villain's money, then – according to the villain – the whole business is a scam, a scam that Marlowe must be in on. The posse run through their scaring tactics. But Marlowe knows nothing about anything. He really doesn't. The villain's girlfriend (not his wife) comes up from outside where she's been left in the Cadillac. She comes up because she was frightened by being alone. To prove how serious he is about getting the dough back, to illustrate his seriousness to Marlowe, the villain takes a Coke bottle from Marlowe's fridge, takes a drink, complains that it's flat, and smashes the bottle into his girlfriend's face (she'd made the mistake of asking for the Coke). The posse bundle her out, and the villain leaves with the threat: That's a person I love, Marlowe. You, I don't even like.

It's an ugly scene, unexpected in its sudden brutality, and it reminds me of Rufus. I think about the moment he damaged himself like that, with the broken glass. We found out later that it was because his girlfriend had left him for another guy. He used to dress in pink satin flares at parties before the 70s were totally retro, he was a very upbeat character like that. It made me think about his inner depths, the suicide incident, you'd never see that side of him. His wrists were still bandaged, Alan said, when he returned one morning a few weeks later to collect his stuff. I missed him. I mean I missed seeing him because I was off that day, and I missed him too, at work. I left the firm to set up The Scanty Sandwich with a couple more disillusionedBoys not long after that. We still speak, me and the other disillusionedBoys, even though there was a bit of cake lost at the time, but we don't really see each other any more, and I never talk about them. It's too painful. I don't much care for success, but failure's worse.

Watching over MarkyBoy and thinking about The Scanty,

and remembering Rufus and the work we all used to do together back then (team-building and all that crap, you can imagine how I liked it, but I felt part of it all the same), was bringing me down. It felt like Spring proper as I sat on the wall holding the half-sandwich, an illusion – because it was the beginning of February. It was as if a season *had* come in in advance. There was sun in the air. But the glint of light from his windscreen and MarkyBoy's place in the scene made it somehow *feel* like Autumn, like any Edward Hopper painting, he looked lonely in that way. There's something about Autumn I don't like, everything dying, and I wanted to cry as well. If you could buy the seasons in advance, you'd be able to sell them on too. You wouldn't have to have Autumn if you didn't want, you could go straight to Winter.

Three schoolgirls pulled in beside me, distracting me from these thoughts. They sat on the wall as they neared the point in their conversation, with each other, and also with a fourth party on their mobile, where the matter had clearly become serious enough that walking and talking was too much and only talking could take place now.

The girl holding the phone was especially animated. Listen, she said, I can't come over to your place, can I, 'cos everybody knows what that would mean.

Her friends nodded agreement. They were about fourteen or fifteen, in uniform, all with long hair and dusky skin. They looked like sisters. The phonee must have responded to her last line by asking what this thing was, the thing that everyone would know what it meant.

They'll know I like you, innit, the mobile girl replied.

The friends giggled. I imagined a happy boy at the other end, hearing this. Having girls tell you that they like you is superb when you're a boy. The next thing he must have asked her was what would be wrong with everyone knowing that she liked him, because she pressed herself into the handset, like she was talking to the boy face to face, and said, Don't want everyone to know, *do I*?

The other pair nodded this through vigorously – it would be wrong for anyone bar themselves to be acquainted with the knowledge. The fall-out from the phone was enough that I could actually hear him ask, Why not?

Because if I came round, then everyone would know I liked you, and I don't want 'em to, like I said, she exasperated, even though this was simply a repeat of her case so far without the addition of further reasoning.

The same lines were knocked back and forth a few times, while the friends huddled in closer either shaking their heads or nodding or giggling or suppressing giggles, as was most appropriate. I felt lucky to have this event happening upon me – they were in their own self-contained pocket – they didn't see me and they didn't see MarkyBoy – they were giving off exuberance which was like a shield to my descending mood. Young love must be as good as life gets, in retrospect, and probably even at the time. It was evident by her answers that the phonee boy hadn't considered suggesting he come over to her instead. In fact, he must've begun acting wounded about her not coming over to him, because her tone dropped into Mae West(ish) and she said, Yeah, I love you, of course I do.

Well, the boy was doing brilliantly here, I almost felt like cheering. I could picture him dunking a chocolate biscuit in celebration of being loved and being told about it, probably even over-dunking, resulting in floating-in-the-tea syndrome (an area of biscuitology that the viscoseBoys thought was Large – on their non-diet days – because they liked slurping the soggy bits out of the cup, if you can believe that). The phone conversation ended. MobileGirl's declaration silenced her friends. Everything went quiet. Love was a serious matter, and they knew it.

What did he say, they asked. He didn't say nothing, she replied.

They walked off. They lived in their own world. I thought about Nat and I wondered if this was what her life was really like, that she lived in her own world with her friends with their codes and rules and what the fuck was I doing trying to get into it, what right did I have anyway? It's sandwiches that make me think that way. They depress me. It's a post-Scanty thing. They never used to. I walked over to MarkyBoy's car. I had a plan to make him feel better.

He still hadn't moved. I tapped on the window. He raised his head and let the window down, it slid electrically, like everything does.

Listen, Mark, I said, I'm sorry to bother you, but you wouldn't have a phone on you, would you? (I don't have one myself.)

He wiped his face on his sleeve and handed it over without speaking.

I called Natalie's work.

'Could I speak to Natalie, please?'

'I'll see if she's at her desk. Who may I say is calling?'

'Winger.'

'Sorry, Mr . . . was that W'gah?'

'Winger.'

'*Winger?*'

'Winger Supply Co.'

'I'll just put you on hold while I locate her extension.'

They had Sade for the hold music. Most unusual. Unexpected. It was Smooth Operator – *His eyes are like angels' but his heart is cold, da da da . . .*

Hi, she said.

Hi, I said.

Calling me at work, eh. What d'you want? she said.

'Is it a bad time?'

'Not necessarily. What d'you want?'

Actually, I wasn't sure now. I was going to tell her that

we couldn't see each other any more, that it wasn't fair for me to get into her life, that Spurs (I'd started feeling sorry for him now, for God's sake) could end up sitting in his car crying like MarkyBoy was, or slashing his wrists like Rufus did, and then after that, if he was still alive, he could have some dickhead like Alan take his job. I was going to tell her she was right, that everything would be too much. That Winganaprair would only be half of it. That we should stop it before it started.

After this I was going to turn to Marky and say, Look – I've got nothing, I've just finished with the first person I've ever loved because I know it won't work – she's already got a boyfriend, all that, everything, it'll just be a fuck-up. I haven't even got a proper job, or a proper commercial ambition, I've only got a c/o address, I've got debts, I can't handle my drugs. I've even been called a waster by a beggar (a beggar said it to me once when I hadn't any change). A *waster*, by a *beggar*. Can you believe that? And, *and*, I've got some serious psychological problems vis-à-vis my legwear.

I thought it might help him to hear this. It might put his problems into perspective.

But then I thought of the words Bernie had made me say. And how it was true that I never *had* felt like this before. And then I thought about the viscoseBoys, of how they treated women and how they still had girlfriends and how clear it was that there must be another way, a better way. And I thought about Antonio and his dryness and his skill, and how he goes through those shitty jobs in order to subsidize his wildlife, his real work; he gives me hope. I thought of Pancho and how he always does that thing with his paw, and how that gives me hope too. And the essence of the brilliant mobile girl and her brilliant friends was fresh on me too.

They only took the time of a break in the connection, these thoughts.

So instead of what I was going to say, I said:

It was nice of you to lend me your dad's trousers.

That's okay, she replied. But I want them back. Did they fit then?

Like a glove, I said.

'Good. Anything else, honey?'

Honey? That's the first time she's called me that. Well, there is just one thing. I think I'd better say it before Bernie lets anything slip.

'Natalie, I think I love you.'

I passed the Nokia in through the window. Nice one, I said. Now I've really fucked it up.

'Why, what did she say?'

She said, What d'you mean, *think*?

MarkyBoy focused on me with intent, and said, You have to tell her outright, otherwise she won't believe you. It's not a sentiment with any room in it for doubt.

He last-number-redialled and pressed the set into my hand.

Diamond life, lover boy . . .

Natalie, I love you.

24

I handed the Nokia back once more. For the second time that day my fingernails were white.

D'you wanna get in the car, he asked.

'This wasn't exactly what I had in mind right now, Marky. (I was cheering *him* up, *that* was the plan.) You were worrying me. You were crying, weren't you?'

'D'you wanna get in the car?'

'I mean . . .'

'Just get in the car, eh.'

'Alright. Alright. Alright.'

It's better furnished than Antonio's flat, with comfier seating. Is this what it is I hate about these cars, that they're just too plush, too easy, there's too much luxury? They're not unlike the foyers from the offices where theBoys work, where the set-up's set up to reassure you that you're a-okay, in a safe place, when of course you're not, prey as you are to anti-head-hunters and suicidists all around.

I passed him the balance of the sandwich. 'D'you fancy it?'

MarkyBoy took it and threw it out the window like a baby discarding a rattle from a pram.

What's the matter then, I asked.

I'm not hungry, he replied. I'll take you for a drive.

It was quiet for the time of day (it was more or less knocking-off time), one of those odd pockets of still silence like you sometimes get round the back of the British Museum, although it was from a side-turning near Mortimer Street that we glid into traffic as MarkyBoy fiddled about under the steering wheel, not looking where he was going, like people don't.

What did she say, he asked.

I wasn't sure what to make of Natalie's response, how to

translate it, I was running the words over in my mind and I didn't want to tell Marky her answer, but I couldn't think of anything better, so I did.

'She said: You can't say that, it's making my head explode.'

He was checking his rear-view mirror. 'Do you make that a good or a bad thing?'

'Not sure. Good?'

'What else did she say?'

'Nothing. We got cut off, the line dropped.'

'Probably a reasonable point for a disconnection. Give you both time to think, wouldn't you say?'

'Yeah. You might be right. Yeah.'

'Would she expect this declaration? Have you warmed her up for it?'

'I kind of . . . well, I did mention Love in an oblique sort of way last night.'

'Would this said obliqueness come under the aegis of warming her up?'

I'd heard MarkyBoy speak before, often enough, in this kind of barristorial manner, but all the same there was some edge in the sound of his voice that was new. I answered the question.

'I'm not sure. We were having a cool time. Together. I mean, well, we'd had an awkward conversation in the restaurant after I'd left you after the football . . .'

MarkyBoy interrupted. Yes, you attracted much disapprobation by that action, he said, at the same time nodding to indicate that I should go on.

' . . . but we were okay by the time I used the word.'

'You were in bed by then?'

'On it.'

'It was after sex?'

I never answer questions like that. Something about me must've said Yes though, because he nodded and said, She might not be totally unprepared for it then; in a sense you've led her to the idea by your use of the word – Love – in the post-coital receptive environment. And by being oblique about it, you've diminished – as much as is possible – the normal pressure that such a moment carries. In short, you haven't done that badly. No?

'Maybe.'

I was beginning to feel like Mark had some specialist knowledge in this area. The way he was speaking was not unlike the psychologist you get on the radio (she comes on after the sport sometimes, on the transistor in the bathroom), he was couching propositions in questions to me in that professional way. Bernie had been doing something similar in the workshop. What was I giving off? Were Natalie's dad's trousers making me look especially in need of counselling or therapy or something?

How did she sound, he asked. Did her voice change after your declaration?

'Well, first there was a silence, then she . . . well, she sounded more or less normal, I think. Although I wouldn't call what she said normal.'

'And how do you feel about her voice not changing?'

'Don't know. What d'you think?'

'She's at work, isn't she?'

'Yeah, yeah.'

'Then it could be difficult for her to talk properly, it's quite possible other people would be listening-in.'

That's true. And she isn't a schoolgirl after all, like the schoolgirls were. Her friends and colleagues wouldn't be giggling and nodding things through, would they? They'd be doing something else. They'd be standing round, or probably sitting on her desk like in a coffee-ad going: You gave him your work number!? Jesus, Nat, how stupid can you get? Well, you can at least get a new mobile and keep your ansaphone on monitor. Mad. How long have you known him? Is it a fortnight? Yeah. Right.

We turned into the main road, the indicator seemed over-loud because the sound deadening was first class; we sat in near-silence, the volume display on the Entertainment System reading oo. We were heading down to Aldwych. I offered Marky a cigarette, but he didn't smoke, which I knew. My offering was a way of requesting an exemption – it was obvious that this was a space where smoking was not normally allowed. Antonio's friend, the one who slept in the tram, told me that in Italy you can smoke anywhere – museums, art galleries, corner shops, clothes shops, even in banks. He said it was virtually compulsory. I'd like to go there, just to see that.

We drove in silence for half a minute, I let the window down so the smoke could drift out. We hadn't gone much further when the traffic came to a standstill. Mark was looking across me at the people coming up from the tube, and he started talking, his voice changing from the clipped delivery of a minute before to something more distant and slow.

'I got married young, y'know. I don't suppose I've ever mentioned it.'

He hadn't. I wondered how much older than me he was. I wouldn't've put him past late twenties.

How old are you now then, I asked.

'Thirty-two in June.'

I glanced at him. You couldn't really tell. He looked good for that age.

'It was nearly ten years ago.'

'You were only twenty-two?'

'Too young I suppose, although no one can persuade you of it at the time.'

'Yeah, you think you know everything when you're young, don't you?'

'Lizzy. Very pretty, extrovert, we weren't much alike.'

He pulled a picture out of his wallet. Redhead.

She was a bit wild, he said. She liked nothing more than

to throw food about in restaurants and at dinner parties.

He laughed softly. I pictured bread rolls arcing through the air as I handed back the photograph. The cars edged forward, bumpers to bumpers, pedestrians squeezing in between, dispatchers cutting us up.

'We went out for a couple of years before we married. Bought our first place in Cricklewood – people thought we were crazy.'

I knew what he meant, Cricklewood's about as cool as Acton.

He was focused, talking to himself, staring through the windscreen. Something in him had dissolved, I might not have been there. The traffic was still barely shifting – it's weird how it can be blocked solid just around the corner from where it's been so empty. He continued, and I took my turn at radio psychologist mode: I dropped into a period of passive listening while he talked it out.

'In the daytime we both worked, hard, and at nights we spent time together doing the place up, stripping wallpaper and sanding floorboards and arguing about paint colours. We sold that house, and we made a tidy sum and we bought a bigger place, near Earls Court. It over-stretched us. I was, I got into . . . well, I suppose you'd have to describe it as scamming – it's not a word I like. I was taking on outside consultancy work and other odds and ends to service the borrowing. Things were tight. I was over-tired, she was over-tired . . .'

He drifted to quiet. You were both over-tired, I said, to let him know that I was keeping up, that I was still with him.

'We were both over-tired, and maybe there wasn't much fun.'

My cigarette had nearly burnt away, and he reached over and took it from me, took a drag and tossed it out of the window.

'We were camping out on the ground floor – sleeping on a baseless futon, all that, while we did the rest of the place up. We'd've been set fair if it'd gone right. Have you seen property prices in SW5 these days?'

I shook my head. He remained staring through the windscreen. I prompted him again. What happened, I asked. How did it not all go right?

'I came home in the late afternoon one day – I'd finished work early, I was going to grout the bathroom tiles – and I found . . . Shit, it sounds so crass, even to me. I found a note she'd left on the mantelpiece. We *had* a mantelpiece by then, at least, so she had somewhere to leave it.'

'What did it say?'

'It said she'd gone. It said that she couldn't stand it any more. It said no more than that.'

I didn't know what to say about this. I let out a big sigh.

'It.' He spat the word out. 'I didn't even know what it was, this It that she couldn't stand.'

No wonder the poor guy's Losing It. I mean, when I first saw him, I thought he might be crying over a fall in the value of the Dow Jones. But, no, it wasn't about work, it was about something more than work. Much more. He was crying for the same reason that Rufus had slashed himself. These things do happen outside work – in real life – don't they, but work is real life too, I suppose, and sometimes the two parts interfere with each other. That's how these scenarios come about. Maybe it's one of the reasons so many people have two different masks, a work one and a home one. Maybe it's because some people have such a shit time at home that maybe for some of them work might be *better*. Hell. I'd never even thought about it like that before.

Mark, I said, that must've been awful.

'Yes. It was. It is.'

'Did you find out what it was then, this It?'

'Well, it was as if she'd disappeared from the face of the Earth. No one would tell me anything – she was like that, she could coerce people into silence. I spoke to her mother on the phone, who said that all she could say was that Lizzy was all right, in the sense that she was well, that she hadn't been abducted or anything. Try not to worry, her mother said. Ha.'

I knew what it meant, his 'Ha'. Try not to worry. That's just the kind of helpful advice you need.

'Have you seen her since?'

'No. She called, took me by surprise, and we arranged to meet, but she didn't turn up. And then we arranged to meet again, at the house, which I was keen for her to see – the place was beginning to look shipshape, you know, I was proud of it. But once more she didn't turn up.'

The traffic was stop-starting. Mark continued his staring through the windscreen. I let loose a volley of questions:

What did you think? I mean, what was going on? Do you know? Have you found out?

'Well, naturally I asked around all our friends. It's amazing how people close down on you. I don't know why it is that they choose to protect the person who's done wrong. People I thought of as good friends all knew nothing.'

He had his foot on the clutch, pressing it to the floor, he was playing the gear stick through the gate, not engaging it, just knocking it back and forth. He was still staring through the windscreen.

'I'd always use the phone to speak to them, I couldn't bear to look them in the eye you know, I felt shame about it, although it would've been better had I had the courage to face them –'

I looked down to his hand. He was whacking the gear stick back and forth now. He was still wearing a ring.

'– because then at least I'd've been able to see them lie, at least I'd've known they were lying.'

He was really upset, and what he was saying was resonating in me, giving me something not unlike déjà-vu, so I lit another cigarette. I think it was to do with something I'd dreamt, or something Natalie might've been saying as we fell to sleep the night before.

The traffic began to shift.

Bastards, he went on. Absolute bastards. Always the same story: Mark? Is that you? I'm so sorry, yes, I heard about it from X. I had no idea anything was wrong between the two of you . . . Has she been in touch? . . . With me? Oh, no. I don't think it would be *me* she'd choose to confide in. Of course I'll let you know if I hear anything. Of *course*.'

It sounds as though Mark's circle are the same lot that Alan and Jenny have round for supper. I suppose they *are*. I felt sorry for him if these people were his friends.

Mark unfixed his stare and we both looked away to the view as we crossed the river. I wondered where we might be going. We turned right and he put his foot down as we moved along the southern embankment where the traffic thinned enough for there to be gaps. Mark started weaving, overtaking and undertaking, kicking the throttle and braking at the last second. The acceleration was intense. It was angry driving and it was a good car for it, I could see that. Perhaps this is why people in jobs like his with lives like his need these cars, for stress relief. I found myself holding tight to the door handle.

'Was there somebody else?'

'It took me nine months to find that out. A woman told me at a party. Drunk. She said everyone knew.'

'Fucking hell.'

'Fucking hell. Indeed.'

'Who was he, the other bloke?' (This was a stupid question, because whoever it was, I wouldn't know them. I didn't even know Lizzy, who, apart from what she was putting MarkyBoy through, I liked the sound of, in outline, I mean, with her bread-throwing good looks.)

'Somebody from her work.'

That's the opposite of me. I'm somebody from not work. Nevertheless, I'm occupying the same position as Lizzy's new bloke vis-à-vis Spurs. Of course, MarkyBoy doesn't know about Spurs, as I never made the speech to him, the one I was going to cheer him up with.

Did you know the guy, I asked.

'I'd met him socially once or twice.'

'Did you want to kill him?'

'Funnily enough, no. Or at least only in an abstract way – I'd think of him sometimes when I was hammer-drilling into a wall.'

I found that an easy image to picture, and not all that abstract, either. We raced a Mercedes off the lights (no contest) and he continued.

'It's not just about wanting to kill somebody. The pain is terrible. I spent hours, days, weeks trying to work out what I'd done. What the It was. I'd lie down on the floor at the end of the day with my feet up on the Workmate, watching the headlights pass across the ceiling, trying to analyse where I went wrong. It must be my fault, that was what I thought. It must be all my fault –'

I looked over at Mark. I didn't think it probably was all his fault. Although I'd assumed he led the dickhead lifestyle, he obviously wasn't one. Why hadn't Alan mentioned any of this to me? Probably because he doesn't like associating with failure, not at any level, even at the level of relationships. But he associates with *me*, and Jenny invites me round. Maybe they're not as bad as I make them out. Mark continued, before I had the chance to say I didn't think it was all his fault.

'The conclusion I reached was that I hadn't expressed to her often enough how I felt about her. I lay on those boards trying to recollect when was the last time that I'd told her I loved her. And do you know what? I couldn't remember.'

We took some back streets and went through a couple of chicanes, and he turned to me and changed the subject for a second:

'Rear-wheel drive, absolutely the best, you know.'

Right, I said.

'Everybody watches the headlights pass across the ceiling, don't they? Do you?'

'Yes.'

'Not everybody talks about it, though, that's the difference. Not everybody *mentions* it.'

I still didn't know where we were going, geographically, yet, indirect as this last line of talk was, I thought he was trying to take me somewhere in my head, trying to lead me to a destination, trying to lead me to an answer, in the radio psychologist manner.

So, I said, telling Natalie I love her was the right thing?

Yes. Yes, he replied. All to the good, all to the good. Completely the right idea. It absolutely can't do any harm anyway. I know that.

We were doing about ninety beside Clapham Common by now.

'Where are we going, Mark?'

'We are going to go and get absolutely plastered. Would you mind?'

It's cool with me.

We pulled in a few hundred yards from the huge pub where we were to spend the next five hours. We paused to watch some teenagers playing a scratch five-a-side on the grass, urchinBoys who didn't give two fucks about who they were in love with, or who was in love with them, or about who didn't love them any more, or about anything at all (including the style of shorts they were wearing). They were the kind of boys who do nothing other than play football, you could tell at a glance. A couple of them were terrific players, one tall, fast one, one bundle-of-tricks short one, the bundle-of-tricks short one setting it up for the fast one to score. It's a common mate pairing, that. We get some like them hanging round our pitch, trying to crash our match. As we watched, I thought that any one of them might've been the recipient of mobileGirl's call. Any one of them could be mobileBoy, the boy who went quiet when mobileGirl said she loved him. Actually, if you don't care about something at their age, the normal response is to make a lot of noise. Perhaps they cared about who loved them more than I thought. Perhaps I was misjudging them.

Beautiful game, football, Mark said.

Beautiful boys, I said.

He looked at me.

You know when you're young and you just don't care about anything and anything's possible as well. That's what I mean, I explained, and then I recited some words, words that put it better:

When I was young, each day was
the beginning of something new,
and each evening ended in the glow
of a new dawn.

Where's that from, Mark asked, giving me the kind of funny look people reserve for other people who can remember poetry.

I read it on a clothing tag, I said. On one of those Snowboard-Style labels. I think it was on a fleece, actually. Not that I really wear that sort of stuff, it doesn't suit me, but I look at it sometimes.

His funny look doubled up; he used it for clothes-talkers as well as for poetry-rememberers. He was wearing the business uniform himself, naturally, but rather than running all my normal prejudices over him, I recalled instead Natalie's homespun truth about it being what's inside that counts.

Another goal was scored and the urchinBoys celebrated with spread-eagle dives. As we watched them, Mark smiled and said, And then we grow up, and then it all goes custard peardrop-shaped.

I guess, I said. D'you want to see if we can get a kick-about with them before we start drinking?

'No. We'll get hammered. And anyway, aren't you aching from last night?'

(I was, but I'd forgotten. Last night seemed ages ago.) Yes I am, I said. By the way, you didn't dead-leg me on purpose, did you?

'I did actually. Sometimes I just get the urge to hurt somebody. Sorry.'

25

At half-past midnight, back at 42, slaughtered, dishing out a large measure into a mug from the only bottle of spirits in the place – the one we never touch, the product from the Dominican Republic with the medical taste and a number, not a name, on the label – I decided it would be a good idea to phone Natalie. I lay on the sofa and began to dial as the room span. But Pancho came and sat on me, and something about him, some look in his spinning eye, stopped me doing it. Pancho, I slurred, what is the thing that I'm trying to say, what is it, the thing about everything and everything, Pancho? What? What all about it, eh? What? The Domniicxan Public, eh? What all abouts that?

Pancho just stared at my trousers, reminding me they were not my own.

'Sorry, Pancho, I've been out drinking again.'

Pancho said, Those aren't your trousers, are they?

I had bad dreams, but I won't go into them. I hate being told about dreams, it's boring. After the bad dreams, the next thing I knew it was the early morning, the horrible horrible early morning of the horrible horrible hangover. Early waking on the horrible horrible early morning of the horrible horrible hangover was where early waking began. A final proof, as if I needed one, that this was the real thing. It was *before* seven, if you can believe that. I've never woken before seven in my life. The phone was where I'd left it, under Pancho. I slid it out. I thought I might give Marky-Boy a wake-up call, the bizarre kind of thought you can have when you're under the influence of the sort of hangover I was under and it's *before* seven. I had his mobile number now. He was sleeping in his car that night, something he sometimes did. It was well equipped for sleeping, the seats dropping back flat, and the cabin and auxiliary areas benefiting from Optional Equipment as follows: a roll-up sleeping bag housed in a special compartment beside the spare wheel, mineral water in a chilled cooler bag which plugged into a special socket in the boot, travel toothpaste, travel toothbrush, shoeshine, washbag, a torch with warning lights in the glove compartment, first-aid cabinet, diamanté hazard triangle, distress flares – the kind you launch into the sky if you're on a ship, not the kind you wear, though they should share the same name – silver thermo wrap sheet, silver thermo kagoul, silver thermo wrap strides (don't ask). In short, the BMW belogoed lot. Mark ran me through it as we staggered about and all of the BMW logos spun in front of my eyes, making me feel sick. There wasn't anything Marky didn't know about that car, and there wasn't anything you could have for that car that that car didn't have. I think he's an obsessive.

But I didn't phone him because I reckoned the sound of the traffic round the common would be at bona fide day-time levels by now; he'd be awake already. More to the point, how had Natalie spent the night? (Which was, of course, the first thought I should have had.) I tapped out the number I'd meant to tap out before Pancho intervened the night before.

Urgh, was the noise with which the phone was answered.

'Natalie?'

'Winger?'

Hey, good morning, I said, sounding cheerful in that way you can before you realize how absolutely dreadfully ill you are. How are you? I inquired.

'Hungover.'

'No, that's me. It's me who's hungover. What d'you mean, hungover? Did you go out last night?' [Who with?]

Oh, God, I'm not even wearing my own hair, she said.

'What?' [I'm not even wearing my own trousers, which is very bad, but that sounds possibly worse]

'Urgh, I've just seen myself in the mirror. Urgh.'

'Listen, I'm sorry about phoning you yesterday and everything, and getting cut off, but I was with MarkyBoy and he's got problems and things, things [ouch, ouch, my head, my head] – things got a bit out of hand. Sorry. What about you?' [Who with? Who with?]

'I met Bernie and Sam for a drink, we went down Bow Basin and talked. I told them there was this boy in my life who'd phoned me and told me he loved me twice, the first time he only thought he loved me and the second time he definitely did because that was all he said. And that after that I hadn't heard from him. I thought he might've done a runner.'

'I was scared. I was scared I might've . . . might've – messed everything up. I had a talk with Mark. What d'you mean, boy?'

'Man. Are you a man?'

'Well . . .'

'We think you're a boy. Bernie calls you the BoyWinger. How d'you mean, messed everything up?'

'It might be too much of a thing to say.'

'It's a lovely thing to say.'

'It's alright?' [Ouch, BoyWinger?]

'No. But it's still a lovely thing to say.'

Natalie, d'you like zabaglione, I asked.

'Oh, Winger, what sort of a question is that?'

'*Do* you?'

Yes, she replied.

'Would you come over here and let me cook for you?'

That'd be cool with me, she said.

'Half past eight, then?'

'Half past eight, yeah. You're learning.'

'Zabaglione, then?'

'Zabaglione.'

We made the arrangement for Thursday, a week and a day ahead – she said work was hectic. It was too far in the future for my liking, but at least I'd see her at football in between times, and I might've got rid of my hangover by then. [Ouch] [Ouch] [Ouch]

I slipped the phone back under Pancho and embarked on the Paracetamol hunt. My head wasn't the only part of me that was in severe pain. I rubbed a nerve under my shoulder blade. I think I'd trapped it by passing out in the wrong position. And my stomach was sore where the Bernie's newly punctured belt had been cutting in. I clattered about, unable to locate Paracetamol, wondering if Mark was suffering similar pain from sleeping in the car, though he shouldn't've, because he told me during the fourth and fifth drinks that he got a better night's sleep in the Beamer than in many hotel rooms (though in fact you actually could book a hotel room from it, from the On Board Computer). It had air-conditioning as standard, for example, he said, which is not always guaranteed in hotel life. He'd talked at length about the level of standard and optional equipment as theBoys always do (we'd become exhausted from talking about personal things) and I found I was happy to show interest, so I asked him what he'd been messing with under the steering wheel as we first pulled away. That's the adjustable steering column, he said – I was raising it back to its normal position. Oh, I said. Why did you have it low in the first place? Best position for what I was doing, he replied.

I thought about this while Mark went for the sixth pints and the sixth chasers. What he'd been doing was weeping, which meant that the car came equipped with a fully adjustable weeping position. Is it optional or standard, the adjustable steering column, I asked, as he placed the drinks down, as the foam heads lapped over the sides.

He looked a bit glassy, but he had the answer to hand. Standard, he replied.

Standard. It would be, wouldn't it.

26

You shouldn't make arrangements with a hangover. When you come out of the hangover it'll become apparent that you've made a mistake. It was three whole days plus most of Monday itself until football on Monday night, then two more plus most of Thursday itself until the dinner on Thursday night. Not ideal. Not at all. I could have rephoned, but I didn't. We had an arrangement, and I'd made the last several phone calls, so I left it.

Antonio keeps a big desk diary by the phone book, a freebie from some chemical suppliers, a page-a-day. Neither of us hardly ever normally uses it, but it does have a heavily doodled, drawn, scribbled and transcribed section from 3 Feb to 10 Feb where I sat in the evenings and at other times of the day with a selection of pens, being cool and waiting for the phone to ring. I've looked back over these doodlings, drawings, scribblings and transcriptions – they form a sort of guide to the condition of my psyche during this period.

Thursday 3/02
Doodlings: Many astral bodies – some New Age suns, lots of Saturns and many moons. Five hearts – some in 3-D, some not, some shaded in with lots of smaller hearts like Bernie's Russian-doll pots, some not.
Drawings: Several pairs of shoes. [?]
Scribblings: None.
Transcriptions: Oh woe is me oh woe is me. Dedah dedah dedah. Fuck.
(A blue Biro day)

Interpretation: I was dealing with my hangover crisis.

Friday 4/02
Doodlings: Musical notes.
Drawing: Picture of a woman skating, in classic skating pose – her hands linked at the base of the back, her body in forward-leaning posture.
Scribblings: Spirally things.
Transcriptions: *(Partial) Lyrics to Today I Fell in Love.*
Am I really hard to please
Perhaps I have such special needs.
(*Line of quavers doodled here.*)
'Cos the feeling was so unexpected
I could hardly keep myself collected
I thought it took a little time to learn about love and
Never did believe in loving on sight.
(*Line of quavers doodled here too.*)
(A fine black Uniball day)

Interpretation: Nat had sent me a card from which I had copied the picture. I was no artist, I was a lovesick fool.

Saturday 5/02
Doodlings: Aeroplanes. Arrows. Clouds.
Drawing: Two telephones with more arrows coming out of them.
Scribblings: Zigzags.
Transcriptions: ANTONIO – HEATHROW. 9.30 A.M. SET ALARMS!!!
(Writ large in RED CAPITALS day)

Interpretation: I drove Antonio to the airport. (Didn't need to set alarms, I woke up early anyway because it was after waking up early had begun). I think the arrows are to do with him and Kate. The telephone drawings meant that Nat had called while I was sitting on the M4 for hours. She left no message, I did a 1471. I didn't call her back (although I half-dialled her number a thousand times), in case Spurs might be there. It was the weekend, after all.

Sunday 6/02
Doodlings: A rectangular border within the edge of the page in funereal black marker, if you can count that as a doodling.
Drawings: A flowery-style vest centred within the rectangular border, decorated with crescent moons and Saturns instead of flowers.
Scribblings: None.
Transcriptions: The word Bollocks written small and repeatedly within and parallel to the border, if you can call that a transcription.
(A funereal black-marker day.)

Interpretation: An extended interpretation is required here.
Extended interpretation: The key to unlocking meaning in this image lies in the vest which stands at the centre of the frame. This was the day I read the piece on American Abstraction, hence, paradigmatically, this was the day upon which I was reborn with access to a specialized art-interpretive language lexicon language. (In fact, this was a whole period in which I did little but read and watch football.)

I gave Pancho his Sunday lunch, and then I walked down to the Tate, inspired as I was by the article, to see the Rothkos. I considered calling Nat, inviting her to a meet-up at the Embankment. She'd seemed interested enough when I mentioned the idea at the Ha Nazdaroveeyeh. But then I imagined her consuming brunch in bed with Spurs, her real boyfriend, and so, metonymically, contextually, and even actually, I didn't (phone). It was a long, grey walk and when I arrived I found the gallery atmosphere was heavy with all the wrong people, misshapen people who were wearing a wholly miserable collection of strides (i.e. tourists). Never go to a gallery on a Sunday, it's a basic rule, and one that I can only imagine I'd broken because being in love had massively disturbed my mind. To create further disruption to it (my mind) (it's important to overdo the parenthesis when you write in the specialized lexicon language), they'd shut the Rothko room. The Rothkos were off on tour somewhere. (Of course they were, it was the hook for the article I'd been reading – the *touring* exhibition of American Abstraction.) I was glad I hadn't phoned Nat. At least I wouldn't be meeting her to show her nothing. So I left the overcrowded gallery interior and sat outside on the grey steps gazing at the grey river. I lit up behind the shielding hand. As I smoked I noticed a girl sitting two steps down to my right wearing a flowery vest very similar to Nat's market-stall flowery top. The sight of this top provoked a recollection of the semi-awake conversation which took place after the fight we had on the clothes art, of which the flowery top was a part (the salad).

We lay together, her front to my back – spooning, as people call it (just too obvious a description for my taste) – in the state of pre-sleep, and Natalie *did* talk. *That* was it. This was the déjà-vu that I felt when Mark was talking about his friends the lying bastards. It *wasn't* a dream.

She said, You know when you know somebody intimately, and they tell you something important or personal and you look them in the eye and straight off you can tell whether they're being honest or lying?

(I must've said, Yeah.)

'Well, I'm worried about it.'

'Why?' (That's right. I said, Why?)

Have you ever skated, Winger, she asked in reply to my Why.

No, I said. Never. (Yes. This was how it went.)

I'm skating on thin ice, she said. If it happens – if he asks me a question and I have to lie – he'll know. He'll look me in the eye and he'll know.

You might have to wear shades, or goggles, or a mask or something, I said.

She rolled on to her back saying, That's not funny.

Sorry, you're right, it's not, I said. I rolled on to my back. 'Have you ever skated, Natalie?'

'I used to, but not for a long while. It's such a feeling. Like being on another planet.'

I propped myself up on my elbow and kissed her instead of answering with another difficult moment unfunny comment-joke.

I feel a bit like that now, a bit skatey, she said.

We stayed lying on our backs. The next thing we knew it was morning.

It's not unusual to forget bits of conversation that occur just before sleep. It's normal.

Summary of extended interpretation: It became clear as I ground my fag out on the Tate steps, and recalled this déjà-vu moment, that since I'd had my mind on the moon and spacemen while I was walking to the Ha Nazdaroveeyeh, then we'd *both* separately had ideas of other planets on our minds that same night (the moon's not strictly a planet, we have to accept that, but for the purposes of this analysis it's as good as). We'd also had unusual methods of human propulsion (skating c/f moon-walking) on our minds that same night too. Hence the central image of the stellar vest – a symbol of body and soul (the soul lies beneath the vest) in collaborative motion. The frame with the internal moat constructed of the single signifier Bollocks is representative of all that confines and constricts the potential freedom of true love. (Thus ends the use of this specialized language lexicon language. I can't say I like it, it's the verbal equivalent of a green checked suit worn with a purple striped shirt, red braces and a yellow spotted bow tie.)

Précis of extended interpretation: It was a Sunday.

Monday 7/02

Doodlings: Circles.

Drawings: A football pitch littered with tactical arrows

showing the movement of fish-footballers. Either side of the pitch are neat, accurate depictions of two types of knife: one bread knife, one fish-filleting knife. Bread rolls for corner flags.
Scribblings: Scrolls.
Transcriptions: None.
(A green Rollerball day. One of Antonio's. Like green clothes, I don't have green pens of my own, obviously.)

STOP PRESS: Match Report and Post-Match Debriefing
Very bad news from the dressing room: Natalie's name did not appear on the team sheet. I was entitled to play a dreadful game, and I did. Where the fuck was she? I was so bad [The boy was piss-poor] that if we'd had a manager he'd've pulled me off before half-time, and if we'd had a crowd I'd've been jeered off even earlier. Also new friend MarkyBoy missing, additionally BearBoy had it in for me for some obscure reason, singling me out for special treatment. Actually, we *did* have our occasional crowd of urchinBoys, in amongst whom there was the unsettling presence of some weirdo making the penultimate trouser faux pas: leather strides. An altogether crappy night. Except: Good news – one of Natalie's team-mates, a blonde, passed me a note on the way off. This is for you, she said, out of the corner of her mouth, sounding like an East German spy (they've got more internationals than Chelsea, her lot). I slipped it down my shorts. Read it straight off at the drinks machine, making a pretence of securing a Lucozade. Folded purple paper, six punch holes torn through. It said:

Sorry, won't see you tonight – got to go up to Manchester (work). Left a message at yours. You need a mobile. See you Thursday for zabagwotsit. Nat XXX
PS Score a hat trick, yeah.

Would the East German give her a match report? Fuck. I hope not. 'Za boy 'ad a nightmare.'

Interpretation: Pancho was starving when I returned home after the match – I'd only been in charge for two days and we were already out of Felinix. The circles indicate the emptiness of the cupboards. I grilled us sole fillets with mushrooms, to share. He adores that. I'm in love, Pancho, I said, while listening to Nat's message over and over: Hello, is anybody there? . . . Winger? . . . No? Oh, well, I'll try'n catch ya later . . . Love. Listen to this, listen to that voice, I said, as Pancho settled into my lap and watched me draw the tactical arrows on the pitch, and the knives, and the scrolls under the knives. He gave a purr of huge approval. The fish and bread and knives indicate that I'd done another production session for the new mag (it's called TopLad). It was a brand new feature with celebs in various biblical poses, in this instance a soap star doing Jesus Feeding the Five Thousand. I was helping out a photographer acquaintance of Ant's. The scrolls are part of the biblical imagery. The football pitch is self-explanatory.

Tuesday 8/02
Doodlings: None.
Drawings: None.
Scribblings: None.
Transcriptions: None.

Interpretation: Did nothing.

Wednesday 9/02
Doodlings: Snowflakes.
Drawings: A picture of Pancho sitting pulling a face in between Batman and Robin.
Scribblings: Whorls.
Transcriptions: None.

(An HB pencil day.)

Interpretation: Made a practice zabaglione. Not bad. Tried a spoonful on Pancho. He pulled a face. They're a trial, cats, aren't they? It's not as though their food either looks or smells nice, unless you grill them some sole avec mushrooms.

Thursday 10/02
Doodlings: None.
Drawings: None.
Scribblings: Big ball of string thing.
Transcriptions: None, though corner of page torn out.
(Red Letter day.)

Interpretation: Made a shopping list and went shopping for dinner ingredients.

27

It was my stepfather who taught me how to cook, or at least how to cook zabaglione. He said the old cliché worked both ways round, that it was the way to a woman's heart too.

I used to stand on a stool beside the cooker watching and helping, peeling things and stirring things. As I got older, he moved me on to more advanced tasks, like zabaglione-whipping. I had to use a manual whisk – he thought the electric ones were unmanly, For fucking queers, as he put it. It was the sort of thing he used to say. Same thing went for recipe books. Make your own life, make your own menu – you don't need no fucking book. He used to say that sort of thing too. He thought Paolo Rossi was a better player than Pelé. He's a bit mad, but he is half Italian and I love him. Some of my favourite times were times spent cooking and arguing the toss over football, ingredients, recipes (of our own, not from books) and other associated international matters.

Zabaglione was one of his specialities, then it became one of our specialities, then when I left home it became one of my specialities. You whip the yolks in a bowl over steam. Gentle heat is important – if it's too hot it'll curdle, but without a little heat it won't work. It takes time and it makes your wrist ache, but it's worth it to see the yolks balloon from the uninspired yellow puddle to the miracle foam cloud. Before I knew about zabaglione, I'd only seen the white of an egg whipped, I didn't know you could do it with the yolk. It's easier to whip the white of course; yolk-whipping is a skill. The only other ingredients are castor sugar and Marsala, for sweetness and flavour (the same as in cookery books actually, I've since checked – there isn't really a serious alternative recipe to this one). Serve it straight off with a cherry on top (you don't really need it, but it gives a focus). Perfetto, as he used to say.

I'd spoken to Natalie earlier in the day, at work. Finally I could call, since we had a date, and though I was more than out of sorts at not seeing her for so long, I *had* received one postcard, one ansaphone message and one note in the last eight days, which wasn't nothing. She sounded a bit apprehensive, like people do when they speak after so much time has passed. I probably sounded apprehensive too. Anyway, dinner was still on as planned, and I gave her apprehensive-sounding directions. She didn't arrive at half-eight, nor at 8.35, nor at 8.40. I was through my 3.5th cigarette of the quarter-hour by the time I heard the fall of her feet on the steps at 8.45, and I paused a few seconds before opening the door as if everything was cool with me. We didn't embrace, we stood off each other like it was the first time we'd met. Which it was, in its way, on my territory and with the love thing and all. She walked round the place noting items and picking things up. All the objects were Antonio's and each time I'd explain this and say where it came from, if I knew. She became irritated.

'It don't get any easier, does it, when where you live isn't yours and what you own isn't yours either.'

'What don't get any easier?'

'Sorting you out.'

Oh, well, that's the way I like it, I lied.

'Is it? And why do you like it like that?'

She'd cocked her head to the side. She was wearing a faux pony-skin poncho, which took me by surprise. It looked well on her, like they can on girls (men shouldn't wear a poncho unless they actually *are* in a Spaghetti Western). It was a sample, she said, a perk of the job. She might have done a twirl, but she didn't. I poured wine and showed her to the table, which is easy to find: it's a versatile pad – the kitchen/dining/living area all being one room. I lit extra candles while I thought about how to answer her double question. It's the problem with lies – even little insignificant ones like this – seeing them through, keeping them intact, defending the position. Not betraying the lie, I suppose. I suppose that would be the best way of putting it.

'I like it like that because it's easier that way.'

'Don't you feel like a nomad?'

'You're the one wearing the poncho.'

Yeah, she said in a flat tone. But don't you feel like a nomad?

'Well. Not really.'

'You don't feel unstable, insecure?'

'Well, how much less secure should I feel than you? I mean, *you* don't have a mortgage and all that . . . *stuff*, do you? Am I any less secure than you?'

'I own my own things and I pay rent.'

'Is it a lot more stable than this, though, really? Do you have a secure tenancy or something?'

'Are you going to be horrible to me?'

I wasn't being horrible to her, I was lying about me, which is different. I was so insecure about more or less everything, that I wouldn't even let on that I had my own tatty bedsit in Kensal Rise with virtually nothing in it because I'd sold most of it at car boot sales just to raise cash, and that I owed three months' rent at least, so in all probability I'd actually been evicted and was technically homeless even though I didn't know it. That was the truth I was concealing. I wanted to kiss her, to show that I wasn't being horrible to her, and to make me feel loved too. So I did. But she wasn't there in the kiss, she was reluctant. I pulled back and looked at her. She didn't give me any clues. This was more than the tactic of a defensive wall. Maybe she'd got a sort of separation anxiety syndrome as a result of us being apart for so long. What to do? I could feel my fingernails were on the point of going. Food is the answer and you know that for sure, as John Lennon would've sung, if it was a song about food that he was singing.

It's dinner time, I said.

Hors-d'oeuvre are best kept simple, from the point of view of both the chef and the client. I presented buffalo mozzarella with tomatoes and basil, and warm bread from the oven, no two-day-old granary baps on the menu that night. No way.

I had a starter like this in Milan last year, she said.

'Did you enjoy it, Signorina?'

'Milan?'

'No, the starter.

'Yeah, it was alright.'

'Were you there for fashion?'

'MmmHmm. Work, yeah.'

'You like jet-setting? How was Manchester?'

'Could be worse. Manchester was sunny, for the first time ever.'

'What sort of story is it going to be this season then?'

'What?'

'Don't you remember, when you told me: it's a lycra story and all that?'

'Ah, yeah. It's gonna be a white story. White's the new black.'

She didn't sound all that happy. I asked her if she was okay.

'Just a bit tired. The suppliers were a pain in the arse – lots of price hassles.'

This reminded me of what Bernie had said about her, which I mentioned.

'Bernie says you could do something different, that you're creative and you should become a designer.'

She put her cutlery down. 'Oh does she?'

She was definitely cross about this. Shit. It was a dimwit thing for me to repeat. Some girls hate other girls having and expressing opinions about them. So I cut in fast, waving my arms, hoping that this might soothe the air, saying, Oh, she was probably responding to something I said.

'Like what? Like what did you say?'

I'm trying to remember, what did I say? I said, moving my head into my hands now like I was thinking hard. I *was* thinking hard. What about mobile phone calls about love, why weren't we talking about that? About *It*.

'The thing is, Winger, I work where there's safe money, you see. Because I need it, like we all need it, and I want to get it without a load of stress and hassle and worry and everything like my dad had, and without it ruining my health like it ruined his.'

She picked up her cutlery and carried on eating, in a mood I could recognize as a furious quiet. I was wondering how I'd got off on such a bad start. I couldn't work it out. Lies, eh?

'What happened then, with your dad?' She hadn't mentioned this before. Not on the firstDate, for sure, and then not after that. That's the way it goes with subjects sometimes, they don't get mentioned, and then you don't know they're even there, it doesn't occur to you to ask. It's not a subject for a firstDate, is it? The firstDate exists in its own time, its own moment, and you'd naturally exclude matters from it that could make you unhappy. It has no history to fuck it up; it can only go wrong if you don't like each other. We *did* like each other, but now we'd got some history, even if it was only a tiny bit.

'Worked hard all his life and it killed him, that's what.'

We both had our cutlery laid down. Where did he work, I asked.

'At Franzi's, out Stratford way.'

'What's Franzi's?'

'Marble merchants.'

'What did he do there?'

'He was a foreman. He had responsibilities.'

'Did he have an accident?'

'Nah. He got ill.'

I topped her glass, I topped my glass. I broke some bread while she toyed with her food and carried on.

'I used to go down there after school sometimes: you know how you do, how you go searching for your parents, where you know you shouldn't and when you know you shouldn't, but you do anyway because you just want to be with them?'

I nodded.

'Well, I'd do that, and it was alright because the men down the yard were alright, they were lovely really, really lovely, and so Dad could be nice to me because of them – they made it okay for him. I mean, he was nice *any*way, but their being nice made it . . . he didn't have to be embarrassed or anything.'

Was it a big place, I asked.

'Not really, there were probably about twenty of them. They all seemed to look the same, the other men, how they do, when you're little.'

I expect they liked you, I said.

'Yeah. They used to call me Princess. They'd call out to Dad: Princess 'as found her way down again. Dad'd come out of his workshop in the corner, covered in dust, shaking his head. The oldest man, who'd been there for ever, Bill, who looked after the office, would lift me up and sit me on the marble and bring me tea and biscuits.'

'How d'you mean, sit you on the marble?'

'It comes in sheets, enormous they are, they rest against each other, all colours and patterns and grains. It seemed to me then that they were the biggest things in the world. And they were, y'know. They were. He'd sit me up there.'

'And you'd watch them work while you had your tea and biscuits?'

'Yeah, out of harm's way.'

'It was dangerous then?'

'Well-dangerous, wasn't it? It killed my dad.'

'Sorry. But dangerous in the ordinary way as well, I mean?'

'There was a machine which cut the marble, the Cutter. It had a huge diamond wheel. It ran on an arm which swung out and they dropped it into the piece they were cutting. It seems uncuttable when you feel it, how cold and hard it is. But it was like a knife through butter.'

'Wow.'

'Wow's right. It's amazing to see. And to hear – it's a soft noise, but loud.'

Bernie's studio was the only spot I could picture which sounded at all like it might've been similar. Only for the dust, really. I filled the glasses.

'They have pipes which send water on to the wheel to keep it cool, the water spurts off like it does if you don't have a mudguard on your back tyre and it sprays up your anorak. The men wear goggles to keep it out of their eyes.'

'It sounds something.'

'Yeah.'

'Sounds like Bernie's place in a way – solid, people making things.'

She went quiet.

'What do they make there anyway? Gravestones or something?'

'Gravestones are one of the things they make. Yes.'

She went more quiet. I was at my absolute peak for saying the wrong thing, my absolute peak. We should be talking about love, and instead I'm making faux pas about gravestones. She fiddles with her food and I just watch her. She dips a piece of bread into her wine and sucks it. And then she carries on talking, in a distracted way.

Sometimes she caught the bus back home on her own, on the days when her dad was working late, and there were plenty of them. 'Mind how you go,' he'd always say as he saw her off. 'Tell your mother to keep the tea warm.' Her mother used to keep the tea warm by placing one plate over the other and leaving it set low in the oven. Other times she'd wait until the end of the day, watching them brush up and hose down, a customer might turn up to collect a piece, and when everything was shut, she'd walk with her dad and he'd hold her hand in his, big and rough and warm. When the bus came she'd sit beside him on the seats at the back on the bottom deck, the ones that face each other. Once in a while, they'd stop off at a café on the way home, on the walk between their stop and their flat, and he'd buy her apple pie with custard and he'd just have a cup of tea. Don't tell your mum, he'd say. The café had a picture of the King of Siam on the wall – that's the king that Yul Brynner played in The King and I. Sitting with him on the bus, holding his hand, the click of the ticket machine – she used to like to keep the ticket. These were her abiding memories. The King and I is her favourite film. I'd been concentrating so intently I had words ringing in my head:

Don't tell your mum.

Apple pie.

Mind how you go.

Princess.

I filled the glasses again and asked the question.

'How did he die, Nat?'

'They call it renal failure on the certificate. It means emphysema. He smoked though, so there's not even any chance of compensation. Four years coming up.'

'That's not long ago really, is it?'

She looked at me. The cold quiet rage with which she'd started talking had dissipated, and she shrank in a way I didn't want to see her shrink. It was this time of year, she said. I think about him every day, but it's worse . . .

I rounded the table and held her. Her tears came in waves. I stroked her hair. An image of Mark in the standard weeping position came across me. What one person needs is another person, not a steering wheel. It's obvious. Obvious.

I stood holding her and when the tears stemmed I said, Listen, you don't have to eat. It's okay. D'you want to just sit down? It's Antonio's sofa, but mine'd be the same if I had one – I'd choose one like this.

She tried a smile. We tried a smile. We sat side by side as she rolled a joint. It helps me, it makes me feel better, she said.

S'alright, you don't have to apologize for anything, I said.

'I'm not apologizing, I'm just saying. What about your parents, Winger?'

'I got a stepfather when I was eight.'

'What happened?'

'Mum and Dad didn't get on, split up. He wasn't about a lot of the time, my stepfather, but neither was my real dad.'

'D'you feel like you don't have a father then?'

'I've never thought about it like that before. I don't know. But I think it's alright. Boys probably get different things from dads than girls.'

'Like what?'

'Well, my stepdad taught me how to make zabaglione, for instance, while at the same time arguing that Paolo Rossi was a better player than Pelé.'

'He never.'

'He did.'

'That's no contest, is it?'

'He wasn't a bad player, Rossi.'

'Yeah but . . .'

'You're right. The 10 on the back of my football shirt is for Pelé.'

'Why don't you have his name there too?'

'I don't like writing on clothes.'

She passed the joint and gave me a look. And asked, Is he from round here then, your stepdad?

'Half, and the other half's Italian. He has Italian tastes. Sharp suits.'

'You keep in touch?'

'Not much, mostly on the phone. They've moved to High Wycombe.'

I don't like to worry them, that's the real reason I hardly phone. My mum'd be sending out food parcels if she knew the full details. I didn't want to tell Nat about any of this either, so instead I asked her if she wanted to go on with the meal. She said she wasn't really hungry. Me neither.

There was an exquisite rack of lamb going to waste here, plus an exquisite range of side dishes and accessories, but I had more important matters to attend to – the state of Natalie's soul, the undiscussed love issue. The state of my own soul, that would mean.

'We could have dessert though – something sweet might be nice.'

Yeah, she said.

'After all, it was zabaglione that brought you here in the first place. D'you know how to make it?'

Course not, she replied.

'Let me show you then.'

'Alright.'

She kissed me. It was better. It felt like we might be on the way back.

One of the outcomes of repeating a process over and over again is that you can do something else while you're at it, usually. It'd be dangerous if you were an astronaut or a marble-cutter, but at zabaglione-making level you can talk about what you're doing as well as talking about other things too, and if you're really pushed you can even work on another dish at the same time: multiTasking, theBoys would call it. As I broke the shells and began whipping, I was self-conscious about my strides – I was wearing a post-deconstructed pair right then, I bought them from a Style Lab the day before. What the fuck was I up to? They felt nice enough against my leg, they were made of a soft cotton material and they hung quite well, but they weren't right, of course they weren't. I was conscious of *them*, but I stayed with *her*, I really really stayed with her, and sometimes when I fitted my little fingertip into the dimple of her smile or tried to soothe the line of her frown with the back of my hand, and we talked and she talked and I talked and she rubbed the small of her back against the worktop and I whipped the sugar and the Marsala into the yolks, I forgot about them completely, my trousers, right there and then, not almost completely, but completely completely. And this is true. And we talked. But we didn't talk about love.

We talked about my past. I don't talk about my past, I just don't, but she started pushing me about it and not letting me get away with sluicing it off like I do, like ducks do, like the Franzi's men must do as the water spins from the diamond wheel and lashes over their goggles. I knew I'd be losing her if I didn't start breaking something, a habit, a pattern of behaviour. Her irritation at not being able to tell anything about me from the objects and furniture would develop into full-blown leaving me. But because I did talk about some part of my past with her – because she'd been telling me about her dad, and because she'd cried and because I loved her, and maybe because I could feel far enough away from it, my past I mean, that I could talk – well, I started moving out of myself in a regressive way. I began to feel like I used to when I was eight, when I lay in bed just after the parent split, and the whole world used to recede. The walls in the hall, which I could see through my bedroom door – which was always kept open – went miles away, and the knock-on effect of this was that I used to feel as though I'd shrunk, that I was made little and slight like a bird, and tight like a heart attack, and it provoked fear in me, and no matter what, I couldn't make it stop until it did so by itself. It was a physical terror – eyes closed or eyes open it was just the same – and I couldn't sleep until it passed. I think it used to happen before the parent split as well. It happened when I was a shepherd in the nativity – that was before that. I was only seven. Maybe it always happened.

I don't know why, but I started there with that, I told Nat about it – the sensation of the fabric of the real world being miles away – and as I told her about it, I began to feel that way again, and it wasn't just the tiny bit of dope smoke kicking in or the energy dip from the wrist-aching effort of zabaglione-whipping, it was something else. The mixing bowl started moving away from me and the whisk went tiny in my hand like a piece from a doll's-house. And then I slumped, sank, and the zabaglione curdled. There's a way of saving it when that happens, it can be saved – just a tablespoon of warm water, that's all it needs – but I wasn't in the right shape to manage it, not at all. I was slumping. I was Losing It.

28

Something in the episode of the curdled zabaglione planted the seed of masktheft. I was frightened of masks when I was little, I'd run away if I ever saw anyone wearing one, and I'd always stay indoors on Halloween.

The regressive feeling progressed from bad to worse and I began hallucinating about the Franzi's men and their facewear as I slumped: visions of begoggled faces spun towards me, the same as the BMW logos had, only worse. Even beginning to talk about my past, who I really am, must've tripped some wire.

Natalie lay me down on Antonio's sofa. I think she stroked my head . . . *before I put on my make-up, I say a little prayer for you.* She must've been singing too, singing me to sleep. A new pattern was beginning to repeat. It turned out the same with Nat as it had with MarkyBoy. They'd each ignited in me some kind of overactive sympathy by the stories they told, then as soon as I'd taken this on board – instead of my helping them out as would've seemed appropriate – *they* ended up dealing with *me*: Mark having to be an Agony Uncle, Nat having to be a Florence Nightingale. Whatever it was in me that was off balance was coming right to the surface.

And it still isn't far off the surface. I watch the urban spaceBoy return to his shop. The silver metallic weave in his strides has them glinting in the sun. The weather's warm, which is not right, it's always cold in February. It occurs to me what it is that's wrong with the trousers that would be suitable for wearing on the moon if it were a warm and fashion-conscious place. The moon has no seasons, does it? It's always cold, because it has no atmosphere. And you'd always be floating out of yourself, because it has no gravity. Inappropriate, those strides. Not made for any known conditions.

The Snowboard Puffa incorporates zip-off sleeves, which I'm tempted to zip off, but what are you supposed to do with them then, where are you supposed to put them when they're zipped off? A bag, that's it, I have to buy a bag, not least for the mask. Come on, get a grip.

I don't like buying bags. I don't even like my own sports bag, which is just plain black with no logo, a virtually impossible object to come by, except from a market stall. I *did* pick it up from a market stall, in fact, from the market next to the knife-sharpener's arch; I wander round while he does his work, otherwise you have to come back two weeks later when he's next there. Anyway, I haven't got my sports bag with me, and the market's too far away, and it's not market day either. The shop that sells the one-man igloo tents and the silver vacuum flasks is only round the corner. It'll have to be that. They have hundreds of thousands of bags there.

I return the mask to my inside pocket and move off keeping my hand on it, walking along in a pose made popular by Lord Nelson. Not cool.

I spent time slow-circling the museum assistant before I stole it. He was at work in the area near the mask's case, on the mezzanine. I circled him from a long distance, and also from a middle distance, and in addition I was mixing it up in midfield, switching wings and moving across him at obliques and tangents. He didn't appear to be paying me any attention, nor me him. From his point of view I suppose I was simply moving in an expected way; I was travelling at the speed of an action replay, like people do in a museum, gliding absorbedly and randomly in and out of the exhibits and display cases. I didn't know he was going to take the mask out, it was simple good timing that, a nice squeeze, but I knew he was going to do something, he had the keys and he had the trolley and he had the equipment, that's why I was keeping him under surveillance. He was wearing a long jacket, like a manila porter's coat only better cut, the uniform of his duties. His strides were typical assistant: brown, too long, many many concertinas too many. His distinguishing feature was his hair, which was combed back and greased up in a retro-50s flick. He was about my age. I'm glad he wasn't an older person, because I'd be feeling irresponsible today if I'd given an older person distress, it'd upset me to think I'd caused a family man with obligations and responsibilities a sleepless night or lost him his job, so he couldn't hold his daughter's hand on the bus home any more. It would absolutely upset me more than the thought of the act of masktheft, that's for certain. I mean, the museum must've stolen the mask in the first place, same as the Elgin Marbles – everyone always goes on about them but you never hear a murmur about all the other little things.

Maybe that's why I prefer art, really, to objects. At least someone's been paid for it, and paid for it properly too. I mean, it's a nice earner, being an artist. This is only true of modern stuff of course, since artists have had agents and hustlers and galleries operating for them instead of patrons. The article about American Abstraction went on about it – art and the marketplace and the CIA and the FBI. There was a political angle on it then, when the Cold War was still on, when the Western bloc took on the Eastern bloc in all manner of quiet ways. Everybody knows about the SpaceraceBoys with their outward-bound strides – Yuri, Buzz, Apollo, Sputnik et cetera. And chess players, everybody knows about them too, sombre-suited, always having a showdown in Reykjavik. Not so many people know that the same thing went on with artists too, but it did. It was all about who owned the top painters, and who owned the most, the best and the biggest modern paintings. America clinched it easy of course, much the same as Premier

League football – who has the most money wins. Nearly all of America's top painters were foreign imports, and actually most of them came from round the Eastern bloc way too. It'd be like England buying up all the top German players to beat Germany in an international. Which is against the rules, of course, and illustrative of one way in which football is fairer than art. It took place in the 50s, all this, when the world was a more dangerous place. In the days before a shop assistant could knock about wearing metallic Capri pants in broad daylight and expect to live.

Though there are paintings at the museum, they're not ones I like, and anyway I'd gone in specifically to look at the mask, like I often did. I'd never analysed it at all properly before, why I did this. It's like a sculpture, the mask, and it's such a small thing – it's little more than a detail in itself, and so often the detail is all I see of anything, except when I miss it completely. It was its tiny-detailed sculpturalness that drew me to it in the first place. But there are lots of other similar icons and *objets* about that I barely notice at all. I've been trying to sort out the why of this. The obvious thing is that none of the other items are masks. I have a theory now: I think I was trying to conquer the fear. Post-zabaglione disaster, I've turned the matter over. A lot. In the immediate aftermath, with the hallucinations about the spinning Franzi's men and their goggles and the lashing water, and walls drifting away, and flashbacks to the nativity, and the whisk receding, the mask emerged somehow as a sort of conclusion to it all. Just as I was waking, I saw an image, like you sometimes do, behind my eyelids, like a film-still. It was an image of this mask. I don't really want to go on about it, otherwise it'll be like telling a dream. I've decided that I look at it to try to conquer fear of everything. That's why. I don't like fear, though I have enough of it. It fucks you up, in the words of the other poem a lot of people like.

Before I went on to the mezzanine, I ate in the basement restaurant, with the broadsheet papers and the still mineral water, in the normal way. I didn't pay in the normal way though, I just walked off, something I don't do, however tempting it is in those places – the staff always being straight-out distracted types who've clearly got something much more interesting to think about than sorting you out a foccacia with bresaola and a peach smoothie (I experimented once with a peach smoothie, it's not really a drink though, is it?). The distracted staff take hours to serve you, and then you sit eating and watching the other clients pulling faces and sighing during their own long wait, and you can become disaffected enough to do the runner. Or rather, the walker: I mean, you don't need to run, nobody's going to give chase.

So I left the broadsheet newspapers and the still mineral water and remnants of foccacia and bresaola behind and casually moved half a floor up the building. I suppose doing the walker prepared me in some way, made me emboldened for the act of theft. Not that I knew anything about what I was going to do until I did it. I was amazed when he took the mask out, and I experienced a reverse of the lying-in-bed-with-the-world-diminishing thing I used to have, and have had again only t6o recently. I could see the mask like it was the size of a football, yet I was still three display cases away, and in actual size it fits into a pocket.

It fits into my pocket.

It's hard and cold and fine in my hand. I can wedge my little fingernail into the eye-hole – it gets caught sharp, like when you put it into your lover's mouth and she nips quick and hard, and it goes white.

Only an hour till I meet Rosie. There's no way I'm considering considering buying strides now, it can't be done,

I've accepted it. But I can check a couple more places on the way, for old times' sake; just five minutes in the Style Lab. The new generation of legwear is so fabulous. Post-apocalypse, postmodern, post-unmodern, post-structural, first-past-the-post-structural, Postman Pat: LoverMan, the choice is yours. How many gizmos does one require, really? Really?

This strap detail at the ankle – this tightening on the Velcro strip – it's absolutely ideal for not letting rats and other rodents up your leg, if you wear it tightened up, which of course you don't, you wear it doing nothing other than hanging loose looking lovely, which is only very ideal for doing nothing other than hanging loose looking lovely. Then what happens is that it gets wet in the rain and conducts water up your calf towards your thigh. Which is simply a new twist on the overriding design fault of the frayed flare. Hopeless, quite hopeless, and you'll Catch Your Death that way, as my Great Auntie would say. By the way, don't forget to note the offset piping in chenille overlay, perfect if you find yourself caught in a military march, we supply a separate bugle or, alternately, for impromptu mail delivery, we supply a delivery bag.

What about these razor-frayed Westwoods? To die for. Urban Red Indian is very very . . . Rubbish?

It's a beautiful shop, but there's something about it I just can't get on with, in the same way there was something about the interior of Marky's car that I couldn't entirely appreciate. Is it too plush? Yes, but no. It can't be *only* that. It's something else.

Anyway, it's not Urban Red Indian I need now, it's more Urban Eskimo. It's made me feel brave, coming in here though, it's about conquering another fear – because this was the place I shopped the day before the horrible horrible day of the horrible horrible *horrible* zabaglione disaster.

29

Post-zabaglione disaster it was dark, I mean the lights had been lowered, the candles had burnt out, Natalie had gone and she'd left me tucked up. She'd found a blanket, one of Antonio's Tibetan items. Pancho was drooling on my chin. I used the blanket to wipe the drool. I found the note she'd left on the table.

We can't do this. It's making me sad and it's making you collapse and it's wrong. We just can't y'know. Sorry n'that.
Nat XXX

I'd failed. I'd really failed. I mean I'd failed on my own terms and nobody should see you do that, it shouldn't happen. What was I doing collapsing and forgetting how to make a zabaglione? *What?*

Where was my pride?

I tried to call her.

Engaged.

I tried to call her.

Engaged.

I tried to call her.

Engaged.

I re-read the note. I examined the paper, a folded and opened purple rectangle with six punch holes torn through where it had been removed from her personal organizer. I re-read the note. It looked as though she'd probably used a blue pen, but the paper made the ink go black like a bruise. I walked around the flat. I re-read the note. It doesn't say she doesn't want to do this, I thought. It doesn't say that. It says, We just can't y'know – which is different.

I re-rang the phone. Engaged. I re-read the note. I re-rang the phone. Engaged. I re-read the note. I re-rang the phone. Bernie answered.

'Is Nat there? Is she there?'

'What, Winger? Is that you?'

'Yeah, Bernie. Yeah.'

'You're having dinner, aren't you? I thought Nat said you were cooking for her. Is there something wrong?'

'She's left. I had a funny attack. She tucked me up on the sofa. I'm alright now (Yeah, sure I was, sitting wearing the Tibetan blanket round my shoulders poncho-style; very un-alright, in fact). Is she there?'

'No. How long ago was this?'

'I don't know.'

'Well, did she take the tube?'

'I don't know.'

'A cab?'

'I don't know.'

'Did she say she was coming here?'

'I don't know.'

'What sort of funny attack did you have, Winger? One that brought on total amnesia?'

'A sort of blackout funny attack. Not funny, in fact.'

'Blackout? Is that something that happens to you?'

'No. No. It never happens. I've been drinking a lot while Nat's been away. It could be retrospective alcohol poisoning, if there is such a thing. D'you think there is?'

'I've never heard of it. So Natalie's left?'

'Yeah.'

'Oh dear.'

'What d'you mean, oh dear?'

'Well. I know she's been having a tough time. I mean oh dear for her. And oh dear for you too.'

'What sort of tough time?'

'Just generally. She's been out of sorts, easily upset, snappy.'

(Right. Good. It wasn't just with me then.)

'Have you seen much of her, Bernie, with her being away, I mean?'

'Not a lot. I'm only talking about the bits I've seen. I don't think the situation between you two is helping, though.'

'What situation?'

'She told us about your declaration.'

'Bernie, you encouraged me to say it.'

'What d'you mean by that?'

'In your workshop.'

'No, I encouraged you to make the admission to yourself. I didn't tell you to do anything.'

'Was it a wrong thing for me to say?'

'No.'

'Are you against it?'

'It doesn't matter, does it?'

'Have you given her advice?'

'All girls talk, Winger. I have my own opinions.'

A telephone silence developed. She wasn't exactly being rude in this silence, but I could feel she wasn't going to be giving out any insightful information.

Will you let her know I called, I said.

'Of course. As soon as she returns.'

'You will?'

'Yes.'

'Don't forget.'

'I won't.'

'Thanks.'

'You're welcome.'

'Thanks, Bernie.'

'It's okay.'

'Thanks.'

'It's okay.'

'Thanks. Bernie, one more thing . . .'

'Yes?'

'You didn't say anything about trousers, did you?'

'You asked me not to, Winger.'

'Okay. Thanks.'

'Bye.'

She put the phone down. I put the phone down.

I went to the sink and drank some water straight from the tap and in doing so I caught a sidelong glance at the saddest sight in the world – the remains of an unsuccessful zabaglione. The distance between glory and the other thing is really just a whip of air. I want to buy the seasons in advance?

Sure.

I can't even make a zabaglione any more.

30

The shop that sells the one-man igloo tents and the silver vacuum flasks is in the street parallel to Style Lab Street. In fact, the shop that sells the one-man igloo tents and the silver vacuum flasks really *is* called Outward Bound. I know this because, to be honest, I've been in here a few times more than I'd normally let on. I've got a kind of sick fascination with the place. One thing my research (is research the right word? No. Hobby? No no no, not that, no way. What? What is the right word? *Passion?* Yeah – that'd be a much better word for it. Passion) has left me sure of is that these shops are the seedbed for the Snowboard Coolwear outlets, like the one Nick runs, where you get the nice vibe. I mean, when you get right down to it, the clothes aren't that much different, they really aren't. What's different is the essence of the ambience. My Great Auntie would feel at home in Outward Bound, and equally and oppositely not so at Nice Vibe.

Time's pressing. I've been in here for minutes now. The moment has come to make direct contact with the serving guy.

I'm looking for a bag to travel north with, I say.

What sort of north, sir, he asks.

Far north, I reply.

He raises the quizzical eyebrow, and I've the feeling he would like to say, Polar expedition? in order to humorously comment on my geographical vaguity. But instead, for assistant-professional-politeness, he tries, Scandinavia? Right first time.

'Right first time.'

The range of possible suitable bag options is extensive, they have a whole wall of them, and if you're unguided you're no better equipped to make a choice than a five-year-old in a sweet shop.

Will you be taking part in any pursuits there, sir? he inquires, as a preamble to establishing whether he could sell me anything else while he was at it. Snowboarding, for instance?

I might play a bit of football, I reply.

Hmm, he says. We don't really deal with snow football boots. A normal studded astroturf would probably be the best we can do.

He directs me to the bag-range that complies with my requirements. They're quite different to clothes shop staff, these people, actually. I have to admit, they're more relaxed. Better, even. Somehow I'm feeling not totally uncomfortable with the man even though he's in the full hill-walking uniform, including beard and waterproof hiking boots, indoors, in the middle of the day. He asks me what I'll be carrying, will I have a football strip, training track-suit, do I need a thermo-vest and so on – we have a special offer on our lycra under-shorts, he says. You footballers wear them under your actual shorts, don't you? Is it business and pleasure combined, your trip, he asks.

Not sure, I reply. Bit of both, I think.

I only have to decline a couple – one pink/purple, one mauve-green – before he settles me on the ideal black bag. It's called a FullSump Flare, it features a multi-zip pocket under the front flap and a detachable accessory pouch. It looks like you should use it to store your mobile, this pouch, but it's immediately clear that it's just the right size for the mask, which makes it the perfect detachable bag-accessory for me. Inside the main compartment there's room enough to accommodate the zipped-off Snowboard Puffa sleeves, leaving enough space for the football kit I don't have with me and a few other wardrobe items which I don't have with me either. There's just the one simple badge on the front which I can remove later with a sharp knife, which I can also buy here (just the most basic Swiss

Army – two blades, a saw, a bottle opener/screwdriver, a tin opener/screwdriver and a tool for removing stones from a horse's hoof; plus, of course, a toothpick, tweezers and a corkscrew. That's your absolute minimum on a Swiss Army knife, it really is. Which is no surprise when you think of Swiss strides). The bag comes with a generous thirty-year guarantee which the label says doesn't cover normal wear and tear or abuse. Oh? What then? Only defects of workmanship or materials. Right.

It's all been so simple so far (I've never purchased anything from Outward Bound before, obviously, or spoken to any of the staff) that it's impossible to resist asking questions about the garments.

What does one ideally wear in a harsh climate, I ask. One can indulge in a bit of BernieSpeak if one wants. It has a certain cool effectiveness.

'Will you be doing anything extreme at all?'

'How d'you mean?'

'Trekking, ice climbing . . . ?'

'I might be doing something extreme, but not really in that field. No. More like, well, more like just walking about a city really, probably, I think.'

'I see. In that case, for body-warmth, you can't really improve on a fleece, sir –'

(I knew he was going to say that.)

'– and for your downstairs, I'd recommend some of these berghaus® undertrousers.'

Downstairs?? I ask you. Let's start with the easy stuff. With the fleeces. I hardly need say how difficult this is for me. You know how the word Muppet is used as an insult, normally thrown by someone like bearBoy at someone like apeBoy to indicate that the one thinks the other a fucking-Prat? Well, I never thought The Muppets were prats, I thought they were quite smart, but they *were* puppets, and they *were* made of a puppet-appropriate fabric, which to me looks very much like a fleece. What I'm saying is that fleece-material is just not an appropriate finish for a human being. If you want to use the word Muppet as an insult, you should call it to someone wearing a fleece.

I try several. The first is obviously the hardest – I mean, just putting it on at all, so uncool, so muppety-puppety – but once inside the attraction is clear (if you like this sort of thing). Try wearing your winceyette pyjamas while simultaneously tucked up snug inside a duckdown sleeping bag, and the whole fleeceThing becomes apparent straight off: it's an obvious appeal to a return to the womb. (I read a bit of Freud too during the earnest period – only in a pop-psycho edition, I don't know any more about him than anybody else, but this is basic.) Anyway, after the trying-on ordeal, my decision, if you could call it that, is that there's something not right about all of them (they're fleeces). But . . . You know, it could be really cold up there, it really could. I'll have to make a phone call. In the meantime, the man says he'll hold the least offensive one behind the counter, it's the only one left in my size.

The good thing about not having a mobile (they're vulgar, that's why not) is that as every other fucker in the world's got one now (Antonio, Rosie, Natalie, my Great Auntie, I've even seen the Poet Laureate on one), it means that public telephones are always free. In fact they're very seldom even pissed over or vandalized any more, that's how bad it's got. Two opinions to take:

1] Rosie.

Rosie says, A fleece, mate? Don't know. I once had a friend who was in a hardcore fleecy gang, she became *very* boring about it, always rattling on about togs and ratings and gradients, one-in-ten, one-in-four, detachable furry linings, bomb-proofing. It's not your style, is it? *Don't* be late for lunch.

2] Nick at Nice Vibes (who I don't know all that well, but this is a unique situation).

Nick says, Believe me, man, a fleece *is* a wardrobe staple.

I knew he was going to say that. Everything's staple with him.

'Are the ones you sell actually cool, though, Nick? Are they? I mean, can you be seen in them?'

Yeah, he says. Of course they're cool, sure they are. But the ones they sell over there are probably warmer, they'll have a tog rating and all that. Bomb-proofing and whathaveyou.

Is it alright for me to buy one then, I ask.

'I'm telling you, man, a fleece is a wardrobe staple. Go For It. Get Out There.'

Get Out There. Okay. But it's not actually all that cool with me, this, to be honest, it really isn't.

31

After the conversation with Bernie, I sat wearing my Tibetan blanket poncho-style waiting for the phone to ring. In order to deflect myself from dwelling on the new and entirely unwelcome feeling of incapability-at-zabaglione-making, I considered instead what Spurs's problem might be. It was a matter I thought about often (along with the feelings of sexual jealousy I was no longer in a position to refuse to recognize), but if I had to think about anything, I'd rather consider *his* problem than the sexual jealousy situation any day. Of course, his problem was a matter outside my remit, and a matter about which I could ask no one else. I mean there was no one else *to* ask. There were the other five-a-siders, of course, but I'd only seen them, I didn't know them. And there was Bernie, but there was also the code of the girls, so that was no-go. I wasted too much on these Spurs's-problem thoughts, they occupied a disproportionate amount of my headSpace, as theBoys' girls say: I just haven't got the headSpace for it, they go. Or: It's cluttering up my headSpace, darling, as they wave their hands in their Sloane-way. It might be funny if they were being ironic, but they're not. It's a joke. I mean, I don't know what the rest of their headSpace is supposed to be used for, I never hear them talk about anything apart from year-round Christmas Shopping and Holidays and Pore Strips.

Anyway, one of the things I'd been trying not to do in my headSpace was to be like Spurs, although of course I didn't know what not being him *was* or could consist of. We don't get on – that was all she said, that was all I knew. Our thing – Nat's and my thing – was so fragile that I just hadn't pushed her on the subject at all. Whenever I'd thought of asking, I'd decided against on the grounds that it would just be too dangerous. So in what way they didn't get on I still hadn't any idea. I sat wrapped in the Tibetan poncho and decided that the time had come to find out. There was lots I'd attributed to him in my mind – all the usual things – repulsive nylon socks with crests and patterns, white-leg-display between sock-top and trouser-hem (whilst in the seated position), comedy ties (theBoys have been known to wear these, it'd kill me if I thought it was even remotely amusing), themed ties, patterned ties, club ties, blazers with shiny buttons, double-breasted suits, button-down shirts with an extra button at the back. Etcetera. But I didn't think it was any of this really. It must be something else. Etcetera.

Et cetera, et cetera, et cetera, as Yul Brynner says in the King and I, as Nat reminded me. She came out with it during her dad soliloquy. 'Working all your life and ruining your health like it ruined his; et cetera, et cetera, et cetera.' That was how she actually said it. Hard on it, Princess. She knew how to be ironic, she understood irony and its deflective use.

Actually, it's that that I can't stand about theBoys' tight-mouthed Girls, actually. No irony. It's their no irony that means they can wear their lousy Kensington frocks with their faces straight. There's no irony in their headSpace because their headSpace is fully occupied with smugness. That's it. It's obvious really. Maybe it's a version of that that I really don't get on with inside the Label Shops and the cabins of BMWs. Yeah. I think that *is* it.

I lit a cigarette. I risked another glance at the zabaglione-wreck. It had to go. I slid it into the bin, feeling a bit sick. Where does the air go? Must be the same place as the wax of the spent candles, I thought, as I gazed at their guttering remains in the aftermath of everything.

Et cetera, et cetera, *et cetera*. It was the first time while we'd been together that she'd been angry, offhand, cross, pissed off, in a bad mood or anything like it. All the time we'd had in each other's company had been more or less cool with us before then, and normally a lot better than even that. What precipitated this change, when I thought back over it, was the mention of Bernie having an opinion about her, about what she should do.

Being in love with someone else's girlfriend wasn't a situation with which I was familiar. And by now I wasn't liking it. Not at all. I'd never had to think this hard before, trying to second-guess everything.

The distinguishing feature of Marlowe in The Long Goodbye is that he gives off a constant air of knackeredness, and I was beginning to figure out that it'd be the persistent second-guessing that went with his job-description that would be the cause of it.

I'd been in so-called love with other people's girlfriends before, everybody has, haven't they – the grass is always greener on the other side et cetera, but usually the other-person's-girlfriend love isn't reciprocated, usually the other person's girlfriend doesn't even know you are in so-called love with her, if you play it right and tight. It's the easiest, safest way of having a relationship – it doesn't cost you, you don't make any investment and you don't even have to do anything at all. It's only a game and even though you think you feel the feelings, the headRush feelings, and the associated painRush feelings, which infiltrate your headSpace, actually you don't. You just carry on worrying about your trousers in the normal way. Life goes on.

But if Nat left me now, as the note implied, I knew I'd end up like Marky, finding myself in the standard weeping position, probably not in a BMW cabin, probably somewhere else – there must be other standard weeping positions in the world – and that life wouldn't be going on. I returned to the sofa and sat with my head between my legs. The phone wasn't going to be ringing now, it was too late. Could she have gone over to see Spurs? Would he have a greater level of competence than me? He must have, it could hardly be worse, could it? I couldn't just sit like that, feeling sorry for myself, so I watched The Long Goodbye again on the video.

There was a revelation in this watching. Marlowe doesn't say, It's cool with me, he says, It's *okay* with me. I don't know how long it was since I'd seen it last, and in fact I've only seen it three times ever before, because I don't think you should over-watch a favourite film, but I'd certainly remembered it wrong. It was an epic mistake to make, though, because he uses the expression about a million times squared.

The first time I *ever* saw it was after a late-night World Cup match I'd been watching with my stepdad (Bulgaria v. Algeria). I didn't even know there was a film coming on following the commercial break, it was past midnight, but it turned out to be a big bonus after the goalless draw. We both liked the way it began, with the cat and everything, but my stepdad was snoring long before the final credits, it was the first time he'd ever gone to sleep before me, so only I saw the way it finished and I had to tell him about it when he woke up. The way it finishes is that Marlowe goes down to Mexico to find that his so-called dead friend is actually still alive. Quite a lot of other stuff has gone on in the meantime. I won't derail you with all the details, but in brief: the writer-guy managed to drown himself – in the sea, rather than in the bottle – he pulled back that heavy glass door and staggered into the surf. Then Marlowe found out that his friend (he's called Terry Lennox, I *can* remember now) was having an affair with the writer-guy's wife, that Lennox *did* murder his own wife (Marlowe spends the film convinced of, and trying to prove, Lennox's innocence), that a lot of money was involved, et cetera, plus twists. (You know how hard it is to keep up with everything in private-eye films with all the interconnected complexities. That's why all private eyes have to be very idiosyncratic characters; it's to keep you in there when you lose the plot.) Anyway, at the end, Marlowe goes down to Mexico to see his old friend Terry Lennox, and because he's grown to despise him now that he knows all about his wife-killing ways (not to mention that he really *did* put Marlowe's own life in danger – by leaving some money in a car he left parked in Marlowe's garage, those Coke-bottle-smashing villains weren't wrong), and because Lennox is officially dead anyway (he paid off some Bandidos to see to the paperwork), Marlowe is quite free to shoot him if he feels so inclined, because it couldn't even be registered as a crime anyway. So he does. First he explains to him his opinion about his wife-killing ways – a very negative opinion, Marlowe was a little in love with Lennox's wife, even if only in the so-called way – and he also mentions how pissed off he is to have had his friendship abused. That's what friends are for, says Lennox. Marlowe, you're a Born Loser, he says. Marlowe likes this as much as I liked being called a waster by the tramp.

So Marlowe gives him the single bullet. And after that he skips back towards the sunset, playing a tune on his mini-mouth-organ (a very late introduction of an idiosyncrasy; it's the only time he does it) while kicking his heels side to side. The writer-guy's wife, reunited with her lover, drives by in an open Jeep, and Marlowe simply nods to her. An enormous look of disconcertment passes over her face as she glances back at Marlowe, and it's going to get worse, that look, when she finds her lover blown away further down the track. That's the end.

Another cigarette. I rubbed my neck against the back of Antonio's sofa, thinking: he doesn't say, It's cool with me, he says, It's *okay* with me. I spent time trying to find any redeeming feature in the unique sloppiness involved in my having got this wrong. I made coffee. I lit another cigarette. I've seen people pull a match up the grain of their jeans to strike a match. Not me. I struck it on the box and sat sniffing the residue on the sandpaper. After a while at this I arrived at a redeeming feature: this meant I had my *own* catch phrase: It's cool with me.

It's cool with me.

I sat drinking coffee and smoking like you do after seeing a favourite film (and watching it did make me feel better, like it should), then I had more coffee and more cigarettes and spent more time thinking about Nat and Spurs. I was left with one distilled thought and a steely-grey dawn. The distilled thought was that the only time I'd seen Natalie upset was precipitated by my letting it be known that her friend had an opinion about her, an opinion about what she should do. I might've been slow coming to it, it might've taken longer than it should've done, but the conclusion I arrived at was that Spurs must have too many opinions about her, about what she should do or shouldn't do – that *that* must be the way in which they didn't get on. At least I wasn't like him. The film had sharpened up my thinking process. And failing to succeed at zabaglione-making just *once* must be a lesser offence than harassing your girlfriend in a heavy-handed way like that, it must be. It is in my book, anyway.

I left it until the TV-video display read 08.00 and then I rang. It was answered straight off. By Bernie, very businesslike.

'Is Natalie there?'

'No.'

'She didn't come back?'

'Yes.'

'She's gone to work then?'

'Not yet.'

'Is she saying she doesn't want to speak to me?'

'I'm saying it for her, as it were.'

'Why?'

'Use your imagination, Winger.'

Bernie put the phone down. Spurs was there. Telling Nat what to do and what not to do, what to wear and what not to wear, et cetera. Hello Hello, we are the TottenhamBoys, Hello Hello, you'll tell us from our noise. I went there once, to White Hart Lane, that's the song. Et cetera, et cetera, et cetera.

Fuck.

I'd been up all night, but I didn't float out of myself like you do normally, I stayed within myself.

I re-read the note. Fuck.

Fuck, fuck, fuck.

32

I had a hard time that morning, re-reading the note and repeatedly saying fuck. It was the sort of experience that's served well in preparing me to deal with the kind of hard time I'm having now, considering the unconsiderable back in Outward Bound. Somewhere deep in my headSpace I know it has to be true that the way to stay warm and to avoid frostbite in the far north will involve wearing more than one item of legwear at a time. Outward Bound man thinks nothing of the suggestion; after all, we've had a conversation already in which it's been acknowledged that people who play football are prepared to do it in the highly specialized instance of wearing lycra under-shorts. But it's like he just totally doesn't understand that there are completely different rules for proper trousers. And neither do the manufacturers. For instance, take a random label on a pair of these long-john *things*:

> The Z400 Series of micro-breathable Fabrics(tm)® provide warmth without weight and are designed to be the middle or outer layer of the Multi-Climate-Controlled Matrix-System.® Z400 micro-breathables provide a bedrock support foundation that will enhance performance however demanding the demands of the environment.

Middle or outer layer? You see what's being implied here – that there could be a *third* layer, an under-under layer. Or even an outer-outer layer. Imagine what that would look like. Or better still, don't. The whole matter is unthinkable; the area deep in my headSpace just won't allow for it. It's bad enough that I'm going to buy a fleece. The rest of my body will have to be cold. I'm not wearing two pairs of strides. I'm just not. The demands can demand all they want.

For garments other than strides, the kind of purchaser I am is the kind of purchaser who will bite the plastic label-holders off (just be vicious with them) and wear the new purchase straight out. Back on the pavement, I feel very odd, conspicuous, very strange indeed. It's not unnatural to feel this way when you're wearing a fleece. I've bought new wrap-around shades too, silver and blue (in order to wear a fleece, you have to add appropriate accessories). They're not unlike the goggles, in their way, they're the same generally oval shape (not a shape I like). And of course, like any other shades, they are something to hide behind.

By now I must look like I'm going somewhere, I must. I bought a hat too – it's in the bag together with the zipped-off sleeves. To be honest, I couldn't even bear to look at myself wearing it, I simply chose the most innocuous bonnet available and pretended it wasn't happening. The bill for the fleece, hat, knife and shades totted up to quite a reasonable amount, though I've paid more for trousers I've never, *ever* worn often enough before.

Alan picked me up in his black BMW on the way to the Rear Window Snooker Club last night. I had to ask him to lend me money on the way. I need a safety buffer in my account. I hated doing it, but as I've never made such a request before, he had to say yes. It's just an understood thing, this, when one of you has money or access to credit, and one of you hasn't. None the less, he was circumspect about the matter, umming and aahing like your assistant bank manager, and after that he introduced a certain amount of cross-questioning to do with needs and entitlements before coming up with an offer that included a complex compound interest rate. Playing my part in this rigmarole was something I found difficult – having to give him the bullshit right answers and so on. I mean, even though he knew he had to say yes, he could still have said no – there'd've been nothing I could do about it if he answered in the unaffirmative. I hate asking anyone for money, that's one reason why I'm such a poor businessman, I even disliked taking money for the sandwiches in the Scanty days. Anyway, at the conclusion of the interview, having no choice, I simply agreed to his outrageous repayment requirements. He still made me sweat, delaying writing the cheque until after the snooker (which of course I had to lose, even if I was going to anyway, under the circumstances). He'll be a millionaire before he's thirty, the way he carries on. I should stop off at a bank. I should pay it in.

Completion of the transaction in Outward Bound hasn't made me happy or anything approaching it. You wouldn't expect it to, having to make necessity purchases like that, it couldn't. But there's more to it. Outward Bound man got a conversation going as we waited for the card to clear:

Are you going away for long, he asked.

Not sure, I replied.

'Are you flying?'

'Yes.'

'There are good deals about at the moment. Who are you going with?'

'Don't know, I haven't booked my ticket yet.'

The credit card machine was one of those with a long built-in pause, time enough for you to begin to worry about it clearing, time for you to develop the expectation that it will be declined. I've got a large limit actually. The Alan cheque is to bring it down to within that limit. One area in which I do tell a lot of lies is in the boxes where you tick your annual earnings on the forms for credit application and enhancement.

When are you going, he asked.

'Today.'

The machine continued its pause. He looked at me. Everybody looks middle-aged in a beard, but I think he actually was middle-aged anyway. There was something in his eye as we awaited the authorization, I was pretty sure it was unease. And I knew why he might feel that way. It was because I was unprepared. I'd entered the shop unprepared – I hadn't read all the specialist Outward Bound magazines about tog ratings and bomb-proofing et cetera. I didn't know dates, times, schedules. I didn't know the whens or the wheres or the whys. Maybe you have to be a student of his look to recognize it as easily as I do, maybe it's one I see too frequently. I've had it from theBoys often enough, when they've been talking about the pensionPlanlifePlan Lifestyle. Do you know that some people stay in a job for thirty years to get a *pension* at the end of it? We had a representative canvas us in The Scanty once. We were busy doing nothing as usual, so we had no shortage of free time in which to give the rep a hearing – in fact we were happy to give him a hearing (one of us insisted he bought a sandwich first). He was difficult to take seriously because he was wearing a spotty bow tie and unmentionable legwear. But still, I gave him a free tea with his sandwich (a *lot* of money was lost on those free teas), and he talked for at least half an hour – it felt like six times that, of course – and when my headSpace was nearing total numb-down, I asked him a question, to check whether or not I was still with him.

If I'm following you right, I said, then even if we were doing really brilliant business, we'd still need to put virtually everything we earn into a pension scheme and even then it'd only just cover us when we retired. If that. Yes?

I'm afraid that's about the size of it, he replied. Self-employment *is* a difficult option, it's the reason why so many professionals – teachers, civil servants – stay put. Once you're a few years into a company pension, it's very difficult to match it independently because of the employer's contribution, you see.

You mean there are people who stay in a job for twenty more years because of the *pension*? I asked.

'Well, they stay in a career, yes. It happens.'

He looked remarkably cheerful about it.

'And what you're saying is that you can't really fund a private pension and have it work properly?' (I wanted to be certain about this.)

'Well . . .'

He continued and continued. He'd talked himself even further out of doing any business with us by confirming and reconfirming that, give or take a detail or two, I'd understood him right. It was the most interesting aspect of him: he seemed determined to be an unsuccessful pension rep. He was an unusually hungry man, he bought a monkfish and mango salsa take-away in pitta as well as the one he ate while he was with us. (What were we up to menu-wise? I don't know: Trying too much? Trying too hard? What? I'd never cook or eat monkfish and mango salsa normally. *Never*. My assessment, at the end, was that we were over-prepared. Over-anxious. I really think we were. I think it was a real problem.) Anyway, his news made us all think, sped us towards the realization that The Scanty might not be the way forward, and even though his being there allowed us to use the till twice in one hour – a new record – we were able to see the sad fact of such record-setting in the correct light. Not only was this level of activity hopeless in the short term, but even if what we all wanted to happen did happen (have clients) it was also going to be hopeless in the long term too.

Outward Bound man's look of unease made me recall the pension rep. Outward Bound man could easily be in the same fix as theBoys and everybody else, pension-wise. That's why he looked at me like that. That's why people look at me like that. I know this. It's for not having made *provisions*. It's for making them question their own take on the world and how they go through it in their hiking trousers. Even if such questioning goes in and out of their headSpaces in under a minute, it's still long enough to put them in touch with something they don't much care for. It's not that they think I've got the meaning of life right or anything. No way. It's that I'm walking about *not* doing the lifeThing in the approved manner. Maybe it embarrasses them, like having a drunk in the family who you know is out on the streets calling people wasters.

It worries *me* that I know I'm like this. I'm trying to take steps to put it right, to change something, to get some balance back. Well, not *back*, more to get some balance *at all*. I wanted to explain this when I re-established communication with Natalie. I let an unhappy long weekend go by, then I called her at work and we arranged to meet for coffee when she knocked off. It seems like another lifetime and a half ago, but in fact it was only the day before I hung those fuckingPrat curtains with Tissy, the day before my first theft.

33

We sat in a single link of a world-wide chain of coffee outlets, the lights bright overhead. They were nothing like the floodlights which lit us when we first met but somehow they reminded me of them. I was more than relieved that at least we could still meet in the aftermath of the zabaglione disaster and the note. As the Mochaccinos were served, I knew I should dispense with any preamble, I didn't think it would help. I thought I should get straight to the point, the point to which my up-all-night thinking and staying within myself had got me.

Listen, Nat, I said. What is it, the not getting on with Spurs, what's it about? In what way do you two not get on?

'I suppose he doesn't always do the right things for me.'

'What like? Like what things?'

'I can't talk to you about this now.'

'When then?'

'I'm not sure. I'm not sure I can at all.'

'Listen, I shouldn't've repeated what Bernie said, about you being creative and that you should be a designer and that. I hope it's alright between you and her. I hope I haven't caused a problem.'

'Caused a problem?' She sounded distracted. 'Did you think it was that that annoyed me?'

I thought so, yeah, I said.

She looked out of the window. She was distracted. I followed her eyes as they followed a dispatch bike weaving through the traffic. She didn't really want to speak, it was obvious, so I carried on.

'I thought I might be behaving like Spurs, I thought it must be that he has opinions about you, about what you should or shouldn't be or should or shouldn't do. Is that it? Is that what he doesn't do right?'

'Might be.'

Her voice softened as she said it. She continued to gaze through the window and I studied her face in the reflection. I couldn't tell whether her eyes softened or not, because her focus wasn't focused, it was moving with the tail-lights of the dispatcher.

By the way, I said, sorry about the zabaglione.

She half-looked my way. 'Worse things happen.'

Maybe, I said, but a failed zabaglione is the saddest sight in world.

She continued her half-looking. Is it? she said. Leaving you on the sofa wasn't all that cheerful either. I shouldn't've gone like that, Winger, but I just couldn't . . . I had like a panic attack too. There was so much going through my mind – you, and what you were saying about feeling small and things falling away and . . .

She glanced away to the disappearing tail-light of the bike.

'Sometimes I look at the sky, you know, and imagine what a dot I am in everything –'

'A tiny part of a tiny part like you were saying about clothes . . .?'

'– like you started me saying, to be exact. Yeah. I remember the conversation. It's frightening, only being that, isn't it, a speck. And my dad. People dying –'

She looked me straight in the eye.

'– to tell you the truth, I never much talk about things like this. They upset me. And you have a way of asking me things and making me think that upsets me too. I did a runner. Sorry.'

What, I said, you do runners, do you?'

'Sometimes.'

'You're not thinking of doing one now?'

She didn't reply, she resumed her gazing out of the window. The dispatch bike had gone. Suddenly I thought about the guy watching the football, the one in the leather trousers, and Natalie's absence that night. They get around, dispatchers, don't they?

Does *he* play football, I asked, *Spurs*?

'Why?'

'What *does* he do?'

'It doesn't matter.'

I didn't want to think about it, who he might have been. Anybody could have said something to him, from one of the offices where they work, tipped him off. I felt he'd been watching *me*, actually, that was how I noticed him at first, he was staring at me as BearBoy barged me into the perimeter fencing. Watching *me* have a crap game. *And* he could've seen the note passed. I really didn't want to go down this road now, I really didn't. My fingernails were going. I changed the subject. I tried to get back on track. I'd meant to tell her that I was going to sort my life out. That I was going to get a proper job so that I could buy us our own sofa to sit on. Only I hadn't actually worked out the details, not precisely. So I changed the subject to another subject, to being in love, since we *still* hadn't talked about that yet, not face to face.

'Natalie. About saying I love you . . .'

'You can't say that, you know. You can't. We haven't even known each other nearly long enough. (She shook her head. She did her snort laugh. I definitely definitely didn't mention it.) I mean . . .'

'Listen. I know, I know. I know it sounds – Oh, *what*, I don't know, too immediate, too obvious, too something – but it's the way I feel. Nat, I spend my whole life trying not to be somebody, trying not to fall into the . . . template, the . . . the . . .'

I trailed off hopelessly. She helped me out. The cutting pattern? she said.

'That's a technical term, isn't it?'

Everybody knows that, she said.

She was right. It's an expression everyone knows from

somewhere. There are other ones, aren't there, ones like casting the die and toeing the line. Cutting pattern. It was a hard sound as it came out of my mouth, as I repeated it back to her, and it sounded right. It brought images into my mind of those drawings with broken lines, of people and of animals, the ones you're supposed to cut out of books when you're little. And paper chains of linked figures all the same, it reminded me of those too.

The cutting pattern. The whole fucking dickhead game, I said.

We stayed looking at each other straight on. That's the first time I've ever heard you swear, she said. Are you angry?

'No. [Well, yes, but with *me*] I swear a lot, Nat, but mostly only to myself. I think that's what love's like.'

'Like what?'

'Another predestined thing you have to do. I don't want to fall in love any more than I want a pensionPlan, any more than I want to follow the recipe out of the book, any more than . . .'

Ah, she interrupted. Love's like the whole dickhead game – not like swearing to yourself?

I had to stop to think. Since I've never even felt like this before, I'm hardly the right person to ask. Which is it more like then, I thought: the whole dickhead game, or swearing to yourself? I didn't [fucking] know.

It doesn't feel much like the whole dickhead game, I said.

It feels like swearing to yourself then, does it, she asked.

'Not to yourself, no.'

I licked the foam off the rim, I bit into the cardboard lip of the cup, and I came up with the answer to how love feels.

'You know those people who have that condition where they can't stop fucking swearing all the fucking time. D'you know the one I mean?'

Yeah, she said. It's called Tourette's syndrome. It's a fucking bastard if you've got it.

'That's what it feels like.'

Fuck me, she said.

Have *you* got it? I asked. (After all, her swearing rate had taken an upturn.)

Me? She hesitated for a second. Fuck no, she replied.

Are you sure, I asked.

'Fucking positive, Winger.'

We emptied the paper cups and reordered. Two more cups of coffee for the road.

I've got to go soon, she said. Listen, I could get on with you, big time. Really. But there's a way in which you trouble me.

'What way?'

'Being anti things.'

'But I'm not. I'm not anti every*thing*. I'm *for* lots of things.'

'Like what?'

'Art. Football. Five-a-side. Cooking. Football. Fashion. Shopping – most of the time, except for trousers.'

Trousers? she said. Why are you always going on about your trousers, Winger?

'I'm not.'

'I'd say you are. You mentioned them on the first date, didn't you?'

'Did I?' (I knew I did, of course.)

'You started a conversation about them when we were walking back from the restaurant –'

'I did, yes.'

'– I had to lend you some 'cos you wouldn't wear your new ones when they were a bit crumpled –'

'That had to be done, though – they weren't just crumpled, they were *bobbling* too.' [And I've still got your dad's]

'– You doodled a pair on that newspaper you left at the flat, first time you came round, with that stuff written around the edges. You're obsessed with trousers, aren't you?'

'No.'

'You are.'

'Has Bernie said something to you?'

'What d'you mean?'

'About trousers.'

'No. Why should she?'

'No reason.'

'Have you spoken to her about them then?'

'No.' [A lie, it's a lie]

'Why d'you mention it then?'

'Nothing, no reason.'

'D'you fancy her?'

'No. No. No. God. No. Don't get me wrong like that. Shit. Alright – trousers give me trouble. I spend half my life [Minimum] worrying about them . . .'

'Why?'

'I don't know, I just do. I told Bernie, well, she kind of talked it out of me, at her studio. That's all.'

'You *did* speak to her about them?'

'Yes.'

'Why did you say you didn't then?'

"Cos of how I feel about you. It'd make me seem stupid, or something. Less than I should be. [Fuck] I don't remember doodling any on the paper.'

'You did. A punk-rock bondage pair.'

'Never. I wouldn't.'

'You did.'

'Really? Yes, that's right, I remember. I *like* drawing, I'm *for* that too – I'm surprised you noticed.'

'Well you shouldn't be. After all, it was the morning after the first night we spent together, the first night I've ever been unfaithful, as a matter of fact.'

'How long have you been with Spurs?'

'Nearly a year.'

For some reason I'd imagined it had been longer than that. We stared into our coffee-foam in the predictable classic coffee-foam staring way. Then she carried on talking, not about Spurs, but about the Evening Standard with the doodled trousers.

'I even kept that paper. It's under my bed. You got nice writin'. What was it about anyway?'

'It was a poem I copied on the way over to see you, off a bus shelter. It had football-commentator speak in it, didn't it – something about the moon and over it, if I remember right.'

'Yeah, and something about the shit and the fan too.'

She gave me a version of her hard look of hard scrutinization as she said this. And then the expression dropped and she just looked miserable instead.

He came round, didn't he, I asked. After you left me, after the zabaglione.

'Yeah. He rode over.'

Rode. He *rode* over. Fuck. It must've been him. Fuck. I thought he'd be a professional or something.

'Was it a close thing? I mean, were you expecting him? I mean, you were over at mine for dinner.'

'Bernie'll always cover for me. She'll do that, she'll cover for people. And I switch my mobile off a lot, he knows that.'

'But having just left me, making the adjustment, slipping into the different life . . .'

'Slipping into the different lie, more like. I didn't smell of you or anything, but . . . ohh, fuck . . .'

She trailed off. It shouldn't be possible to look miserable and sad when you're wearing a Mochaccino-foam moustache, but she did. As sad as a failed zabaglione. Sadder, in fact.

I had to pick it up eventually:

'First time you've been unfaithful?'

'Yeah.'

She stood up. Listen, she said, I can't do this. I can't. I'm gonna go, she said. Don't call me or anything, *please*.

I stood up too.

Okay, I said. Just one thing: I licked my finger and reached towards her and wiped the foam moustache away.

That's better, I said.

She turned and she didn't look back. She walked out on silver trainers, which normally I can't stand. They'd be the best I could do for finding something about her not to adore. They wouldn't be anything like enough. I didn't think I'd managed to explain anything at all, nothing that helped anyway. And I'd lied about my trousers to someone I should have been able to be truthful with. To the only person it mattered about. *And* been found out. Fuck. Fucking, fucking fuck.

I sat back down with the two half-empty cups at the one round marble table wondering if it would do as a standard weeping position. The overhead lights were too bright for it. I walked through the sliding door of the coffee outlet. Out on the street, the weather had the decency to begin to rain.

34

When I was out on the street in short trousers – which I never was, of course, I wouldn't be seen dead in them – there was a park near where we lived, and in the middle of the park they'd built a long tall glasshouse where tropical plants grew. A winding path wound through the glasshouse, and in the middle, to one side, there was a wishing well. The shop where Rosie works reminds me of it. The floor is made from the same sort of cold, perspiring stone, and your voice slightly echoes in here, same as it did in the glasshouse.

Outward Bound took longer than expected, but I didn't linger elsewhere. Even if I'd bought a pair of Urban Eskimos from the Directional Casualwear range at the Style Lab, I wouldn't've put them on, I know that. They'd just be killing space in the FullSump Flare. Actually, to get to the point and be honest about this now, I'm wearing Natalie's dad's trousers, like I virtually always have done since I've had them. It was a pair of newish black Firetraps that were giving me trouble at the snooker last night, but I was only wearing them because I didn't want Alan to see these; they're nothing to do with him or his Lifestyle. It's good that I'm wearing them. I mean, they really *don't* fit. I think it's a sort of progress.

Rosie's on the phone, a length of ribbon clenched in one corner of her mouth while she arranges a spray on the marble counter. She gestures at me with her eyes: Be with you in a minute.

Having received her two verbal warnings vis-à-vis timekeeping, as a matter of fact I *am* on time, which is a sort of progress too. Being there when I said I'd be there, it's positive.

The flowers are set out in grandstand formation at the

front, arranged in buckets and copper urns. The window is bowed, a green tint to the glass. It's one of my favourite windows. I sniff my way about while I wait. I used to think all flowers had perfume but it's amazing how many don't.

You can tell when Rosie's phone call is coming to an end, it's when she says, Is there a message? She has some past sell-by Valentine Special cards on the marble top next to the phone: Cupid in the right-hand corner, releasing his arrow. I pick them up and ruffle them like a flick book while I wait. We missed Valentine's day, me and Nat, not by much, but we missed it. I couldn't have written a message. And anyway flowers should speak for themselves. Cupid fires and refires. Lyrics come into my head. *People carry roses, make promises by the hour, My love she laughs like the flowers, Valentines can't buy her.* It's that Bob Dylan song again, I don't think I've even thought about it since the firstDate.

D'you know this song, I ask Rosie, singing her the words as she puts the phone down.

Love Minus Zero, Dylan, she says. I see you bought the fleece then.

'Does it look bad?'

'It looks new-fleecy.'

'That *is* bad, isn't it?'

'I've seen worse.'

'Have you?'

'Yeah.'

'Where?'

'All over the place. On old people. Is that a new bag too?'

I fiddle about with the strap, which is already twisted, like bag-straps always are.

'Yeah. I got it from the fleece shop.'

She looks me up and down, but she doesn't say anything about the new bag and fleece in combination with the zipped-off Snowboard Puffa and Natalie's dad's trousers, she knows me better than that. She doesn't want another long conversation, and neither do I.

Are you going somewhere? Is this what you want to talk about? she says.

'Yeah.'

'Let's get a move on. We'll get a table at Astravoid, I can manage an hour.'

All the boys notice her as we walk down the street, she's one of those girls who dresses without trying. The part of her that gives trouble is her hair, she goes through more hairstyle changes than I've got strides, if you can believe that, and she's usually wearing a new tint too. She conducts tint-experiments on her quiet nights in. Her hair turned greeny-orange once after she'd tried some highlighting, which was not the idea, but she lived with it and changed the colour of her nail varnish to aquamarine to make it look deliberate. That's the kind of person she is, and I admire her for it. It'd kill me, having to walk about with the wrong colour hair, I'd have to wear a hat, which'd hardly be any better, in fact it'd be worse. I'd have to stay in.

There's no time to waste, so I begin straight off, talking and walking.

'Natalie and me . . . we stopped seeing each other ten days ago.'

'How can you be so precise?'

'It was the day after Valentine's day.'

'Bad timing.'

'Yeah.'

'So that's why you've been hiding; *that*'s why you haven't phoned.'

'Yeah. She finished with me, sort of. That would be the accurate way of putting it, I suppose.'

'Shit.'

'Shit is it.'

'You must be upset.'

'You could say that.' (I kept Rosie well informed, in the early days, the only days there were really, before my retreat.)

'What have you been doing then?'

'Nothing. Scamming, reading, playing snooker. Smoking. Doing pull-ups on the bedroom door-frame. I can do thirty now. Suffering very downbeat hangovers. Watching the lights pass across the ceiling. Standard weeping.'

Poor boy, she said.

'Oh, and I've started up a new sideline: I nicked a mask from a museum yesterday.'

'Yeah, right.'

'Yeah right, but I did actually.'

'Really?'

'Really.'

'So that was all the intrigue on the phone this morning. What sort of mask?'

'I'll show it to you at Astravoid.'

'Can't you show it to me now?'

'Not in the street, Rosie, it's dangerous.'

'Uh huh. It would be, mask-exposure on a public highway. Have you called Natalie, have you spoken at all?'

'Yes but too late. Bernie answered. Nat's gone away. She's been in the Far East, Buying Fall.'

'Buying Fall?'

'That's what they call it, in fashion, they buy Winter and Fall.'

'Uh huh. So what're you planning?'

'I'm going to find her.'

'Find her?'

'Yeah.'

'In a fleece and a *bodywarmer*?'

'It's a puffa jacket with the sleeves zipped off; it isn't what you just called it. Anyway, it's necessary.'

'For the Far East!? It's not even necessary for this weather.'

We part company as we pass either side of an old couple blocking the pavement like they do. Neither of them is wearing a fleece, a point I point out to Rosie as we reconvene.

That's because a fleece isn't *necessary* for this weather, she replies. That's because it's a nice day for the time of year.

'It's unseasonably nice if you ask me. Nat's not in the Far East any more, she's in the far north, she's in Finland.'

'Finland!? Wow. It will be freezing up there.'

'Exactly.'

'Fair enough, I'll give you the fleece. *Why* is she in Finland?'

'I'm not sure. I don't know. I think it's to do with football. Some of her team-mates are Finnish.'

'Did Bernie tell you where she was?'

'Yeah.'

'Nat's keeping in touch with Bernie then, while she's away?'

'She's called in a couple of times, that's all.'

'Will Bernie tell Nat what you're going to do, if she calls in again. Did you tell Bernie what you were planning?'

'No, I thought it was best not to mention it, and it was hard enough getting the information out of her at all. D'you think it's the right thing, Rosie?'

Astŕavoid is in front of us.

It's romantic, she says, as the door slides open. It's a romantic gesture. Any girl's going to like a bloke chasing her to Finland, aren't they, unless he's a psycho. And you're not a psycho. *Are you?*

'I hope not.'

'Natalie won't think you are, will she, that's what I mean. You haven't done anything mad that I should know about, have you?'

To put her mind at rest, and to double-treble-check this for myself (it's not like I haven't gone through it in my head a million times since), I tell her about the conversation me and Nat had at the coffee outlet. I tell her about the part when Nat said, Fuck no – that she fucking positively didn't have Tourette's syndrome, and how in context this meant that she did love me too. And then I tell her again, I run it past her twice, because I don't think I explain it properly the first time, what with all the swearing and the Mochaccino moustache and absolutely all the details included. She ends up nodding after the second telling, saying that it's possible that it *does* mean that – provided it was an intense conversation and that we were both concentrating – otherwise it could simply mean that she didn't have fucking Tourette's syndrome.

'It *was* an intense conversation. It was.'

'What's up with her then?'

'It's the Spurs thing.'

She nods again. Girls aren't anything like as good at being unfaithful as boys are, she says. Or as good at chucking them. She might've run away and hoped that only one of you'd still be here when she got back.

'D'you think so?'

'It's not impossible. Sometimes it's really hard to face these things.'

'Can you be in love with two people at once, Rosie?'

'No.'

'So if I've got the Tourette's right, she'll be happy to see me when I get there?'

'Yes. I think so. Yes.'

'Right.' (At least count the whole idea as being cool then.)

'But how are you going to find her?'

'Well, I know she's in Helsinki, I know that much, I mean I don't have to search the whole country. I'm hoping she's got her mobile with her. And I'm hoping it'll be switched on. It'll work in Finland, won't it?'

'I reckon. Nokia's base is up there after all.'

'Is it?'

'Yep.'

'Not Japan?'

'No.'

'Sounds Japanese.'

'Things ain't always what they sound, are they?'

'That's true.'

'Like you, for instance.'

'How d'you mean?'

'You don't sound like a maskthief. Where is it then?'

Ah. I pass it to her in the detachable accessory pouch, slipping it under the table, and I tell her the whole thing about that too. She opens it on her knee, looks down, glances across, looks down, glances across. At the end of me telling her the whole thing she gives me her Very Funny Look.

I feel like I've shown her my clothes art, or my Moon and Saturn Vest in Funereal Frame from the diary. I ended up quite liking that – I've sat by the phone more since, but I haven't felt like drawing anything else. I feel like I want her to approve.

'D'you like it?'

It's giving me something like a déjà-vu, she says.

'How?'

'I don't know, something . . .'

'Something what?'

'Something like . . .tulips.'

'Tulips?'

'Yeah. Tulips aren't what they used to be.'

'How?'

'The leaves are too thin, the green's not green enough. It's like that. It's too fragile, it's too fragile to be a mask.'

She slips it back. She's not wrong. She looks at me with her curious look. D'you think it's worth a lot? she says.

'I've no idea, though the thought has crossed my mind. What d'you reckon?'

Who knows? she says. Must be at least a few grand, mustn't it? Could be tens of thousands. You might find a buyer for that in Finland, huh, pay off your debts, make a fresh start.

'It's an Eskimo mask, Rosie. They don't have Eskimos in Finland, do they?'

'No, but they have snow. It's for snow. That was what you said, didn't you?'

'Yeah.'

Well then, she says, as the crêpes arrive. When she says, Well then, that's like a full stop for her, she's really made her point.

Where are you going to get a flight? she says.

'Dunno. D'you know a good travel agent?'

'Have you got money for a ticket then, and currency?'

'I've still got credit on the card which I pay off with all the other cards. Just about. And Alan lent me a cheque to top it.'

'Alan?'

'Yeah. Don't ask.'

'You've got your passport?'

'Yeah.'

We haven't got time to sit here, she says. She picks up her crêpe, wraps it in her napkin. Let's sort it out now, she says. You'll never get there on your own. Finland, wow, she says, Helsinki – I've always liked the sound of that, it's exotic, like Istanbul, isn't it? Come on – let's move.

35

I remember about all *my* déjà-vus as she takes me to the travel agent. She says they're a good sign, she says it means everything's connecting up; they're a form of spiritual communication, she says. I'm prepared to take this from her – I didn't trust the drunk who said the mark on my eye was a sign.

They're not all bad, drunks, she says.

She doesn't have to tell *me*. She stops and takes a look at it, stretches my eyelids between her thumb and finger.

'It's just a tiny little scratch.'

Is it a form of spiritual communication as well, I ask.

'No.'

We walk on, eating crêpes and spilling filling. But while we're on the subject of communication, she says, How will you call Natalie when you get there?

'Phone.'

'D'you think you'll be able to work a Finnish public phone?'

'Well . . .'

'How will you understand the instructions, how will you find the right change?'

'Well, I can't call from here, Rosie. I have to get there, I have to do it for *real*.'

You can have mine, she says.

'But Rosie, that International Roaming doesn't work, I can never get through to Antonio on it. And what will *you* do?'

I'll manage, she says.

At the travel agent's, while they do all the computing about reservations and times, we sit on the comfy chairs by the free coffee and Rosie demonstrates Use of the Mobile

Phone. She calls Antonio. She says for him not to worry, that she knows he only eats F-E-L-I-N-I-X, that I'm off to Helsinki, that she's taken the keys, that she knows it won't be double-locked, and that she'll see him when he gets back. She laughs a couple of times, saying, No, then saying, Oh Yeah? And then she puts me on.

'Ant?'

Finland? he says. She really must be the Goddess of the East Chip Butty. How's Pancho?

'Drooling. He's fine.'

'Good, well don't waste the battery, by the sound of things you're gonna need it. How'd Arsenal get on?'

'One–nil.'

'Zat's my boys. What you wearing then?'

'A fleece.'

You're coming on, he says.

'I know, I've even got a bag called a FullSump *Flare*, if you can believe that.'

Excellent. Good luck, he says.

'Thanks.'

Rosie does her stuff, which means that even though we're quoted a totally unreasonable amount we step outside having paid less. While we're waiting for a yellow light, I ask her what she was laughing about with Ant. What was the No and Oh Yeah?

'He asked me were you wearing any of his clothes.'

'That was the No, right?'

'Right.'

'And the Oh Yeah?'

'That's between me and him.'

The taxi pulls up. Take it easy, she says, as she kisses me in. And I kiss her back and no mistake. She's helped me out here, she really has.

Take him to the Piccadilly Line, she says to the driver. Don't let him persuade you to go to Heathrow, he can't afford it.

Use of the mobile, no. 1: pretend to be on it as refuge from the driver. I hold it to my ear, murmuring and thinking. As she was paying for the tickets ('I won the lottery at the weekend, keep your credit for when you arrive, there might be an emergency') she also mentioned that she wasn't my mum, and that she expected me to be better organized once I'd sorted out my love life.

I'm going to sort out my life life too, I said. I am. Everything's going to be cool.

The luggage label's bothering me as I try to attach it to the FullSump Flare. And it's not just that I can't tie it properly, and it's not just having a mobile in my hand while I'm at it. It's something else.

'. . . I dunno, seems like every alteration what they make's designed to slow you down, it'll all grind to a halt one day, you mark my words. There you go, mate, Eight-thirty. Ta. Your girlfriend's right, you're better off on the tube. State of that M4 . . .'

36

I hate the tube but the cabbie and my girlfriend were both right, it's the best chance of catching the plane (4.40, Terminal 4). I hate the litter down in the valley beside the tracks as much as anything – like you need litter underground, like there isn't enough out there on the surface.

Nobody ever used to speak to each other, did they, you used to get the dead subterranean silence, it was perfectly normal, but that's all changed now, since half the population of the carriage is on the phone. You overhear one side of the world's most banal conversations, but none the less it's the only place I don't mind mobile use. When people are actually talking at all it's like human life does carry on, it's comforting. And of course, now I'm a user myself, I have to mind it even less.

As you step out at Heathrow with your FullSump Flare slung over your back and your rolled-up copy of TopLad tucked under your arm (which you've bought to see whether you've got a stylist's credit for the blindin' Biscuit-Babes shoot – as sad a way as there is to check that you do really exist), it's not like you're anywhere near the plane. Oh no. Five miles of moving pavement to go. Actually, you cover most of this ground after you've checked in and nearly shat yourself wondering if the Customs scanner X-ray is going to read your stolen mask as a terrorist device. It doesn't.

Do you know what they do on planes now? Instead of showing a film on the drop-down video screen, you get to see what's going on on the exterior, they must have a camera on the outside. So you get the pilot's-eye view as you pull on to the runway, taxi, position, hold, taxi and take off. As you rise you look out of the window, you look to the screen and you see the same diminishing landscape from a different point of view. It's a slightly different colour on the screen, the same as any film. It's not quite the colour of real life. It must really freak you out if you have fear of flying. It's real life I'm doing now, though, this. This *is* the colour of real life, Natalie. It must be.

They show route maps for the rest of the flight, only returning you to the outside camera as you approach the Finnish area.

Even if you've absolutely no reason to come here, you should fly over anyway just to see this view.

Snow on white islands and black sea, that's all there is, the world in black and white, like films used to be when you'd've known for sure they *weren't* the colour of real life. And even though it's up there on screen, your fellow passengers crane to the windows like zoo visitors trying to catch a glimpse of the baby panda. The nearer you get, the bigger the white islands become until you're dropping down into the Nordic night, falling close enough to notice that the tail-lights of the cars flow red through the white; so you can see that even the motorways are snow-covered. The view through the window looks a lot colder than the view on the screen, because snow glitters the glass. The view through the window *is* the real colour, and it looks the real temperature *too*.

The plane slows after touchdown and the captain gives out the local time – 20.00 hours, two hours later than it should be.

What was it she said, the night of the firstDate? Stretching time forwards, backwards or something? I said it was like losing it altogether, did I? A different kind of losing it. We were talking about flexitime. 'I suppose you make it up on the way back.' That was it, that was what she said. The two hours aren't lost and gone for ever, are they? If I do this right maybe I can make them up on the way back, and some other lost time too.

The captain gives out the temperature. Minus 10 with a wind-chill factor of 16, whatever that means. My fellow passengers – an alarmingly healthy-looking crew – begin to retrieve their outerwear layers from the overhead lockers. Puffa jackets emerge in all the ludicrous permutations of colour / finish known to man (at least mine's black, same as my new fleece). There are duckdown scarves, goosedown scarves, Thermo, ExtremeThermo, Extra ExtremeThermo and Super Extra ExtremeThermo gloves, and a selection of very stupid hats including one with tiger ears; in addition, something I've never seen before – a selection of animal fur coats. It makes you feel decidedly uneasy about just how chilly minus 10 with a wind-chill factor of 16 might feel.

I'll tell you – for a start, *don't* even think about using a soft word like chilly. To be honest, there isn't really a proper descriptive name for it. Try this: once you've checked through, wander out on to the concourse and light up behind the shielding hand, but *don't* try it without gloves for more than the square root of an eighth of a microsecond if you want to keep your fingers. Do I have gloves, Extreme, Mega Extreme or otherwise? Am I a glove wearer? Of course not, even given my fingernail problem. Half a drag and I'm back inside, crying, looking for the appropriate shop in the hall. Airport clothes are the worst in the world, everybody knows that, but this is another *emergency*.

The staff in the airport glove-vending outlet speak English and smile.

The taxi driver might speak English but he doesn't smile, and he doesn't actually speak at all apart from inquiring where it is I want to go as he opens the door of the Merc. Foreign cabs are always Mercs, aren't they? I've no idea where I want to go. I try thinking up an answer as he pads round the bonnet, as he waits in his seat, as the low hum of an indecipherable tongue plays on the radio. He checks me through his rear-view until he's had enough of the silence then offers his suggestion.

'Centre?'

'Okay. Centre.'

It's not right to land in another country on your own. You feel like you should have somebody with you, or at least have somebody to meet you, even if it's only somebody you don't know, one of those people holding up a piece of cardboard with your name written in marker pen.

The low indecipherable tongue changes to music, a version of Delilah, a song which sounds colder sung by the local Tom Jones, but at least it's a welcome of some sort, like seeing the only other person you know at a party, even if it's someone you don't like. We pull away from the terminal building, which is silver, with snow falling on it. There's snow all round, falling and lying. You never see anything like this back home, nothing at all; it's like driving through a Christmas card.

The taxi moves at a different volume, the tyres roll in a cushioned crunch. It bothers me how it holds the road when it doesn't have snow chains like I thought it would (in fact, as we enter traffic, I notice none of the cars have snow chains like I thought they would. I was looking forward to seeing that). The taxi driver drives at a normal speed, in a normal taxi style, and so does everyone else. I can't work it out. The back end slides slightly on corners, and each time we stop as the lights go red we're into a gentle skid. Each stop should be a crash, yet somehow it isn't.

As the centre approaches, as the buildings close in, it's clear by the awkward gait of the walks on display that a pedestrian needs to be double insulated, at least.

There's a cushioning against your quick frozen footfall as you disembark, taxi to pavement. Everything's cushioned. Everything's cold beyond an appropriate descriptive word. It's not funny this, it's really not. Cool with me? No, it's way beyond that.

37

Right. Long john things. If you ever need your mind focusing, step into factor 16 wind chill at the junction of two broad thoroughfares where the wind chills converge from both directions to create a combined chill factor of minus 32, and it'll happen right away. On *this* corner (Pohjoisesplanadi – learning the language is clearly out of the question if that's supposed to be a street name), the corner where the taxi driver's abandoned me, stands a department store, and as I'm in Europe proper now, it's open, even though it's late. It must be half-past eight, local time. Half-past eight.

Department stores are the same everywhere, you get coated in a blast of warm air as you enter and then it's always the perfume counters first. I take a spray of something from the perfume counters as usual, but before that I stand warming in the warm blast for five minutes, which isn't usual but is the sensible response. Being cold makes you sensible.

Okay. It's been some ordeal in those fitting rooms, but I'm outside and I'm wearing them. I'm wearing under-trouser leg-warmers decorated with pictures of ice-skating and skiing people wearing stupid hats. They're worse than almost anything – bearBoy's red chinos, Alan's jogging pants, the viscoseBoys' viscose monstrosities – forget it. I could hardly be more ashamed if Tissy had run me up a fuckingPrat pair from the offcuts of her floral curtains. I know they're not on view, I *know* that, but tout de même. Tout de fucking même. *And* I'm wearing a stupid hat of my own. *And* I'm still shivering.

The architecture is a mix of the old fancy and the new brutal, I'll tell you that while I'm walking very very fast indeed, but don't expect much travelogue, because my eyes are too cold and I don't do travelogue.

Nearest bar?

38

Freezing and bizarrely clad as I am, some standards have to be maintained. Rule one of arriving abroad has to be applied: never enter the *first* bar you see – it's always either the Fascist Front bar or the gay bar and it can only cause you trouble. The first bar I like the look of (the second bar I see) is called SoDa, an orange, blue, steel and predominantly glass place, with gas-candles either side of the snow-covered step to help prevent you tripping as you go in. You enter through the world's heaviest triple-glazed door. At last; a door that doesn't slide in front of you. 'Drag,' is the word they've chosen to write where normally you see the word Pull, and it *is* the right word. It must be a Viking test of strength or something. Lucky I've been doing my door-frame pull-ups. Inside, it has a vibe which Nick at Nice Vibes would like – they're playing (I think) Norwegian Ambient House, and the air flickers, lit by the votives on the long bar top and the fat church candles on the round tables.

It's a bar, a regular bar which sells alcohol, but on the counter you can get hot drinks as well: chocolate, tea and coffee. Very sensible. Everybody speaks English, same as at the airport, same as in the taxi, same as at the Kämp Gallery (that's what the department store was called, a gallery: maybe it's shopping that's the new art, not clothes). While I wait to order, I take my first studied proper look at Finnish people. Nobody in SoDa is wearing reindeer-skin galoshes, which I thought might be the case, and in fact strides in general tend towards regular khaki-fatigue. Like I'm in a position to comment anyway, any more, considering what I've got on. Jumpers with buttons down the shoulder, like my Great Auntie used to knit me (to wear under my shepherd's outfit in the Sunday school play), are in fashion, which *is* bad, and some of the girls are wearing furry Alice bands with detachable ear-muffs, which puts the hat with tiger ears from the plane into a new perspective. The non-Alice-band-wearing bar-person serves me a vodka, cold with frosting on the glass, and I toast a silent Ha! Nazdaroveeyeh! (I know they're not Russians, but Russia must be close) to the SoDa people. I like them, they don't give too much of a shit what they wear, they've moved on.

The truly noteworthy feature isn't the garment, it's the mobile.

Everybody's on one, it makes even our use of them look completely half-hearted. The Finnish mobile comes with every sort of cover accessory you could dream of, including bearskin and simulated snow. Like you need a simulated snow cover, I think, as I watch a worker scrape frozen, compacted sheets of the real thing off the pavement. It must be a full-time job, that, ideal for a hard man who likes keeping his mind permanently focused. It's no exaggeration to state that I'm the only person here not on the phone. Nokia must have something to do with it; it must be like the sort of patriotic purchasing you get in France, where I've only ever seen them drive Citroëns or Renaults. Groups sit around tables all talking, but not to each other, unless they're doing it via the satellite.

I take a bite of the fish pastry which came free with the vodka. It tastes a lot better than that herring bap I had last night. It's the right idea, this free food provision, probably part of the Finnish NHS – if you didn't eat in this climate, you'd faint. And what if you fainted out on the street? You'd die.

Where do homeless people sleep here? Doorways are out of the question. If there was an abandoned tram available it'd be like the inside of a fridge. How would Antonio's friend have begun a recovery in this?

Anyway. Right. Natalie.

Rosie *wrote down* instructions for me, but I still can't make the fuckingPrat thing fucking work, the fucker. Four attempts at International Roaming have provided four no contacts with any service provider. I sit with it held uselessly in my hand and stare at the ill-tied, battered luggage label hanging from the FullSump. It's a long rectangle, the ticket, so the image underneath the Finnair logo is stretched into the wrong shape, but I've worked out what it is. It's a Rothko. That's what it was that was bothering me.

You shouldn't use art for a luggage label. You just shouldn't.

Mind you. Maybe it means that *this* is where the Rothkos are. Maybe it means that. The article on the Abstract Expressionism, it was about a touring exhibition, wasn't it? It would make sense. It would be another of Rosie's spiritual connections. Another connection. Everything's connected. Everything's connecting; everything except me and the fucking Nokia, that is.

It's a black and white Rothko, the one they've used, from his late period. That'd make sense too. Out there through SoDa's triple-glazed window, it's the same.

'Hei.'

He's been cruising the tables. I noticed him in the triple-glazed reflection while tightening the Puffa-sleeves/Puffa-body zips (trying to eliminate wind-ingress for my return to the wind-chill factor). I thought he was selling something.

'Hei. D'you have a cigarette?'

'Hclp yourself.'

Ah, Kiitos – thank you, he says. I thought I would never get one. I've been trying to quit, but just walking past the window and seeing people smoking – you know how it is . . .

He gestures back to the room. They're all too busy talking on the phone to listen to a question from somebody actually in front of them, that's all it is.

The mobile's very popular here, I say.

'C-phone. That's what we call them.'

'C-phone?'

'Cellular. There's a special language we use, it's called C-talk.'

'What's that then?'

A strange speech pattern, a bit awkward, he says. It's odd, you know, we Finns, we Finnish men especially, were the least communicative race in the world before all this; you sit in the sauna beside someone you've played hockey with for twenty years and he never says a word to you. Unless he's pissed. But then he's not in the sauna.

'Everyone's been friendly so far.'

'How long have you been here?'

'About an hour.'

That long, huh? So why are you here, he asks. It's not the holiday season.

He pulls back the other chair and sits down. I tell him about it, he's one of those guys with in-built listening time, as long as you keep him supplied with cigarettes and vodka.

I give him the short version. He interrupts only once, to say that he's never believed in the romantic ideal of love. It makes me think. It makes me think that maybe it's the only thing I do believe in. When I ask him his name, he tells me and then he draws it, how it should look. He walks to the counter and comes back with the chocolate-powder shaker for the Mochaccinos, and sprinkles it over the table-top, and in the zigzagged, shadowed and highlighted manner of graffiti artists everywhere, he illustrates his tag. His name's Chilli. When I ask him where he executes his work, he says all over. Sometimes straight on to the surface of the snow, so it's just temporary and will melt away.

'How's it going to melt in this weather?'

'It thaws in the spring.'

I tell him about my temporary clothes art. And when I tell him what it was called, he slaps his arm across my back, and laughs and says, Soul brother, because his favourite place to tag right now is on the perspex over a *particular* series of advertisements, ones for Nokia with a picture of a smiling young girl, and copy that says: I want to be everywhere, with everyone, all the time, now and ever.

Isn't that bollocks? he says. It's another one of your Damien Hirst's titles, isn't it?

'I think so, yeah. I've heard of it.'

I don't think it's that bad, as a title. I want to be with Natalie all the time everywhere now and for ever. But actually I want to be with her right now.

Chilli, I ask, d'you think you could get me a connection on this fucking thing.

'Of course.'

What *is* wrong with me? A single attempt and the service provider and I are as one. The server name shows up in the display: FIN. He takes his leave.

As he stands, he says, It's not your real name is it, Winger?

'It's like yours. It's a tag.'

I guessed, he says. A cigarette for the road?

He might as well have a supply, now he's quit quitting. I take a full pack of my duty-free prices from the Snowboard Puffa inside pocket, where I've loaded a couple for convenience.

What's that there, he asks, touching the label.

'It's a bus stop poem. They have them in England. They have them written on the perspex over the advertising.'

'D'you write them?'

'No, I pick them up when I see them, that's all. Somebody else writes them.'

39

I watch him walk away past the window. You have to adjust your eye, because the first image you read is the interior of SoDa reflected back. It's so black and white and dark outside, it makes a fishtank of the inside. It reminds me of the house in The Long Goodbye, the writer's beach house. As the writer staggers to the sea to drown, Marlowe's inside talking to the writer's wife, and the focus cuts between the two of them and him, back and forth, back and forth, through the picture-window door; if you look closely (you will on your fourth viewing, when you watch it as you stay awake all night after you've fucked up a zabaglione) you'll see that all of them – Marlowe, the writer, the writer's wife – reflect in the glass together.

FIN.

Key Natalie's number.

'The Vodaphone user you are calling is currently unavailable. Please leave a message.'

'Natalie, this is Winger. I'm in SoDa – S-O-D-A – in Helsinki. I've come to see you. Please call me. The number is 01379 621 9867.'

While I wait for the phone to ring (yeah, right), I score what I can remember of The Long Goodbye song into the fat side of the table-candle with the tip of the tool for removing stones from horses' hooves.

There's a long goodbye, and it happens every day
When some passer-by invites your eye to come her way.

That's all I can remember, all there's room for, too. A fall of wax rolls over the capital T. A burning candle, it's like a fried egg, isn't it? Once it's melted, you can't do anything else with it, the state of the raw material has changed. Irrevocably.

Downstairs, it's a kind of vault. Maybe it used to be a bank, this place. I hope so, it'd be like Bernie and the credit cards, a better use for it. There's a pool room next to the toilets where I stand and watch two men play. It's just the same as back home, no women and it doesn't smell right and it looks solitary. I've never considered it before, that snooker's a solitary game. The men don't look like all the other Finnish upstairs either, they're wearing checked shirts, like builders. Maybe they're off-duty ice-clearers. One of them looks my way. It's quiet down here, away from the C-talk and the Norwegian Ambient, but a noise has started, seven repeated notes rolling over and over. Fuck. It's humming in my pocket, took me a second to feel it, the vibration has to pass through the leg-warmers. I Say a Little Prayer. Rosie never told me it had a tune for a tone.

40

Just press the tick button, that's all you have to do to get connected. My nail is white.

'Hello?'

'Hello.'

'Winger, is that you?'

'*Natalie?*'

'Yeah, it's me.'

'It's me as well. Natalie, I'm gonna sort everything out. I've got a plan. I've been missing you. Nat, I've come to see you.'

'You haven't *really* come to see me, have you?'

'Nat, I'm in Helsinki. It's fucking freezing, isn't it?'

'Is this the sort of season you'd buy in advance, Winger?'

'I'd buy any season in advance if . . . Natalie, are you here, are you?'

'Yeah.'

'Where are you?'

'Got your message, took a taxi. Where are *you*? I don't see you.'

I've been standing dead still, rooted, watching but not seeing the men play out their frame.

'Winger? You still there?'

'Nat, I'm just coming. I'm coming up.'

I can't see her. Flickering flames, reflections, stupid hats. I can't see her.

'Winger, you look like shit.'

Through the window. Silver trainers, silver quilted strides, silver Puffa, silver hat. Eyes shining blue.

'One of us has to look like shit. Is it the fleece or the hat?

You gave me the strides, they must be okay.'

'It's the shades, Winger. Why are you wearing them?'

'Stay right where you are. Don't move.'

The reverse of Drag is Shove.

She takes my shades off. I won't describe the kiss. It's better to give you the maths of it. It takes place on a corner where the combined wind-chill factors are double minus sixteen and the actual temperature is minus ten.

41

Winger, this ain't kissing weather, our lips'll freeze together, she says. C'mon, *inside*, she says.

'Right.'

We sit down at my old table.

'What's all this mess, Winger?'

I tell her what all this mess is as we drink hot chocolate. I tell her about fuckingPrat curtains and nights spent not sleeping and steely grey dawns and distilled thoughts.

Winger, she says, what's that mark on your eye?'

'It's a sign.'

'Of what?'

I open the jacket and show her the bus stop poem. It's something to do with this, I say.

Heart stood still, she says. That's right, that, she says. What's it got to do with wearing shades?

'Nothing. I've been wearing them because I thought this table was going to become a standard weeping position.'

She doesn't say, What? to this, she says, Winger – [ ] Just like that, like she knows, even though I haven't mentioned nothing to her about no standard weeping position, never ever before. She returns to examining more of the mess, squeezing the flakes of wax which have fallen from the candle-writing.

'This is your writin, is it?'

I explain, and sing her the tune to the words to The Long Goodbye.

She takes my knife and scratches Long Hello deep into the wax and hands it back.

'Where are you staying, Nat? Is it somewhere with a kitchen?'

She says she's staying with Sini, one of the footballers, and what about the kitchen?

'I think I'm ready for another shot at the North Face of the Zabaglione . . . Have you been playing football then?'

'No. It's not the right season for it. I've been skating.'

'Skating? Have you been feeling like you're on another planet, like you said.'

'Yeah.'

'Me too.'

She wears a chocolate moustache. A happy one. What will we do now, I ask.

'We'll get a taxi. Sini said you could stay, I told her about you.'

'Is she the one who gave me your note?'

'Yeah. Even though you played a crap game, she thought you were alright.'

'I should have been substituted.'

'She said you played a crap game 'cos I wasn't there.'

'Very perceptive.'

'It made me think.'

'It was a bad night. Marky didn't show either and there was somebody watching from the edge, somebody wearing leather trousers.'

'I know. He's a dispatch rider.'

'I thought he might be.'

'How?'

'By watching you at the coffee shop. By putting two and two together and making four for once. By thinking what I'd do if I'd heard anything and I was him.'

'Yeah, I had to go sicknote that night, you're right. One of your lot had mentioned something about a boys v the girls match. He overheard it while he was on a job. He didn't like the sound of it.'

'It's a stupid idea.'

'I know, we'd hammer you.'

'He saw who I was then?'

'Yeah. He called you a lot of names, and me some too. I defended you, and not just your football, and well . . . it didn't get any better, let's put it like that.'

She holds my hand. A nice squeeze. My nails are getting their colour back.

It's good to see you, she says.

You could say that for me too, squared to the power of minus n squared.

The taxi slides up.

On the road out of the centre, I show her the mask.

'Where d'you get that?'

I tell her.

'Winger, is this your plan, becoming a bloody thief?'

'No.'

'What is it then?'

'I'll tell you about it later.'

The driver half-turns, he's been watching us in the rear-view.

'Tourist?'

I've certainly got the legwear for it. 'Yeah.'

Do you see the exhibition, he asks, the Rothkos?

It's all connecting. It's all connected. 'No. Are they here?'

It finished at the weekend, he says.

I ask Natalie did she see it.

Yeah, she says.

'And . . .?'

'I liked them. I'm surprised you do though – that repeat of the same *shape*, over and over – specially considering what you were saying, about templates. Patterns.'

'Don't you do it in skating, find the perfect groove and stay in it?'

Yeah, she says.

'Some patterns are like that, aren't they, Nat, perfect grooves.'

And some have to be broken, she says.
'Yeah. You're right.'

The driver swings on the bends in slow recklessness. I lean forward.
'How d'you grip the road?'
Spikes, he says.
'Spikes?'
'Yeah, we have spikes in the tyres.'
Spikes in the tyres. You can't see them, but they dig in.
We all go quiet. He begins swinging wider on every corner, loosening up, skating.
Cool driving, Natalie says. You're the best cabbie yet, she says.
'You like this style?'
He can see we do. At our destination, he turns a full pirouette in front of Sini's parents' log cabin. Olé.
I fumble about, looking for money.
Let me see that, he says.
I hand it over.
'Rare. It's Panuk. About AD 500.'
'Panuk?'
'Distant ancestors.'
'Would you like it?'

His lights recede into the blue-black night.
That was nice of you, she says.
It doesn't belong to me, and it's too fragile to be a mask. And anyway, I don't think I need one any more.
'Maybe it came from up here in the first place.'
'Yeah. Maybe it did. I hope so. Things should be able to go back to where they came from.'

I lose my footing as we turn to the steps up to the cabin.
They're not really the right shoes for this climate, are they? she says.

'Can we talk about that, Nat, I'd like to – because I've always had problems with footwear . . .'

'And my dad's trousers hardly look warm enough either.'

'They're not. I'm wearing under-trousers. It's a nightmare – they're a nightmare, but I'm going to show you them. It'll be a big step for me, a very big step.'

'A big step, eh. It's cool with me.'

'That's my line.'

'I know. I've been using it.'

'Really?'

'Yeah.'

'It's cool with me.'

'It's cool with me.'

'Can we go inside, it's freezing out here.'

'Fucking freezing.'

'Bloody fucking freezing.'

'Bloody fucking bloody fucking freezing.'

'Bloody fucking bloody fucking bloody fucking freezing.'

But it's cool with us.

ACKNOWLEDGEMENTS

For assistance, encouragement and inside information given knowingly and unknowingly along the way, thanks to: Bumble, Marion Catlin, Pele Cox, Rosie Edwards, Karen Fisk, Diane Foster-Watson, Kate Gerova, Ben Keane, Riitta Keurulainen, Andrew Motion, Lizzie Robinson, Dominique Roggo, Andrew 'SmuttyBoy' Smith, John Street, George Szirtes, Emma Warden and Fie Wilson.

For trade service and retail therapy, thanks to: Doddy, David Findlay, Elvis and Dennis at The Blue Jean Co., and to Nick Snell, Robin Norton and the Dogfish Massive at Dogfish.

For professional handling, thanks to my agent Derek Johns and to my editor Julian Loose. Charles Boyle at Faber deserves a particular accolade for smartening me up.

Special thanks to Marion Forsyth.

Extra special thanks to David Hill for editorial excellence, and to Trezza Azzopardi for editorial excellence and more.

A selected list of titles available from
Faber and Faber Ltd

Paul Auster	*The New York Trilogy*	0-571-15223-6
Peter Carey	*Jack Maggs*	0-571-19377-3
Peter Carey	*Oscar and Lucinda*	0-571-15304-6
Peter Carey	*True History of the Kelly Gang*	0-571-20987-4
Mavis Cheek	*Mrs Fytton's Country Life*	0-571-20541-0
Joseph Connolly	*Summer Things*	0-571-19574-1
Michael Dibdin	*Dead Lagoon*	0-571-17347-0
Giles Foden	*The Last King of Scotland*	0-571-19564-4
Michael Frayn	*Headlong*	0-571-20147-4
William Golding	*Lord of the Flies*	0-571-19147-9
Andrew Greig	*That Summer*	0-571-20473-2
Kazuo Ishiguro	*The Remains of the Day*	0-571-15491-3
Kazuo Ishiguro	*When We Were Orphans*	0-571-20516-X
P. D. James	*An Unsuitable Job for a Woman*	0-571-20389-2
Barbara Kingsolver	*The Poisonwood Bible*	0-571-20175-X
Barbara Kingsolver	*Prodigal Summer*	0-571-20648-4
Milan Kundera	*Immortality*	0-571-14456-X
Milan Kundera	*The Unbearable Lightness of Being*	0-571-13539-0
Hanif Kureishi	*The Buddha of Suburbia*	0-571-14274-5
Hanif Kureishi	*Intimacy*	0-571-19570-9
John Lanchester	*Mr Phillips*	0-571-20171-7
John McGahern	*Amongst Women*	0-571-16160-X
Rohinton Mistry	*A Fine Balance*	0-571-17936-3
Lorrie Moore	*Birds of America*	0-571-19727-2
Andrew O'Hagan	*Our Fathers*	0-571-20106-7
Sylvia Plath	*The Bell Jar*	0-571-08178-9
Jane Smiley	*Horse Heaven*	0-571-20560-7
Banana Yoshimoto	*Kitchen*	0-571-17104-4

In case of difficulty in purchasing any Faber title through normal channels, books can be purchased from:

Bookpost, PO BOX 29, Douglas, Isle of Man, IM99 1BQ

Credit cards accepted. Please telephone 01624 836000, fax 01624 837033
Internet www.bookpost.co.uk *or* email bookshop@enterprise.net for details.